GREEN LIGHT FOR MURDER

GREEN LIGHT FOR MURDER

HEYWOOD GOULD

FINKELSTEIN
MEMORIAL LIBRARY
SPRING VALLEY, NY

TYRUS
BOOKS

F+W Media, Inc.

Published by
TYRUS BOOKS
an imprint of F+W Media, Inc.
10151 Carver Road, Suite 200, Blue Ash, Ohio, 45242. U.S.A.
www.tyrusbooks.com

Hardcover ISBN 10: 1-4405-6122-2
Hardcover ISBN 13: 978-1-4405-6122-1
Trade Paperback ISBN 10: 1-4405-6123-0
Trade Paperback ISBN 13: 978-1-4405-6123-8
eISBN 10: 1-4405-6124-9
eISBN 13: 978-1-4405-6124-5

Printed in the United States of America.

10   9   8   7   6   5   4   3   2   1

*This book is available at quantity discounts for bulk purchases.
For information, please call 1-800-289-0963.*

To Patricia.

Cast of Characters

The Madman	*Jay Braffner*
The Poet	*Detective Tommy Veasy*
The Producer	*Lester Tarsis*
The Partner	*Detective Cheri Tingley*
Chief of Police	*George Jonas*
Squad Commander	*Felipe Mineo*
Producers	*Dave Kessel*
	Mitch Helfand
	Gary London
Staff Writers	*Sean O'Meara*
	Noah Lippman
Mr. Tarsis's Assistant	*Eloise Gruber*
Editor	*Elliot Kriegsfeld*
Assistant Editor	*Zack Toledano*
Social Worker	*Alison Sobel*
Explosive Effects	*Roy Farkas*

FADE UP ON ...

THE MADMAN AND HIS IMAGINARY FILM CREW

Jay Braffner is in the wine cellar of producer Dave Kessel's Malibu beach house. Outside, an exterminating crew is draping a blue termite tent over the roof. Inside, the film crew in Jay's head is executing his instructions.'

"Best crew I ever had, Dave," Jay says. "I think it and they do it."

The script appears in flaming letters in his mind.

"Tight TWO SHOT of Braffner and Kessel."

The answer comes back:

("tight two shot, boss.")

"Full crew, Dave," Jay says. "Showed up in my head one morning. Young, eager to learn. No overtime, no meal penalties because they don't eat. No muttering behind my back. Best of all, no teamsters . . ."

Jay calls: "Let the tent billow."

("tent's billowing boss.")

"Remember how I tried to sell you this shot on *Autocop*, Dave?" he asks.

Kessel shakes his head.

Jay pulls a pair of latex gloves over his thick wrists. "The script had a boring murder on a suburban street. Let's put a blue termite tent over the house," I said. "The murderer is disguised in an exterminator's uniform. He ties the victim up and leaves him to die when they turn on the gas. Remember, Dave?"

Kessel's bloodshot eyes bulge above the black gaffer tape covering his nose and mouth.

"You blew me off, Dave," Jay says. "Artsy fartsy, you said. Three months later the exact same scene showed up in another episode with Lester Tarsis's name on it . . ."

Kessel writhes and struggles with muffled pleas.

"That's it Dave, beg for your life," Jay says. "That'll play great."

He twists Kessel's head toward the window where the blue tent is settling gently like a giant bedspread. "Now we cut to this morning. I'm trying to think of a cool, cinematic way to kill you. I see the termite truck in front of your house and I realize the movie gods are sending me a message. So I get a uniform and disguise myself as an exterminator."

Kessel tries to elbow his way free, but Jay puts him in a headlock. "Bayside High Wrestling, Dave. City champs . . ." He squeezes so hard Kessel's cheekbones crack. "Stop fighting and I'll let go." Kessel gets very still. Jay rips the tape off his mouth and he explodes in gulping breaths.

"For Chrissake, Jay, that was 1995."

"Seems like yesterday to me," Jay says.

"What did I do so bad to you?"

"You stole my ideas and gave them to Lester Tarsis."

Kessel sobs. "I didn't have any ideas of my own. Do I deserve to die for that?"

"If you did, Hollywood would be a ghost town," Jay says. "You're dying because you screwed me."

"Lester made me do it, Jay. He's the one you should be after."

"Lester's on my list, too, Dave."

Jay reaches onto the wine rack for a bottle of Armagnac and holds the label up to the light. "Chateau de Laubade, 1922. My mother was born in 1922. It took me eight years in analysis to uncover my primal memories of seeing her screwing somebody while my dad was at Yonkers Raceway. By then she was dead and I couldn't ask her if the guy was my Uncle Willie. See, I thought it was him because I had an olfactory sense memory of his cheap cigars that came up whenever I had sex. It was giving me serious performance issues . . ."

Kessel blubbers. "Lester had us at each other's throats, Jay."

Jay pops the cork. "The TV money kept pouring in, Dave. Lester bought income properties in the Valley. I pissed mine away on coke and bimbos. You assembled the most famous collection of vintage Armagnac in the world. Made the cover of *Gourmet Magazine* . . ."

Kessel dribbles green bile out of the corner of his mouth. "Gimme a break, Jay . . ."

"This is film noir, Dave, no happy endings." Jay grabs Kessel by the back of the neck and jams the bottle down his throat. "Let's drink a last toast to you and your fabulous collection."

Kessel gags and sputters: "No Jay!"

Jay lifts Kessel by the seat of his pants and the back of his collar and rams him into the rack. Bottles tumble, bouncing off his head.

"Take Two, Dave," Jay says. He takes a crow hop and rams him into the rack again.

Kessel goes limp. Jay eases him down to the floor, giving terse commands to the crew. "PAN DOWN and PUSH IN to a TIGHT SHOT as Jay takes the tape off Kessel's wrists and ankles . . ."

("Panning . . .")

"TIGHT ON JAY as he pours the rest of the booze over Kessel to make it look like a drunken accident . . ."

("Tight on Jay.")

Jay closes the wine cellar door and walks quickly down the hall. "See how the sun shines through the tarp," he says. "Has anyone ever made a shot through the tent of a fumigated house?"

("no one but you boss.")

Jay slips through the back door and scrambles out from under the tent. Two exterminators in blue uniforms are standing by the pool.

"Thought I heard a dog barking in the house," Jay says. "Must have been next door."

From the beach he watches as they wind thick ropes around the tent and turn on the gas. Nobody sees him shedding the exterminator's uniform and putting it in a Trader Joe's shopping bag. He strips down to his black Speedo and trudges through the burning sand to the cool shore where he splashes water on the back of his neck. "Just another over-the-hill, over-tanned, pony-tailed New York transplant," he confides to the crew. "Thousands of us came out here to make it big. We look alike, think alike. Love the beach, the blondes, the free parking. Meet one of us, you've met us all. But there's one big difference . . ."

The crew supplies the answer.

("you are a great filmmaker.")

"Thank you," Jay says.

DISSOLVE TO:

THE POET MAKING LOVE

Five miles down the Pacific Coast Highway in a cluttered studio on a beach block in Venice, Detective Tommy Veasy, La Playita PD, is reciting an impromptu poem to his partner, Detective Cheri Tingley:

To be a police romancer
You must keep the requests selective
To get the desired answer
From the sensual detective . . .

"I feel like I'm being undressed by Snoop Dogg," Detective Tingley says, raising her arms.

Detective Veasy unclips her sequin halter top. "I was thinking more Lord Byron."

Tingley arches her back so he can slip off her jeans. "You recite poetry to distract me, but I know you're taking off my clothes."

"That's because you're a trained law enforcement professional . . ."

"Silly shirt," she says, pulling at his buttons. "Palm trees and coconuts . . ."

"Hey, that's my Tommy Bahama knockoff. Fourteen fifty at Costco . . ."

"Funny, when you see somebody naked for the first time, it's never the way you thought it was going to be." She grazes her nail over his nipple. "What does that line mean: *to get the desired answer?*"

"That if I say the wrong thing I'll lose the moment."

Tingley sits up. "You think you talked me into this? I knew I would be coming back to your place all along. Even got my mom to sit with my son."

Veasy blows gently over her body.

"Did you ever notice how the slightest puff of air can make a woman's breasts quiver?"

"Nobody in the squad can know about this," Tingley says.

"You mean I don't get to brag about my conquest? Anyway, it's too late."

Tingley sits up again. "What do you mean?"

10

"Something passes between people who are having a love affair. The energy flow changes. Others can sense it."

She lies back down. "I don't care about energy flow. Just as long you don't write a poem about it and post it on the department website."

Veasy slides his nose over her neck.

"What are you doing?"

"Breathing you in."

Tingley puts her hands behind her head. "Oh God, this is why I've been putting it off."

"Why?"

"Because I was afraid I was going to like it."

"Don't worry," Veasy says.

He rises over her.

"I'll make it as brief and unpleasant as possible."

THE NEXT MORNING

The crew squeezes into Jay Braffner's tiny bedroom, as he gets ready to pitch a show.

("dusty . . .")

"I was in the psycho ward for a year, but the house went on as if I was here," Jay says. "I was on auto pay for the mortgage, phone, and the Internet. The Directors Guild direct deposited my residuals. The mail was dropped inside the door. Jay Braffner's life continued without Jay Braffner . . . You can call me the Invisible Madman."

("great title . . .")

"When I walked in yesterday it was as if I had never left. I was knee-deep in Victoria's Secret catalogues . . ."

("defining moment.")

"*Nobody* knows I was gone. So let's hit the ground running . . . Action . . ."

("rolling . . .")

Jay slips into a safari jacket. "This is the famous drop dead meeting. Most deals are presold by the big players, but the network has to take meetings with old guys like me to make it look like they're running an open marketplace . . ."

The crew is impressed.

("so that's how it works . . .")

"CAMERA, follow me," Jay orders.

It's a short walk down a narrow hall to the living room. Faces from his past appear like sconces in the wall. Dead friends glide by in the shadows.

"In the old days I would have been pitching to a guy just like me," Jay says. "Same age, New York type guy. A guy I could talk to. Hang out with at Dan Tana's. He'd have an assistant, a 'D' girl, for 'Development,'—but really for D-cup (*pause for laughter*)—taking notes, skirt hiked to shoot me some panty peek. If I sold the idea she'd flash me the cleavage signal while stamping my parking pass and I'd ask her out for drinks . . ."

(wait for the admiring murmurs to die down.)

"Six o'clock," Jay says. "I pick her up in my '76 MG . . . Drive out of the lot with the top down. Guard at the gate waves. 'Night Mr. Braffner . . . Cruise down Cahuenga, rolling a joint with one hand— little trick that never fails to impress—people flashing the 'Peace' sign from passing cars. Stop at Roy's on Sunset where I know I'll get a big hello. The bartender comes over on cue . . . Two Bombay Martinis, Eric, straight up, extra olives. I slip her the vial when she goes to the john. Always a heavy hitter in one of the booths. She comes back, eyeballs polished and gushes: Warren Beatty's here . . ."

"I order a big meal for form's sake. She's too wired to eat. More actors coming over. She's knocked out . . . Isn't that . . . ? I saw him in . . . Now wash down a 'lude with a Remy Martin. She's giggling, clinging to my arm like it's driftwood from the Titanic. My Jacuzzi or yours? Can't wait for the hot tub to fill up. Bumping in the darkness, blind as cavefish. Next thing we know the sun is burning hot stripes on the sheets. She panics. Left her car at the studio. *Ta da* . . . ! I come up with a C-note and Beverly Hills Cab. Taxi home, freshen up, and taxi to the studio, darlin'. My treat 'cause you're great. The second she's gone I can't remember her face. Draw the blinds, blast the AC, and settle into the musky sheets for a beauty sleep . . ."

(*"must have been a fun time."*)

"Everybody was working," Jay says. "Stifled, frustrated, underpaid, and undermined . . . But working . . ."

He smiles bravely. "Oh well, can't dwell on past glory." He takes a breath, pastes on a smile, and enters the empty room. "Hi, is this the lion's den? You called for a Christian?" No laugh. "Diversity TV," he confides, pointing to the empty chairs. "There's the Ivy League black chick who thinks I'm just another obsolete white man. A gay guy who is Googling me on his iPhone because he hasn't a clue who I am. A pasty-faced snot flicker, MA in film studies who sneers at everything I ever did. And a severe chick with glasses, who hates me at first sight because I look like the professor who groped her in the American Lit seminar . . . Or didn't . . ."

(*let the helpless laughter subside.*)

"Normally, I couldn't sell *American Idol* in this room," Jay says. "But I'm about to blow their minds. Watch . . ." He clears his throat to get their attention. "There are two questions everybody asks in this town," he begins. "One: How did that asshole get that job . . . ?"

(*hiccup of a laugh from the gay guy.*)

"And Two: Why has nobody ever murdered a producer?"

Chairs creak.

"If they move toward you they're sold," Jay says. "If they sit back, you're a loser . . ."

He jumps up to pull focus.

"Nobody can answer Question One. Nobody can explain why so many morons are given power in this town . . ."

(nods of assent.)

"But I can answer Question Two. Somebody has finally murdered a producer . . . Me."

Jaws drop. "I'm about simplicity so I call the show *I Murder a Producer.*"

(they like the title.)

"In case you're wondering I already have one episode in the can, I Murder Dave Kessel. Dave was an all-night shoot so I'm a little tired and probably look like crap. I don't do the powder pick-me-up thing anymore."

(knowing smiles.)

"Tonight I'm going to shoot I Murder Mitch Helfand. And tomorrow we'll do I Murder Gary London . . ."

They edge even closer. They're hooked.

"I know you guys like to launch big," Jay says. "So on Monday . . . On camera . . . For your pilot episode . . . I'm going to murder Lester Tarsis and the entire staff of his syndicated show, *She, Queen of the Jungle* . . . Don't ask me how, but trust me, it'll be explosive."

ESTABLISH THE LONELY COMMANDER

Let's see if the lovebirds fly in together.

George Jonas, Chief of the La Playita PD, is sitting by his office window waiting for Veasy and Tingley arrive.

Headquarters is a short walk from Veasy's place on the beach. He strolls into the building a little before seven. Tingley drives in a few minutes later, turning off the PCH like she was coming from her home in Tarzana.

They really think they're fooling me.

A month ago Detective Walsh, his spy on the squad, came to him with the news that Veasy had codenamed him "Owl" for his habit of blinking and squinting in meetings. It's a tic he's had since childhood, a little mild Tourette's actually. He has it controlled with haloperidol, but it pops up sometimes when he's under stress.

It started him thinking about what else Veasy was saying about him. And once you open that can of worms . . .

Jonas has been seeing Detective Tingley out of school. He doesn't have to ask Walsh if that's generally known—can't keep a secret around a bunch of detectives. Doesn't have to ask if it's gotten around that Veasy has seduced her away from him.

Everyone knows.

Jonas is sensitive about his appearance. He's bald with a fringe of hair over his ears and a trim brush mustache—the best choice after years of experimenting with the shaven head and goatee look, the close-cropped beard, even a hair weave. He's in the gym every morning at five. Has his uniforms tailored. Wears a short-sleeved tunic to show his guns. Stuck at five-ten, can't hope for a growth spurt at his age. Too late for lifts, the squad would notice the difference. And he'd soon have another codename.

Veasy's gotta be six-three. He was a football hero in high school. Hasn't gained a pound or lost a step since then. Hasn't lost a hair since he was fifteen, either. The squad jokes about him, say he looks like Superman with a hangover.

Why do the troops always love the guy who hates the boss?

Jonas checks the closed circuit cameras. Tingley is walking through the garage. Even has a change of clothes.

Bitch thought of everything.

She disappears from view. A couple of seconds and she still doesn't reappear. Veasy hasn't shown either.

"Any blind spots on our video surveillance?" Jonas asks the officer at the desk.

"Cameras are all pointing in one direction. Guess if you pressed against the wall under a camera you wouldn't be seen."

That's it. They met in the blind spot. Flattened against the wall. Kissed and giggled at their little trick.

A second later he sees Tingley on the stairway camera. Then on the lobby camera. Then, she walks right by him.

"Morning."

Veasy appears in the stairwell camera and then in the lobby.

"Morning, Chief."

Lieutenant Sergeant Mineo, the squad commander, is in the conference room, shuffling reports. "Morning, Chief . . ."

Standing at the coffee machine Jonas watches the detectives file in. "Mornin' Chief . . ." No smirks in his direction.

Cops are good actors.

Jonas had been discreet, waited until he sensed she was receptive. That first night he had taken her to the French bistro in Altadena, deep in the Valley where they wouldn't see anybody they knew. Quiet booth. She was impressed. "I never knew you were such a gourmet."

"Working overseas you learn how to eat well," he said.

That got a raised eyebrow. "Overseas?"

So he hinted at the top-secret missions. "This is between us, okay?"

A few more dates. He knew all the cool out-of-the-way places. Then, when she took his arm walking back to the car, when the good night kiss lingered, he invited her for dinner. He made Beef Wellington with a layer of pâté and a perfect crust. Nice bottle of Cabernet. She was knocked out. "I can't cook this way. How am I going to reciprocate?"

"We'll think of something," he said.

Fifteen minutes after he took the Cialis he felt the blood flowing in a cool current right into his balls.

She was what he needed. Round, comfortable. Big nipples that went rock hard at his touch. Ass like a pillow. A natural, she moved with him like they had been doing it for years.

"Well well," she said, staring up at the ceiling in a daze.

The bitch was totally faking it.

She was a new promotion from Community Affairs. "I'm going to put Tingley with Veasy, Chief," Mineo said. "Some of these other guys have an attitude about women on the job . . ."

Made sense to partner a rookie with an experienced detective. Jonas didn't want to cause suspicion by blocking it. "Sure, let them work together," he said. "Maybe she'll learn something."

One afternoon they came in laughing. He watched from his glassed-in office. Their desks were next to each other, but he saw Veasy texting. Saw her pick up her cell and blush to the roots of her light blonde hair.

They went out for drinks with the squad, but always seemed to pair off like they were hiding in the crowd. Little touches as they passed.

He backed off. Didn't make a date, waiting for her to invite him. But two weeks passed. So he sent her a text about dinner. And she texted back: "Can't get a sitter." She left early. As soon as she was out of the building, Veasy got a call on his cell and smiled.

Secret fucking rendezvous, huh?

For nine years Veasy was the rock star of the La Playita PD, the genius who made all the big cases. Then came the Encarnación murder. Ten-year-old girl, kidnapped, raped, mutilated. The worst homicide in the history of La Playita.

Veasy couldn't crack it. After months with no leads he got a hunch suspect. Trailed him out of jurisdiction to a house in Redondo Beach and almost beat him to death trying to get a confession. Redondo cops had to pull him off the guy.

Mineo had friends on the Redondo PD and got the charge knocked down to harassment. The La Playita City Council put Veasy on an indefinite medical. Even approved his prescription for medical marijuana. He was still on leave when Jonas was hired.

"We're saving a spot for Detective Veasy," Ludwig, City Manager, told Jonas. "You'll have to work shorthanded until he gets back."

He didn't want to start the job with a bad taste so he played it nice. "Sure, it'll be a challenge for the rest of the squad."

He met Veasy for the first time three months later at the "welcome home" party the squad threw for him. They shook hands, sized each other up, and it's been total war ever since.

Jonas sits at the head of the conference table and murmurs into his mini recorder. "Thursday, the tenth, seven-thirty, squad meeting . . ."

He watches the two of them as Mineo drones over the day's work. All business. No secret looks.

They think they're so slick.

"Missing Person," Mineo says. "Alison Sobel. Outpatient Services at Harbor UCLA Psychiatric Center . . . Left her office to visit patients in La Playita . . . Didn't call in . . . Hasn't reported for work . . . Driving a charcoal Honda Civic, plate number GEU479Z . . . Boyfriend reported her missing."

"Do we have a list of the patients she was visiting?" Jonas asks.

"Working on it," Mineo says. "Here's a new one on me. Accidental death by termite gas . . . David Scott Kessel, TV producer. They were tenting his house yesterday afternoon. Crew found him in his wine cellar this morning."

"Interesting," Veasy says. He taps his teeth with a pencil. "No signs of a struggle?"

"Head wounds incurred when he fell into the metal wine rack. His ex-wife says he had gone in to remove his vintage Armagnac collection. Looks like he had a few drinks and passed out. No one was seen entering or leaving . . ."

"Mr. Kessel entered, but never left," Veasy says. "I'll have a chat with the exterminators."

The squad looks at Jonas. Veasy is claiming the case before it is officially assigned. A definite breach.

Don't take the bait.

Jonas shakes his head, curtly.

"It's an accident until proven otherwise. I don't want to carry an unsolved homicide on the books."

Veasy scribbles in his notebook.

Act amused.

"A little poem Veasy?"

Veasy closes the book. "Just wanted to jot a few thoughts before I forgot them."

"Share them with us. If they're not too private . . ."

"Actually I was inspired by something you said, Boss." Veasy opens the notebook and reads:

"There is no crime in La Playita
Our neighbors are so kind and gentle.
We don't even have mosquitahs
And death is always accidental . . ."

Not a sound.

They better not laugh.

Veasy closes the notebook.

"It's just a first draft," he says.

INTERIOR—THE MADMAN'S GARAGE

"Action!" Jay says. And begins to narrate:

"We push through a smoky haze of dust and spider webs and discover Braffner bent over a splintered work table under a sputtering, naked bulb—behind smudged windows."

(*"classic noir imagery."*)

"Thank you," Jay says. He draws on his latex gloves. Pours distilled water over a mound of RDX explosive powder.

"This is the scene Lester wouldn't let me shoot," he says.

He adds the chemical binder.

"He said the gag was too complicated. I told him I could shoot it in quick cuts just like we're doing it now . . ."

Takes a pestle and mixes it into a slurry.

"He said the audience wouldn't buy it. I told him it had been all over the headlines. The Mossad had used it on some guy in Israel . . ."

He fashions the slurry into a lump of C4 plastic explosive that looks like silly putty. Buries a fuse wire in it and shapes the clay around the wire until only an inch or two is showing.

"He said I was being defensive. I said I was fighting for what I believed in . . ."

He attaches the wire to the blasting cap.

"Four months later it was the teaser in an *Autocop* episode. Some guy picks up his office phone and boom! The whole place goes up. The credit was: Written by Lester Tarsis . . ."

(*"idea thief."*)

Jay attaches the blasting cap to a sim card.

"That was the drill. You pitched an idea to Lester in the privacy of his office. He stole it. You didn't get credit, but you got another assignment. Every idea you let him steal you got another job . . . You made money and had a big rep and got laid a lot, which to Lester was the highest reward. Who could ask for anything more than money and sex?"

Jay packs the explosive in a Halliburton attaché case.

"I broke the rule. I fought for my vision. I demanded recognition for my work. I elevated the form. Lester hated the idea that there could be an art to doing TV. He hated me for inspiring the cast and crew. He kicked me off his shows and badmouthed me around town, scaring other people with stories about my stubbornness and drug abuse. I admit I had a problem with cocaine."

("who didn't?")

"There were a few stints in rehab. An unfortunate automobile accident in which a young actress was killed . . ."

("it's a car culture, shit happens.")

"My exile was supposed to last forever . . . But like the Count of Monte Cristo I've returned."

Jay snaps the case shut.

"Early Monday morning I plant an explosive in the phone and another under the desk . . . A few hours later, I call the office. Lester picks up the phone. Lester, I say, this is what you always ask for—a dynamite ending . . . Then I blow the crap out of him and his staff . . ."

("orgasmic.")

"Thank you," says Jay.

AN ACTUARIAL FACT

Alton Burg, President of Universal Extermination, paces uneasily in Dave Kessel's wine cellar. "There has never been a murder in the history of the extermination business," he says.

"Don't tell that to the termites," Veasy says. He rips the yellow crime scene tape away from the doorway. "This is useless," he says. "The scene's compromised. Exterminators, cops, paramedics trampling in and out . . ."

"It read like an accident at the time," Tingley says.

"A corpse is presumed murdered until proven otherwise . . ."

Burg pleads his case to Tingley. "My family has been in this business for over fifty years. We pay the lowest casualty insurance premium in California. You know why? Because no one is ever hurt on our jobs."

"You mean you've never had a fatality of any kind?" she asks.

"We had an incident in 1994. Woman crawled back under the tent to get her parakeet. But it turned out to be a suicide . . ."

"The woman or the parakeet?" Veasy asks.

"You're better than that, Detective Veasy," Tingley says. "What time did your men find the body, Mr. Burg?"

Burg checks the work order. "We tented and secured at four in the afternoon. Started the Vicane at five-fifteen. We wait sixteen hours before going in so it would be somewhere around eight or nine the next morning."

"Somewhere isn't good enough," Veasy says. "We need to know exactly when your crew entered the house and who discovered the body. Find out if anything unusual occurred . . ."

"This was a routine job like all the others," Burg says. "The house was empty when we released the gas."

"Except for Dave Kessel."

"He must have gotten in after we inspected."

"Or while the gas was being piped in," Veasy says.

"That's impossible. The house was locked and tented."

"Mr. Kessel or a person unknown knew that lethal gas was about to be pumped into the house. And sneaked in anyway, which signifies intent to a policeman."

Burg blinks anxiously as Veasy scribbles in his notebook. "My guys are very upset about this. I'm going to have to send some of them for counseling."

Outside, Tingley lets out the laugh she's been holding in.

"Counseling? My God, who knew that exterminators were so sensitive?"

"Notice the big glasses and the hairy fingers," Veasy says. "Weird buzzing voice. Are we sure he's human?"

"You made him nervous taking all those notes."

Veasy shows her what he wrote.

The crime is rare,
The motive hidden
The answer will not come unbidden

"That guy's hiding something," he says.

LOCATION SCOUT

Jay comes out of his house with a green bucket, a pool rake, cargo shorts, and a pair of Topsiders. He poses for the crew.

("perfect disguise.")

"Thank you," Jay says.

He drives to Garland Street in La Playita and stops in front of Mitch Helfand's hacienda-style mansion.

"Classic Hollywood," he says. "Gotta be a hundred years old. Mitch says it was built by silent movie vamp Theda Bara. Sometimes he says it was Pola Negri . . . Sometimes Clara Bow. He says he bought it from Dick Powell's estate. Or Shirley Temple. Everybody knows he got it dirt cheap in a foreclosure deal after a flop producer named Jerry Nadel walked away from it. Everybody dabbles in real estate out here."

("biting insight.")

Jay has to stoop to walk under the stone archway. He points to a dented Chevy Astro in the driveway.

"What does this tell you?"

("the housekeeper's at home.")

The wrought iron knocker is in the shape of a conquistador's profile. The nose is chipped from constant banging. The door opens a crack and a little brown lady peeks out.

Jay waves the rake.

"Pool man," he says.

She closes the door.

Jay leads the crew along the narrow stone path past the high bushes—"Mitch likes to keep things private"—to the old flagstone patio in the backyard. He turns to check light direction.

"We'll be here around sunset," he says. "Won't need to do any rigging. Coupla bounce boards to shape the light . . ."

("master at work.")

Jay points to the pool, sun glittering off the blue water.

"Most of the action will take place here," he says.

SMELLS LIKE MURDER

"Up the Santa Monica Freeway the cars come and go," Veasy says. "But nobody's talking about Michelangelo."

He's in the conference room of La Playita Police Headquarters watching the rush hour traffic crawl east toward LA.

Tingley is on the phone with an indignant mom whose son was busted for pot on the La Playita High School campus.

"The undercover officer observed him hiding under the backstop on the baseball field, ma'am," she says. "The school nurse reported him to be sweaty and disoriented . . ."

"Sounds like a case of masturbation in the first degree," Veasy says.

Mineo, dark, serious, and heavyset, is going through Veasy's report for the third time. He got his promotion for killing two *cholos* who tried to shoot their way out of a traffic stop. To him police work is violent confrontation, not elegant detection.

"I don't see a homicide here, Tommy."

"The idea was to make it look like an accident," says Veasy. "Murderers will do that, the little sneaks . . ."

Jonas appears at the door as if he'd been outside listening. "Good afternoon." He puts his digital mini recorder on the conference table and whispers into the mike: "Wednesday, the 11th, 5:45 P.M. Detectives Veasy, Tingley, and Lieutenant Mineo present to discuss the death of David Kessel." Then he turns to Veasy. "Give me a quick summary of the incident, Detective Veasy."

"It's in the report . . ."

"In case you didn't notice, Detective, I'm recording . . ."

Veasy pinches his throat and sings a few "mi mi mi's."

Jonas squints and blinks. "Some of us want to go home," he says.

"Yes sir," Veasy says and checks his notes. "Exterminators were doing a postfumigation inspection. They found three billion termites and one producer, or *vice versa* . . ."

Jonas looks at the detectives, daring them to laugh. "Paramedics report a deep gash on his head," he says. "Like he had fallen and knocked himself unconscious."

"Or was knocked unconscious and left to die," Veasy says.

"What was he doing there?" Jonas asks.

"House was sold and fumigation was part of the deal. Kessel had gone to get his collection of vintage Armagnac. There was an empty bottle by the body . . ."

"Don't the exterminators do an inspection before they tent the house?" Jonas asks.

"They say they did. The wine cellar is in a converted closet in the maid's room off the kitchen. They say they looked and he wasn't there."

Jonas looks at Mineo. "Autopsy?"

Mineo shuffles papers. "Asphyxiation by inhalation of Vicane gas. Head wound consistent with a fall. Gut full of alcohol . . ."

"So he was selling the house because . . ."

Veasy points to his report. "Disposal of community property for a divorce . . ."

"So Kessel goes back for his brandy collection," Jonas says. "Has a few and gets sentimental. Bangs his head against the metal wine rack and suffocates on termite gas. It looks like negligence leading to an accidental death, but you say it's a homicide . . . Why?"

"The empty bottle of Armagnac was standing by the corpse . . ."

A flush spreads across Jonas's bald dome. "That your reason?"

"If you drink a whole bottle of booze and bang your head against the wine rack, the bottle will fall and roll some distance away from your body. It won't stand there like a good little clue waiting to be discovered."

"Maybe he finished the bottle, put it down, and then banged his head," Jonas says.

"Maybe," Veasy says. "But the report says he had booze on his pants and shoes like somebody poured it on him to make it look like he was drunk."

"Or he was so drunk he poured it on himself," Jonas says.

"The guy was a connoisseur. He would never get that drunk . . ."

Jonas shrugs as if that point doesn't even deserve answering. "Security cameras?"

"Don't cover the whole area, only front and back doors," says Mineo. "Show only termite guys in blue uniforms. No report of any suspicious persons around the house before tenting . . ."

"I'd like to interview each member of the team individually," Veasy says. "I think the owner is lying."

"Just getting his story straight for the lawsuit," Jonas says. "Kessel have any legal issues? Threats, restraining orders?"

"Nothing. Can't put my finger on it. It just smells like murder."

Jonas clenches his fist. Muscles bulge in his forearm. "Unusual venue, no witnesses, no motive, no clue except for your nose . . . "

"I'd like to keep it open for a week or two," Veasy says. "The case, I mean. Not my nose."

EXTERIOR—MITCH HELFAND'S HOUSE—NIGHT.

Jay made a wardrobe change. He's doing the Perry Ellis thing, white linen slacks and sea-green silk shirt.

"I am the CAMERA," he tells the crew. "It's my point of view."

Party time. Cars are parked at crazy angles in the driveway. "Mitch's formula for success hasn't changed in thirty-five years," Jay says. "Tons of drugs, young chicks for the few old cronies who are still around. If this were the '80s he'd be sure to have a deal by the end of the night."

Jay walks up the gravel driveway. "Motown and laughter," he says. "The party noise is mocking me. Daring me to go through with this."

The door is open. It's a step down into a living room the size of a hotel lobby. "Spanish-Moorish, mish mash," Jay says. "Old wood, exposed beams . . ."

There are at least fifty people in the room. "In the old days I would have known everybody here. I'd get big hellos. The party girls would whisper: that's Jay Braffner, he's a big director. After that I'd have my pick . . ."

Jay stops to compose a sequence. "SWISH PANS, PUSH INS to TIGHT CLOSE UPS . . . Make it very free form. Like action painting on film . . ."

("action painting on film. love it . . .")

In the kitchen Mitch Helfand is dropping sliced avocados into a wooden salad bowl. He's a scruffy little guy, crinkly gray hair, stick arms, and a pot belly. Saggy cutoffs and scuffs. A crew T-shirt from his latest movie *Zombie Smugglers*. A girl in a bikini is slicing lemons next to him.

"Jay Braffner, I thought you were dead," Mitch says.

"Only in television," Jay says.

It's an old joke, but a young crew. Jay pauses to let the chuckles die down.

"Still playing the oldies, Mitch."

"Can't dance to Fitty Cent." Mitch puts his arm around the hottie. "Besides, Marvin Gaye is new to her . . ."

"I love Marvin Gaye," she protests.

Jay holds up the bag. "Pot luck?"

Mitch's eyes widen. Sixty-three years old and still a Hoover. "I thought you were off it."

"Just dried out so I could get wet again. Met a guy in rehab who gets a care package from *La Familia* . . ."

"I'm trying to taper," Mitch says.

"Okay." Jay pockets the bag.

"I said taper, not quit."

"I wanna come, too," the hottie pouts.

"Bad luck, three snouts in the trough," Mitch says. "Let's go to my office."

Jay swipes a bottle of Mumms out of a washbasin full of ice and follows Mitch out to the converted garage in the backyard.

"This new?"

"Yeah. Need a place to get away when the kids are visiting."

Nice little hideaway overlooking the pool. Kitchenette, sleeping area, office space.

"You're gonna love this," Mitch says. He turns on the television. "Closed circuit. I can see every room in the house." Flicks to the bedroom. "Cool, huh? Sometimes I watch my housekeeper screwing the gardener." He giggles. "They do it fast, like guppies . . ."

He puts an album cover on the table. Rick James, *Superfreak*.

"You're living in the past, Mitch," Jay says.

"I'm so old I'm new again," says Mitch. "These cheapo horror movies are like the crap we did for Galaxy, only they open huge and get the first-string reviewers . . . May I?"

He dips his pinky into the bag.

"Don't be so delicate," Jay says. He dumps the bag onto the album. "Go for it, baby . . ."

Mitch finds a knife and cuts the pile into lines.

"Still love the ritual," Jay says.

Mitch rolls up a dollar bill and takes a pachyderm snort.

"PUSH IN to a CLOSE UP," Jay whispers. He draws the latex gloves tightly over his hands. Mitch does the other nostril, then looks up with watering eyes.

"Man, when you fall off the wagon you do it from the penthouse."

"Typical TV line, Mitch," Jay says. "If you think about it too long it won't make any sense."

"Maybe no sense, but a lotta dollars. Good, huh? Think I'll use it . . . May I refresh?"

Jay gives a little bow. "Be my guest . . ."

Mitch snorts two fat lines and falls back onto the couch. "Jesus, Jay . . ."

Jay twists the champagne cork. "Want some bubbly, Mitch?"

Mitch turns green and doubles over. Now he realizes he's in trouble. "What did you give me?"

"Little bit of everything," Jay says. "The shrinks in the hospital give me quite a pharmacopoeia to keep me docile . . ." He pops the cork. "Wash it down with a slug of the bubbly . . ."

"I gotta heave, Jay." Mitch tries to get up, but Jay shoves him down.

"Mitch, you're dead, do I have to draw you a picture?" He jams the bottle into Mitch's mouth and holds it down as Mitch flails, blood and vomit streaming out of the sides of his mouth.

"I guess I'm sorry about you," Jay says. "You were just a clown who got the coke and the chicks . . . But when I wanted to shoot the party scene with seventy-five extras, you only booked ten and it looked like shit. When I said I wanted to knock the victim out with toxic dope and drown him in his pool, you told me the network would never let you use narcotics in a show. Then a few months later I'm watching *Miami Vice* and a bad guy is given poisoned coke and drowns in a pool. And guess who has the writing credit . . . Lester Tarsis."

Mitch makes weird choking noises for a while. Then he gets quiet.

Jay draws the blinds and turns off the light. He sits in the dark, waiting for the party to end. After awhile Mitch's hottie comes to the door and looks in. She knocks . . . "Mitch?" Then she walks back to the house. Doors slam. Cars drive away.

Jay surfs the closed circuit TV until he sees a shot of the pool. He finds a power strip behind the couch and yanks every plug. "No trace of yours truly," he says. "I'll plug it back in when I'm finished."

He slings Mitch over his shoulder like a sack of potatoes, carries him to the deep end of the pool, and dumps him in.

Mitch's head bangs against the edge. His blood spreads darkly through the blue floodlit water.

"Blood in the pool," Jay says. "Timeless noir metaphor."

("brilliant," the crew whispers.)

"Thank you," says Jay.

PILLOW TALK

"Mmm . . ."

Tingley awakens with a sigh of well-being. She stretches and reaches across the bed, pouting drowsily when Veasy isn't there. There is a tap. She turns. A little brown man is at the window, grinning with a mouth full of gold teeth.

Tingley screams:

"Veasy!"

She rolls over, reaching for her pistol in the pile of clothes on the floor.

"Don't shoot, hon," Veasy says. "It's only Gabriel, the maintenance guy."

Tingley ducks under the bed. "Tell him to go away . . ."

Veasy doesn't even look up from his computer. "If you throw him a moon he'll move on. Give him a little boob bounce and butt bobble . . ."

"Is that what your other girls do?"

"Nah, mostly it's me in my boxers. He gets the real show from the tranny hooker a few windows down."

"That's very reassuring." Tingley waves at the man. "Va . . . Va . . . Policía . . ." She flashes her badge. He raises his hands in mock surrender. "How can you live in a dump like this?" she asks.

"You kiddin', this is the best place in LA. Downtown Venice, a block from the beach. Got my espresso, pizza, barbecue, Chinese, all in walking distance . . . Bars on the boardwalk where I can commune with kindred spirits . . ."

"Cops should live around people who understand them."

"That's the Simi Valley syndrome, Cheri. Circle the wagons against the hostile world . . ."

She goes into the bathroom and comes right out again.

"Stinks in there."

"Dude, it's a toilet . . ."

"I mean of weed. It'll get on my skin . . ."

"Use the loofah."

She stands behind him as he takes a last puff.

"Can't get out of bed without it?"

"I'd rather not . . ."

He reaches around and strokes her calf. Her brown eyes soften. She tousles his black hair.

"You need a real home, Tommy."

"Home is where when you have to go there, they have to take you in," Veasy says. "Robert Frost . . ."

"You're white as a ghost. Need more time in the sun."

"Jonas has a nice detail planned for me on the Pier pointing the tourists at the Porta Potties . . ."

"He's on your case," Tingley says. "You're not his kind of cop."

"He's not a fan of my poetry, either."

Tingley kneads his shoulders.

"Why the sudden silence?" Veasy asks. "Do you agree with him?"

Tingley sighs as if she knew this would come up. "For a cop to start reciting stuff is like a weird outburst from a suspect. One of the warning signs of possible aberrant behavior . . ."

"That's one of the best descriptions of poetry I've ever heard."

"He can use it against you, Tommy," Tingley says.

"Not to be corny but poetry saved my life," Veasy says. "Nothing worked for me. The drugs made me crazier, the shrinks sat there all smug like they knew it all when they had never even pulled a guy over for expired plates, let alone tried to find a child killer . . ."

"The Encarnación case?"

"They thought I could talk my way to mental health. It was like asking Humpty Dumpty to put himself back together."

"Because it was a little girl?"

"No. Because I couldn't solve it."

"Motiveless crimes of opportunity are the hardest to crack," she says. "Oh God, I sound like a textbook . . ."

"It's true, there's a clock ticking on a psycho killing. You either figure it out in a few days or you have to wait years and hope to get lucky . . ."

"Happens to every cop."

"Not to me," Veasy says. "I was batting a thousand until then. But then I realized the other cases had been easy, most cases are. Suddenly, someone kills an innocent little girl and I can't find him. I wasn't so special after all. That's what pissed me off . . ."

Tingley turns and starts to make the bed so he won't see the tears in her eyes.

"I went through the whole playbook on this one," Veasy says. "Checked the registered sex offenders in the area. They all had alibis. Went to Theory Two: somebody passing through, a homeless drifter, a tourist, a guy on a business trip. Checked the shelters, the hotels, travel agencies, junkets, groups . . . Twenty hour days, hundreds of names . . . Nothing . . .

"Went back to the scene. People saw Nina—that was her name— on the street. A second later she was gone. Ten people and not one of them remembered a stranger . . . Cleared the neighbors. A lotta times it's a relative or friend, even the dad or mom . . . Not this time . . ."

Tingley squeezes by, eyes averted, to get into the kitchenette.

"I wanted to hypnotize the witnesses," Veasy says. "City Attorney said they had to sign releases. Took time to round the people up. Meanwhile I'm going nuts. I can see this guy getting farther away. I'm checking the wires to see if another child homicide has been reported. Nothing . . ."

Tingley scrubs at a rust spot in the kitchen sink.

"Then, I got a break. Put ten people under. One witness, retired Navy, remembers seeing the meter reader walking through the backyards. A guy like the mailman who you see but don't notice. Nobody had mentioned him first time around, but then some of them are like: oh yeah, the gas guy . . ."

"I find out from the gas company who was working that day. The guy had quit a week after the murder and moved to Redondo Beach. He had a record of domestic disputes. His ex-wife had made a complaint that he was molesting his stepdaughter.

"I couldn't sleep that night. Next morning I drove out to Redondo. Forgot to check in with the local cops. The guy was living on unemployment at his mother's house off the beach. Little weasel, unshaven, scraggly, bad B.O. Nervous at first, can't lull him with small talk. But he gets vicious about his ex-wife. The bitch made that molesting story up, he says . . . There's murder in his eyes for sure . . . I've seen enough . . . He's my guy . . ."

"I run to get a search warrant, but the court is closed. Come back and sit in the car outside his house. Around midnight I see a flame flare in the dark kitchen. I break down the door and catch him burning a pile of photos at the sink. Burn my hand trying to put the fire out. Too late . . ."

"I get on him. What were you burning? Nothing, I don't have to tell you nothing. I'm shakin' him, throwin' him around pretty good. His mother calls the cops . . ."

Veasy breaks off. "The rest is public record," he says. "Redondo PD wanted to crucify me, but Mineo knew people and Streeter talked them into a suspension and a shrinkage. Put me on an indefinite. Said I would have to show progress before they'd let me back on the job . . .

"I refused medication. Shrinks are on a God trip like cops. They don't like it when you argue. They wouldn't clear me . . ."

"They sent me to a poetry therapy class. Me and some burnt-out Iraq vets. This old lady, Doctor Deutsch, I have political problems with the police, she told me. I have political problems with shrinks, I said. I was angry, wanted to shock her so I told her the truth. I can't sleep. I keep seeing the nude body of little Nina Encarnación, hogtied with a dirty rag shoved in her mouth. It was the first time I had ever told that to anybody . . ."

"You do better with women," Tingley says.

"She told me to write a poem about it," Veasy says. "Make sure it rhymes, she said. I want Robert Louis Stevenson, not T. S. Eliot. Made me think about what had really happened. What was really going on in my mind . . . Got me started reading the other lonely nutjobs, Baudelaire, Rimbaud—Emily Dickinson . . . She gave me the 80–20 ratio . . ."

"What's that?"

"You spend 80 percent of your time in reality, 20 percent in fantasy. If those percentages change, you're in trouble. So I spread the 20 percent through the day, writing these little poems . . ."

"What happened to your suspect?" Tingley asks.

"Disappeared. His mom claimed she didn't know where he went. Was he at it again? Who knows? I tried to keep tabs, but hundreds of little girls disappear every year . . ."

"Do you still see the little girl?" Tingley asks.

"Every night," Veasy says. "If I get high enough and read some poetry, the image fades . . ."

Tingley is tearless and ready to come out of the kitchen. "I'm not saying you should stop," she says. "Just don't do it around the boss."

"I don't care what he thinks."

"Why go out of your way to antagonize him?"

"Because he's a bully. He became a cop so he could push people around. Set 'em up. Trap 'em. Turn 'em. Use his power to get sexual favors . . ."

Tingley slaps him in the head. "Okay, so you guessed it . . ."

Veasy slides his hand under her leg and cups her buttock. "I got jealous vibes from him yesterday. You two have a history?"

"I've got my boob in your ear and you want to talk about Jonas?"

"You can always put your boob back . . ."

She steps away. "He was very discreet. Coffee after work to discuss a case. A call on my day off . . . I could see it coming. These guys melt down when their marriages break up. They have to prove they're men again. It wasn't about me."

"Don't be so modest," Veasy says.

"After a few dates he was like, when is this bitch gonna give it up? I could see the hammer hanging over my head. Sudden demotion down to uniform—budget thing, Cheri, sorry . . ."

"So you made the two-backed beast," Veasy says.

"I've got nine years in. One more year and I'm vested at Detective pay. I've got the pension and medical care for me and my little boy."

"And how was your night of love?"

Tingley slides a pot of coffee out from under the Krupp. "How old is this?"

"Younger than me because I made it . . . Answer the question."

"He's got a nice condo in Culver City. Very neat and soulless like him . . . Working fireplace."

"Was he good?" Veasy asks.

"Technically very good," Tingley says with a thoughtful look. "A performer. He watches to see how you react. He wants applause. There's not much in it for him."

"Is he better than me?"

"You're a selfish prick. But I'm here, aren't I?" She blinks and turns away. "Now you think I'm a whore."

"I'm not the judge, ma'am, only the arresting officer." Veasy's phone rings. He checks Caller ID. "It's Mineo . . . Hey boss . . . Okay . . ." Scribbles an address. "Tell 'em not to move the body this time." He disconnects.

"Interesting . . ."

"What now?" Tingley asks.

"Another suspicious death. Mitchell Helfand. And guess what, he's a producer."

AN ULTIMATUM

Jonas's first official act as Chief of La Playita PD was to take down a marijuana operation on the Venice boardwalk. He sent undercovers into Dwayne's, the old surfer bar, and came out with nine kilos, a few guns, and $33,000 in cash. During the raid Dwayne hit one of his officers with a bar stool and had to be tased. He was in his late eighties, but the officer required medical treatment and two weeks convalescent leave.

Jonas didn't expect a heavy sentence for the old man, but he was surprised when the City Attorney accepted a misdemeanor plea, time served, one night in jail, and no supervised probation.

"This isn't a few loose joints, Mr. Streeter," he said. "It's a serious distribution operation plus resisting arrest and assaulting a police officer."

Streeter hardly looked up from his Blackberry. "Dwayne's has been open since 1958," he said. "Dwayne himself is a Venice legend. Did you check out those autographed photos behind the bar? Legendary surfers, movie stars, politicians, everybody wants his picture in Dwayne's."

City Manager Ludwig started packing his attaché case, a dismissive gesture that would become all too familiar to Jonas. "Marijuana enforcement is a poor use of our slender resources," he said. "It's not popular with people here. Frankly, Chief, I don't know why you chose this for your first major operation."

"I wanted to make a statement to the community," Jonas said. "To show that we would enforce the law no matter who was involved."

Streeter's look of quiet scorn would become familiar as well.

"And did you expect the community to rise up as one and give you a round of applause?"

"Tourists come to the La Playita Boardwalk from all over the world," Ludwig said. "They love the unlicensed tattoo parlors, the tacky souvenir vendors, the whores and pervs, the homeless weirdos. Our shady little town is a hundred million dollar industry and you want to turn it into Disneyland."

Streeter slid a copy of his contract across the table. "The agreement that you so obsessively negotiated clearly states that you will engage in no undercover investigation without prior approval of the City Attorney. In the future we expect full compliance."

That was a year ago. Things have gone downhill since then. He hasn't adapted to the lay-back beach town culture. Isn't invited to speak to community groups or throw out the first ball of the Little League season. He's got two years left on his contract. They won't fire him—the city can't afford to pay him off and hire another Chief. Plus, he has developed a constituency of his own, a hard core of pro-life, fundamentalist twelve-steppers who vote as a bloc and resent the tree-hugging metrosexuals who run the city. They would love to hear that the Administration is protecting an unstable, pot-smoking detective.

They better not try to shove Veasy down my throat.

He waits until the Friday morning meeting is over. Until Ludwig, the City Manager, has drawn a thick black Sharpie line through every item on the agenda. City Attorney Streeter has already closed his laptop and packed his attaché case.

"What's the statute of limitation on pity?" he asks.

They look at each other like now what does this guy want?

"Depends on what kind of pity," Streeter says. "Pity in the first degree . . . Pity larceny . . ."

"I want to know how long I'm going to be stuck with Tommy Veasy."

Ludwig raises an eyebrow. "He's been back nine months. Isn't this kind of old news?"

"Not to me. I inherited the guy . . ."

"He had a temporary breakdown," Ludwig says.

"It was the Encarnación homicide," Streeter says. "I'm a father. Little girl kidnapped and murdered. I almost went south on that case myself . . ."

"But you didn't," Jonas says. "You didn't attack a suspect out of your jurisdiction and almost beat him to death, trying to get a confession. Veasy was judged emotionally unfit for the job. Under California regs he was supposed to be terminated, but you made me take him back."

"He was cleared for duty," Streeter says.

"He was reinstated without proper vetting . . ."

"Veasy's made a good record since coming back on the job," Streeter says. He looks at Jonas, suspiciously. "You were okay with it. Why are you changing your mind?"

"Because he's gotten worse. He's undermining my authority."

"In what way?"

"He's unstable. Writes poetry . . ."

"That's not a terminative offense," Ludwig says.

"His responses are not predictable. I have to know how my people are going to react in a given situation . . ."

"I understand your concern," Streeter says. "But as long as he doesn't go outside of department guidelines, there's nothing we can do."

Jonas fights off a wave of irritation.

Can't make this seem like a personal vendetta.

"He's disruptive. Argues about case strategy. He's insubordinate . . ."

"Are you saying he disobeys direct orders?" Streeter asks.

"Not in an obvious way. He just works cases his own way, no matter how I've instructed him. He sneers at me behind my back. Turns the others against me . . . I think he's having an affair with one of my detectives . . ."

"Male or female?" Ludwig asks.

"I'd like to be taken seriously, if that's okay," Jonas says.

Streeter turns to Ludwig. "I could bring a fraternization complaint . . ."

Ludwig waves him off. "This is the twenty-first century. I'm not going to fire two competent detectives, male or female, for having an affair."

Jonas reaches into his case and shuts off the recorder he's been hiding. Then, he leans forward and lowers his voice. "Look, I know there's no love lost here. I know Chief Hoenig quietly retired after it came out that seventeen restaurants on Main Street had been issued illegal outdoor permits and eleven prominent civilians had police parking passes . . ."

"Hoenig had reached retirement age," Ludwig says.

"And I know that I'm the hero DEA agent, who was brought in to clean up Dodge. But only on paper . . ."

"If we didn't like you we wouldn't have hired you," Streeter says.

"You hired the resumé, not the man. You wanted an outsider, a book cop with a clean record who would make you look like reformers, but wouldn't change anything."

Puzzled looks.

"Why such tough talk?" Ludwig asks.

"You've been shooting me down on everything from budget to operations, making it very clear that I'm a lame duck around here."

"No one's ever said that . . ."

"I've cut the crime rate and increased convictions. I have a right to run my department . . ."

"But not as an absolute monarch," Ludwig says.

"I come to you with a simple personnel request . . ."

Streeter gets up. "I've got a staff meeting."

"Veasy is vested," Ludwig says. "He can't be fired unless he gets drunk or rapes a teenager or is dangerously incompetent . . ."

"He's admitting to smoking marijuana," Jonas says.

"It was prescribed by the doctors," Streeter says. "He was officially off the job. He stopped when he was reinstated."

"He's still smoking and you know it," Jonas says.

"Now you're accusing the City Attorney of abetting a felony," Streeter says. "What have *you* been smoking?"

Back in his office, Jonas sees the Helfand report and gets Mineo on the phone.

"Did you send Veasy out on that Helfand job?"

"He's there now."

"Get him off it," Jonas says. "I don't want him on any high-profile cases."

BANISHED TO A BURGLARY

"The chained dog slobbers at death's fetid stink,
  Anxious to unleash
  His predator's kink . . ."
"The neighbor's dog wouldn't shut up," the young cop says. "He almost choked on his chain trying to jump the fence."

Mitch Helfand's body is floating face-down in the pool. Veasy crouches to check a patch of discolored water. "Blood . . ."

"Pretty bad gash on his forehead," the young cop says. "Must have hit his head when he fell in."

Veasy gestures toward the house. "Anybody home?"

"Not now," the young cop says. "They were partying pretty hearty last night. We found cocaine residue, roaches, empty bottles . . ."

"Used condoms?"

"No . . ."

"That means it was a party, not an orgy."

"Detective Veasy just lost interest," Tingley says.

Veasy walks down the path to Helfand's office. Stops to examine something. "Looks like puke over here." Walks further down. "Puke mixed with blood."

"We found drug residue in the *casita* as well," the young cop says.

"*Casita*," Veasy says. "Means little house . . . Pretty language . . ."

"Also an empty bottle of champagne . . ."

"In an ice bucket?"

"No . . ."

"That means Helfand brought it from the main house," Veasy says. "Wanted to be alone with somebody . . ."

"He could have had a bottle in the fridge," Tingley says.

Veasy wags a finger at her. "Don't confuse me with the facts, Detective . . ."

The rusty gate squeaks. Mineo walks in, followed by Detectives Walsh and Guest.

"Backup?" Veasy asks.

"Pinch hitters," says Mineo. "We'll clean up here. There was a home invasion on 21st. Old lady got roughed up pretty bad."

"In other words I'm being pulled off a possible homicide," Veasy says.

Mineo pulls open the gate. "In those words," he says.

Veasy stands his ground. "Can I get Crime Scene to bag the party debris in the main house?"

"This isn't your case, remember?" Mineo says.

"Slipped my mind," Veasy says. "Also, the bottle of champagne in the *casita*. And a few globs of bloody puke on the walk . . ."

Mineo moves in closer and whispers, "In addition to short-term memory loss, I've heard that overuse of marijuana makes you deaf . . ."

Veasy cocks his head. "Come again?"

CREW CALL

In the roaring blackness Jay's calf muscle cramps up.

"Ahh, Christ . . . !"

Shadows flit across his bedroom wall.

("nine A.M., Mr. Braffner.")

"Can't you see I'm in pain . . . ?"

He writhes and slams the bed in agony.

("title sequence, sir.")

Jay stiffens his leg and points his toe until the spasm in his calf subsides. "Symptom of advancing age . . ."

("we're rolling, sir.")

"I know, the show must go on." He takes a breath. The script scrolls down in his mind.

"Open on BLACK SCREEN. We hear the spatter of rain on a tin roof. But as we FADE UP we see it is coffee dripping into a pot."

("cool reveal.")

Jay rolls off the bed. "CAMERA, follow me into the bathroom." He takes a beat to let the dolly catch up.

"Braffner is so tall he has to duck to see his face in the medicine cabinet mirror. He has the deep-set, wounded eyes of a poet, along with the bent, spent body of an ex-athlete, paying with arthritic knees and compressed vertebrae for his early years of gridiron glory . . ."

("eloquent.")

"Thank you," Jay says. "CAMERA, follow me down the hall into the kitchen."

Jay slashes the green mold off a sesame bagel and crams the good parts in the toaster.

But then he sees something in his eye line and shouts:

"CUT!"

Miss Sobel, the social worker, is sitting at the kitchen table staring at him in astonishment, the phone cord still wound tightly around her neck. Nice girl. She came to see how he was doing. *Those meds working, Mr. Braffner? No more voices in your head? No more nighttime visitors? Make sure you keep taking them now that you're on your own. Have something in the morning—bagel or a bowl of oatmeal so you don't irritate your stomach.* Just as she was leaving he had let it slip about the movie. Her eyes got big. Then, she got real casual like they always do when they're about to steal your idea. *Movie? That's great. What's it about?*

He had pulled the old joke. *If I tell you I'll have to kill you.* But she persisted, fiddling in her pocket book like she could care less, but he knew she was recording everything so she could steal it later. *C'mon, tell me, Mr. Braffner.*

So he told her.

"The social worker is collateral damage and not part of the story," Jay says. "I'm going to remove her from the set when I have a chance. Keep her out of the shot for now."

("anything you say, chief . . .")

THE HOME INVASION THAT
WENT TERRIBLY WRONG

*"Chic boutiques
Botox freaks . . ."*
Veasy snaps his fingers as they roll past the clothing stores on Grove
Avenue, the upscale shopping street of La Playita.
*"Welcome to the land of the stealthy wealthy.
Their streets are calmed
By towering palms . . ."*
"You ever get any of this published?" Tingley asks.
"There isn't a huge market for light verse. I might try Hallmark."
Tingley goes north on Margarita. "Those palms were trucked in from
the desert, placed equidistant to one another, and pruned to uniform
heights," she says. "They're supposed to add another quarter of a mil to
the value of the house. But it's not happening in this market."
"Tingley, you are a veritable compendium," Veasy says.
*"The uniform palm's no balm
In the golden Gilead
By the sea . . ."*
They stop in front a gloomy Tudor on 21st Street. It's the oldest
house on a block where Persian mini-palaces mingle with Streamline
split-levels, Eames knockoffs, and pseudo-modern chunks of stone and
glass.
A cop greets them. "Victim is Helen Brownlee. Age 78 . . . Perpetrator
escaped, no witnesses."
A La Playita FD ambulance is in the driveway. A warning sign—
"This premises is protected by ADCOM Systems, Armed Response"—
has been kicked over on the lawn.
They find Mrs. Brownlee under a Tiffany lamp in a room of dark
mahogany. She is holding an ice bag to a purple bruise on her cheekbone.
A studio photo of a young naval officer is on the table next to her.
There's a bandaged splint on her left ring finger.

"The scumbag must have pulled off her wedding band," Veasy whispers. He sits down next to her. "I'm Detective Veasy, Mrs. Brownlee."

She winces as if speaking is painful. "I don't know why I pay all this money for private security services when a man like this can just roam the streets doing whatever he pleases . . ."

"Can you tell me what happened?" Veasy asks.

"He rang the bell and said he was from the city and had to come into the house to turn off the water. He was wearing a La Playita Water Department cap so I thought he was alright. But when I let him in, he bent my fingers back and said take me to the safe. I told him we didn't have a safe and didn't keep a lot of money in the house. He slapped me. I'll kill you if you don't take me to the safe, he said."

"Show me what happened next."

Mrs. Brownlee gets up. Veasy takes her arm, but she pulls away. "I'm fine . . ."

She walks unsteadily up thickly piled steps. In the bedroom, a paramedic is kneeling by a shrunken old man in a Barcalounger.

"Get out," the man screeches. "Get out . . ."

"His heart is going like a jackhammer," the paramedic says, opening his bag.

"Don't give him anything," Mrs. Brownlee says, sharply. "He'll tire himself out after awhile."

"That the handsome naval officer in the picture downstairs?" Veasy asks.

"My husband, yes. He's got dementia. Gets stuck on a word or a phrase like a broken record. Strangers upset him. He started screaming. Shut him up, the man said. He's senile, I told him. I gave him my jewel box and three hundred dollars I keep for the housekeeper to buy groceries. Take me to the safe, he said. We don't have a safe, I told him. That's when he hit me. I must have passed out because the next thing I was on the floor and he had his hands around my husband's neck. Better tell me or I'll kill him. You can kill everybody in the house and we still won't have a safe, I told him. He kicked me in the ribs. If you tell anybody what I look like I'll come back and kill the both of you, he said."

She passes a trembling hand over her eyes. "I heard him slam the door and I broke down, sobbing on the floor. My husband was screaming, but I couldn't get up to help him . . ."

"Sit down, Mrs. Brownlee," Veasy says. He takes her arm and walks her to the bed. Then, in a gentle voice: "We're going to take you to the hospital for X-rays . . ."

She tries to get up. "I'm not leaving my husband . . ."

"Then we'll take him with us. Got room for two?" he asks the paramedic.

"They're not gonna like havin' a feeb in the ER."

"Police emergency." Veasy eases Mrs. Brownlee back on her brocade spread and puts a throw pillow under her feet.

"Is your jewelry insured?" he asks.

"We've got the homeowner's policy, but it's only my mother's pearls and some costume jewelry. With all the rich people on this block I don't know why he picked on us."

"Just relax, now," Veasy says. He strokes her cheek. She closes her eyes. Her lids flutter like a kitten's. He leans close to her and in a caressing, hypnotic voice . . .

"Can you remember what the man looked like?"

"Just ordinary," she says. "Pale and sweaty like he'd been sick."

"Now get a good picture of him in your head. Tell me: what color are his eyes?"

"Blue, but kind of bloodshot like he'd been drinking. He was chewing gum . . ."

"And is he old or young?"

"In his forties, maybe . . ."

"Okay, Helen, rest now." Veasy kisses her lightly on the forehead. "We'll get your stuff back for you . . ."

Tingley watches from the doorway. "That kiss could be considered elder abuse."

"Ever notice how old people live converging lives?" Veasy says. "It doesn't matter who you are or what you were, the road to the grave narrows and everybody ends up on the same path. In bed. In pain. Alone . . ."

"You should send that to Hallmark," Tingley says.

Outside, babies squall in carriages, petulant toddlers fuss and whine. The nannies, timid brown women, watch Veasy with resigned looks, expecting the worst.

"*No soy la migra*," Veasy says to the women. "*Soy su mejor amigo, la policía* . . ."

They smile.

"They got your joke," Tingley says.

"The oppressed invented irony. *Ha visto un hombre extraño aquí?*" he asks.

A young woman steps forward and says in perfect English: "There's been a man in a red van parked here for a couple of days now."

"*Él trabaja aquí?*" Veasy asks.

"No," she says. "He just sat here for an hour or two . . . When we were leaving we saw him drive by again."

Veasy bows. "*Gracias señorita.*"

She half-curtsies. "*Por nada, señor.*"

"Natural aristocrat," Veasy says as they walk to the car. "All she needs is a fan and a plunging neckline and she could play a Contessa . . ."

"And you can be Zorro jumping through the window of her boudoir in the moonlight."

They watch as Mr. Brownlee, strapped to a gurney and holding Mrs. Brownlee's hand, is wheeled to the ambulance.

"A man in a red van stakes out the house for a few days," Veasy says. "He's in his forties, pale like he's been where the sun don't shine. Takes a drink for motivation . . ."

"In other words, a pro," Tingley says.

"Definitely a pro. He spends all this time and energy casing the house, planning the score. He demands the safe, only there is no safe and nothing to steal . . ."

"He had bad information," Tingley says.

"Or he went to the wrong address."

"Flopped the numbers?"

"Maybe . . ."

Veasy taps his teeth with his pen. "Interesting . . ."

"I hate it when you get thoughtful," says Tingley.

"Say it's a contract burglary. The client writes down the address for him. He's out here for a coupla days. Sees an old lady coming and going. Only, it isn't the old lady he's supposed to hit."

"So we look for another old lady up the block . . ."

"Or around the corner. You know why they put a Place with the same number next to a Street?"

"Because they miscounted the streets and had to add one between 21st and 22nd."

"Give this girl a purple lollipop," Veasy says.

"Why does that sound obscene coming from you?"

"Let's see if there's an old lady at 468 21st Place," Veasy says.

They drive around the corner. There are no uniform palms on 21st Place, just a motley collection of neglected trees. The old houses outnumber the new. Shingled bungalows with scraggly lawns.

Veasy starts rapping:

"Tear downs.
They lower the assessment
To create an investment
And the wrecks become specs . . .
That's what going west meant."

468 is an old California Craftsman. Broken bell. Veasy thumps the wrought iron knocker. The door opens on the chain and a white-haired, watery-eyed old woman peeks out.

Veasy holds up the badge. "La Playita police, ma'am. There was a robbery on Twenty-first Street and we're just checking to see if anybody saw anything suspicious . . ."

"It was at Helen Brownlee's, wasn't it?" the woman says.

"Do you know her?"

"Only for fifty years. We were co-founders of Wilshire Baptist."

"Can we come in for a moment . . . ?"

The woman's voice cracks. "Stay where you are. That robber told Helen he was with the water department . . ."

"We're real, ma'am." Veasy hands the woman his card. "You can call headquarters to check us out."

Tingley steps around Veasy. "Has anybody tried to get into the house?"

"Nobody but you."

"Anybody try to break into your safe?" Veasy asks.

"No and they won't either. They'll never find it."

"Live here a long time?" Tingley asks.

"Fifty-seven years in this house. My husband passed away seven years ago."

Tingley offers her card. "Do you have anybody who can come stay with you?"

"I called my daughter in Thousand Oaks. My son's in Portland . . . You can come back tomorrow and talk to whoever shows up."

No parting words. The door slams in their faces.

"How much you think they paid for that house fifty-seven years ago?" Veasy asks.

"Twelve thousand, tops," Tingley says. "It's a double lot, worth over a million, even in this market . . ."

"Your house appreciates
While you deteriorate."

Veasy taps his teeth . . . Tingley slaps at his hand. "Irritating habit . . ."

"I've got a theory," he says. "Our burglar . . ."

Tingley interrupts: ". . . was hired by someone to hit the safe and make it look like a home invasion. He cased 468 Twenty-first Street instead of Twenty-first Place. It's a common mistake, delivery people make it all the time . . ."

"Give a woman your body and the next thing you know she's reading your mind," Veasy says.

CRIME WAVE IN PARADISE

Veasy likes the La Rica Taco Truck; Tingley prefers Tokyo Ramen. They flip a coin and he wins.

A line of laborers is waiting at La Rica as they pull up.

"If you want the best *tamales* / Follow the *ilegales*." Veasy puts the blue light on the dashboard. They see cop and melt away.

He takes a matchbook out of his pocket. "Time for an apéritif . . ."

"What is this, a test of my loyalty?" Tingley says.

Veasy opens the door. "Loyalty not required. I'll take a quick walk."

"Marijuana stays in your system for thirty days," Tingley says.

"I hope so."

"What if Jonas pulls a random drug test?"

"He'll have to fire half the force."

"What if he singles you out?"

"He can't risk an obvious show of personal bias."

"What if he has cause?"

"He won't . . ." Veasy leans forward and kisses her on the cheek. "As long as you don't give me up . . ."

Tingley looks the other way as he digs a tiny roach out of the matchbook.

"This makes me a better cop, you know. Most criminals are high on something. This puts me on their wavelength, helps me think the way they do . . ."

"That sounds like the kind of excuse a criminal would make," Tingley says.

"See, it works. I'm already thinking like a criminal."

A siren bleeps. Mineo pulls up alongside and rolls down his window.

"Busy day," he says. "We got a dognapping on Wilshire. Old man lost his Lab . . . Anything on that home invasion?"

"There's more there than meets the eye," Veasy says.

"We don't think it was a simple crime of opportunity," Tingley says.

"We? Now he's got you drinkin' the Kool-Aid."

Mineo rolls the window up and pulls away, shaking his head.

THE MADMAN PLOTS HIS
NEXT MURDER

"It's called shoe leather in the trade," Jay says. "It's watching a killer set up a hit. If you do it well it keeps the audience entertained while you move the plot . . ."

("you always do it well.")

"Thank you."

Jay drives along the Pacific Coast Highway. "More Hollywood geography. If the beach is on your left you're going north into Malibu and stardom. If it's on your right you've had your fifteen minutes. Hope you saved your money, pal. Now get the fuck out of town."

He turns onto Chautauqua Street and drives up the hill into Palisades.

"Palisades," he narrates. "Place of refuge for the cream of European intelligentsia fleeing the Nazis. Thomas Mann, Lion Feuchtwanger, Igor Stravinsky to name a few . . . Not to mention the English super-esthetes, Huxley, Isherwood . . . Now home to stock swindlers and hack producers . . ."

("bitterly ironic.")

"Producer Gary London lives on a boulevard of lifeless mansions along the bluffs over the ocean. It's like a bomb wiped out all the white people and left their artifacts . . ."

("apt metaphor.")

"The men are at the office. The women in yoga. The kiddies in preschool. You could sacrifice a goat in the middle of the street and nobody would notice. The only cars in the driveways are the rusty old wrecks of the housekeepers."

Jay rings the bell. A small brown lady in a flowered skirt opens the door.

"I'm from Modern Modems," Jay says. "You had some trouble with your Internet connection?"

She shrugs.

"*Dónde están los* computers?" he asks.

("he's even bilingual.")

"Housekeeper Spanish 101," Jay says.

The brown lady leads him through the house to an office in the back. An iMac with a seventeen-inch terminal is on a stainless steel desk with a glass top.

"It's not green to leave the computer on," Jay says. He opens a new Word file and types:

"Three days with no calls. People I've known for thirty years won't return . . . I'm a leper in this town . . . My career is over . . . Everything's going to shit . . ."

He leaves the file "Untitled . . ."

("perfect suicide note.")

"Thank you," Jay says. "Now all we need is the suicide to go with it."

THE COMMANDER SETS A TRAP

Jonas was a hall monitor in middle school. He was a ref for the Youth Soccer League and loved chasing parents off the field. Fresh out of Yorba Linda High, he joined the local PD and spent his first year pepper-spraying protesters in front of the Richard Nixon Memorial Library.

Most of the guys were happy with the life of a small town cop—all the power with none of the risk. But Jonas wanted adventure. He volunteered to infiltrate a meth ring that was operating in neighboring Placentia. They were cooking the stuff in an abandoned Ranger's cabin in Chino State Forest. One night he was spotted by a kid he'd busted for drag racing. "He's a cop, get him!" the kid shouted. Jonas fired a shot into a two-gallon plastic jar of pseudoephedrine hydrochloride. The solution burst into flame. He jumped through a window a second before the stove exploded and the cabin erupted. He called for backup, listening to the screams of the kids trapped inside.

The bust got him a rep as a daredevil and an appointment to the DEA. Even after his hair fell out he looked like a bald young guy, so he could still make buys on college campuses. He liked setting up the suburban wannabes, who thought they were bigtime dealers, and the cool girls who had always highhatted him in high school. Then, somebody put his photo on a website called "Bodysnatchers" with a warning: "Do not sell drugs to this man."

He was transferred to opium interdiction in Istanbul. His favorite move was to plant GPS devices in bags of heroin and drive across the border to Armenia, pretending to be a clueless American smuggler. He'd have a UMV hovering overhead, sending back live video feeds as he bribed the border cops with cash and drugs. Then they would follow the signals back to the barracks and headquarters to bust the generals and customs chiefs as they took their cut. This got him a commendation from the State Department, but no love from the locals. One morning, three motorcyclists pumped sixty bullets into his Suburban, killing his Kurdish driver. He hit the floor and sustained minor lacerations from flying glass, but that was enough to get him early retirement on disability, and he went back to police work.

The DEA is the pit bull of narcotics enforcement. Underfunded, undermanned, and generally mistrusted by the FBI, CIA, ATF, and ICE, it has to lie and cheat to come up with cases that they can't preempt. So even though it is illegal to carry out video surveillance without a warrant, Jonas knows they're watching every medical marijuana store in the state. He calls Romero, the head of the LA office.

"I'm calling in that favor you owe me," he says.

"What favor?" Romero says.

"The one I'm doing you allowing you to operate all over my jurisdiction without officially informing me. You're making buys on the boardwalk, trying to track back to some cartel stooge you're working on. You've got cameras on the medical marijuana store on Venice . . ."

"Oh, you mean *that* favor," Romero says.

"I'm gonna e-mail you a picture of one of my guys," Jonas says. "Tell me if he turns up on your tapes."

"Fax me the photo," Romero says. "DHS is moderating my e-mail."

EXTERIOR—GARY LONDON'S HOUSE—THURSDAY NIGHT

"Nobody looks twice at a man with a dog," Jay says. "I used this gag in a *Murder, She Wrote* and we got these jokey letters from cops saying: thanks, you just gave the bad guys a new trick."

("cops loved that show . . .")

That afternoon he had approached an old Lab with whitened jowls tied up outside the Von's Supermarket on Wilshire and bought its loyalty with raw hamburger. The mutt gobbled it up, licked Jay's fingers in gratitude, and followed him home hoping for more. "Typical Hollywood whore," Jay said, scratching him under the chin.

Now, at nightfall, he takes the dog out. It's an eight-mile walk from his bungalow in Mar Vista to Granada Way, the last block in La Playita. He passes houses where no lights burn. Sees no one for miles. Dressed in black with a black dog he arrives unnoticed at Gary London's house and instructs the crew: "No lights. We'll have enough ambient illumination from the moon, the street lamps, and the little spill from Gary's motion sensor . . . Braffner's looming shadow will morph into his dark form prowling the driveway."

("scary reveal . . .")

"Thank you," Jay says.

Headlights like two burning eyes bounce over the curb. The garage door rises. A black Porsche Panamera rolls in. Gary London, black silk shirt, black slacks, white Nikes, gets out. Armani glasses, trim salt and pepper beard . . . A little man, fastidious about his appearance. He looks up as the shadow looms over the car.

"Long time, huh Gary?" Jay says.

Gary blinks. "Is that Jay Braffner?" He tries to keep it light. "Long time no see."

"I've been playing musical mental hospitals, Gary," Jay says. "Going from one facility to the next. Getting a little crazier each time." He puts a large, latexed hand on Gary's shoulder. "I was wondering if you had read my script."

Gary shrinks as Jay towers over him. "I've been pretty slammed . . ."

"It's a little retro, but I think it'll resonate. About a guy who bounces from detox to rehab, frazzled with meds, brooding about his life and deciding to take revenge on all the jealous little shits who took him down. There's a great scene where the guy kills a producer by faking a suicide. Sound familiar?"

Gary goes for his pocket, but Jay grabs his hand.

"Got one of those panic buttons, Gary? I thought they were only for old ladies who fell in the bathtub . . ."

"For God's sake, Jay," Gary says in a strangled voice. Jay twists his arm behind his back. "Let's sit in your car, Gary." He slams Gary against the door. "Get in . . ." Grabs the bottle of champagne he brought in with him and slides into the passenger seat.

Gary searches frantically through a pile of scripts in the back seat. "It's here somewhere, Jay," he says. "It was on my list to read . . . I was just talking about you to Rafi at dinner . . ."

Jay slaps him hard with his open hand, sending his head crashing against the window.

"There is no script, Gary," Jay says. "You're lying like you lied when you told Lester you had written that carbon monoxide scene . . ."

"Lester had us all plotting against each other . . . Me and Mitch . . ."

"Don't speak ill of the dead, Gary."

Gary's face scrunches with terror. "My God, Jay, did you . . . ?"

Jay grabs Gary by the hair and pulls his head back. "Let's make it a phony suicide, I said. Let's knock the guy out and put him in a car with the motor running. Remember what you said, Gary?"

"It's been a long time, Jay . . ."

"Bawrrring, you said. Then, you pitched the idea to Lester and when I said you had stolen it, you said I was trying to cover up for being too loaded to shoot the big chase scene . . ."

Gary pleads. "I was trying to survive, Jay. Lester had told me I was on thin ice. You had a million ideas, you could afford to give me one."

"Only you didn't ask my permission, Gary."

"But I made up for it, didn't I? I booked you on the show . . ."

"Because Lester told you to give me a shot so he could keep on picking my brain," Jay says. "You're a lying little no-talent weasel, Gary. You never did anything without sticking your nose up Lester's ass first to take his temperature . . . And speaking of asses . . ." Jay sniffs. "I thought I had you scared shitless, Gary, but I guess I was wrong."

Jay turns to the crew.

"Off screen champagne pop," he orders.

("POP!" goes the prop man.)

Jay jams the bottle down Gary's throat. Gary gags and sputters and pulls his head away and sobs:

"Send me your script, Jay."

"Can't steal this one, Gary," Jay says. "This movie is all in my mind."

"I've got a deal at Weinstein. I'll make it happen."

"Famous last words," Jay says.

He slams Gary's head into the steering wheel. Lets him slump unconscious, against the door. Finds the car keys in his pocket.

"PUSH IN tighter," Jay says. "Let's see the keys turning in the ignition. Hear the motor roaring . . ."

("keys turning, motor roaring!")

Jay hits the remote. The garage door starts to creak down. He steps through the smoke and slides under the door onto the driveway as the door closes.

"Get a shot of the smoke seeping under the garage door," Jay says.

("done . . .")

The old black Lab is sleeping under a tree. It totters to its feet at his approach. "Can't be seen with a stolen dog," Jay says.

(anxious whispers.)

"I'll take him back where I got him. His owner will find him tomorrow."

(sighs of relief.)

Jay laughs. "Hey I know the TV rules. Kill as many people as you want, but don't ever harm an animal."

He leads the Lab into the cool night air. "Look at that big, starry western sky." He takes a deep breath.

"God, I love this town," he says.

VEASY THROWS A CURVE

Jonas watches them through the glass windows of his office.

Gotta get through this meeting.

His neck had gone into spasm when he saw the report on Gary London. It had to be suicide. Champagne to get his courage up, motor running, death by carbon monoxide poisoning, suicide note found on his computer. But with Dave Kessel and Mitchell Helfand, that made three producers dead in a week. Probably a statistical oddity, but he could see Veasy snickering with his little clique.

The loneliness of command. All great generals faced it. You were supposed to be the smartest and the bravest. The troops watched you like a hawk for the slightest sign of weakness, always ready to mock.

Get in there and man up.

Jonas picks up his files and his recorder and walks into the conference room.

"Good morning . . ."

Mumbles in return. Then silence. Expectant looks. Just waiting for the Gary London thing to come up.

Deal with it as an accident. Hit the big case first.

He opens a folder. "All other cases are hereby on the back burner until we solve this home invasion. This is a repetitive-compulsive crime. The perp will stay with it until he is caught or decides to move on. We have a lot of seniors who are easy prey. So I want to get him off the street before he strikes again . . ."

He points at Captain Moritz, chief of patrol. "Flood the area with a uniform presence, patrols on the street 24–7." Moritz nods and makes a note. He points at Mineo. "I want detectives canvassing every block so the people in the neighborhood know we're on this and won't let it happen again."

Mineo nods, his jaw muscles fluttering.

They hate it when I point at them.

"Uh Chief," Veasy says.

He's going to bring up the London thing.

"I'm not so sure our guy is a serial home invader."

Another challenge?
Is he bucking me on every case?
"Why is that?" Jonas asks.
Tingley leans back and tries to catch Veasy's eye.
Trying to shut him up.
"For one thing the description doesn't fit the profile," Veasy says. "Daytime home invaders play young and preppy so they can gain access to the houses. They often work with a female accomplice and pretend to be selling magazines or need to call triple A for a jump because their phone is dead. This guy is older, a little seedy, and seems to have been drinking. Also, he was wearing a water department cap . . ."

"So that was his Trojan horse," Jonas says.

"But unless he works for the water department he had to get that cap, which means he had to plan this score."

Don't let him provoke you.

"Maybe he's had the cap for years. Maybe he found it. Maybe he stole it or maybe he's a bitter employee of the water department now embarked on a life of crime . . ."

"Housekeepers say they saw a red van in front of the house the day before and on the day of the robbery. Sounds like he was casing it."

Can't get into a pissing contest.

"Home invasions are often carefully planned," he says.

"Usually by insiders," Veasy says. "Gardeners, domestic help, relatives, even neighbors—people who know what they're after. This guy planned the score and then came up empty. He kept asking Mrs. Brownlee for the safe, but she doesn't have one . . ."

"Maybe he was just taking a stab. Most seniors have safes or lockboxes."

Veasy has the secret smile of a poker player who just pulled a check-raise. "On a hunch, we went around the corner to 468 21st Place. There's an elderly widow living there. She does have a safe . . ."

Jonas drums his fingers to show impatience. "And your point is?"

"I think our guy was hired to hit 468 21st Place and make it look like a home invasion, but went to 468 21st Street by mistake."

"A home invasion to the wrong home?"

"Two of the same numbered streets. It's a common mistake. Delivery people make it all the time."

Stay in control. Demonstrate concern with the larger issue.

"The important thing here is to reassure the neighborhood," Jonas says. "Veasy, you go out with Mineo. Hit every house and make sure you talk to residents, not housekeepers. I want people to know we're on this. Tingley, you stay here and work that dope ring at the high school. See if there's gang involvement."

Tingley looks like she's about to burst into tears.

That's right, bitch. I'm breaking up your beautiful friendship.

Then, keeping his tone casual: "Anything new on that dead producer?"

"Which one?" Veasy asks, doodling on his pad.

Don't take the bait.

"Gary London," he says.

Mineo shuffles papers. "Waiting for the pathologist's report."

"The missing social worker?"

Detective Walsh checks his notes. "Still missing. Boyfriend says she usually calls at least twice a day . . ."

"One piece of good news," Moritz says. "The guy who reported his dog missing found it in the same place he left it."

"A prank?" Jonas asks.

"He doesn't know who did it or why."

"Interesting," Veasy says. He taps his teeth with his pencil. "Why would somebody take a guy's dog, keep it for the night, and then return it the next day?"

"The dog is back, Veasy," Jonas says. He looks around the room with mock incredulity. "I think we can safely say the case is closed."

They could make points forever by shooting him a smile. But nobody cracks.

They really hate my guts.

THREE CASE PILEUP

Mineo turns onto the 10 Freeway. "You really think this was a contract burglary or are you just sticking it to the boss?"

"Both," Veasy says.

"And do you really think some dude's running around killing producers?"

"He won't stop killin' / Until we chill him."

"Serial killers, botched home invasions. What's next in your marijuana mind, alien invaders?"

"They've been here for years."

"Not in our sleepy little beach town," Mineo says.

"This ain't no marijuana modality / This is sho'nuf reality."

Two patrol cars speed by them, sirens blaring.

"I suppose those guys are going to get old Mrs. Doheny's cat out of a tree," Veasy says. "Why don't you drive past the street where the orange groves used to be? Oh, because that's where the Graveyard Crips and the Kansas Posse had a shootout over the multimillion-dollar drug trade on the pier. Or the bungalows that Douglas Aircraft built for its workers after World War Two. That's where the coyotes kept a whorehouse with the Guatemalan girls they smuggled in." He pokes Mineo. "Cut the myopia / You ain't livin' in utopia."

Up ahead the patrol cars have pulled over a pickup truck full of Mexican workers. The cops are approaching, guns drawn. The driver of the pickup steps out with his hands over his head.

"You'll get yourself in trouble cryin' serial killer," Mineo says.

"Better to cry / Than to deny . . . Three well-known, otherwise healthy producers die under mysterious circumstances in a three-day period . . ."

"Three older guys, drug problems, divorce and career issues," Mineo says. "Just another day in LA . . ."

Veasy persists. "These deaths are too similar in too many respects."

"They're not similar at all. Kessel passed out in his house and was killed by termite poison. The autopsy on Helfand listed seven different drugs present in his system . . ."

"Kessel was a collector. He would never guzzle a whole bottle of vintage armagnac, even if his marriage was breaking up. Helfand was a hardcore partier. He wouldn't mix and match like a college binger. They found Oxycodone in his nostrils, Lexapro, Xanax, and cocaine . . . Tequila, champagne, Ativan in his gut . . . Anyway, two dead producers is a coincidence. Three is a pattern . . ."

"Gary London killed himself," Mineo says. "Dude sat in his Porsche with the motor running. No witnesses . . ."

"He had no motive," Veasy says.

"His latest picture was a flop. His option at Warner's hadn't been picked up . . ."

"If that was a motive we'd have dead producers washing up all over . . ."

"His wife found a suicide note on his computer."

"The murderer could have written that."

"Snuck into the bedroom while she was asleep?"

"What odds you givin' she was zonked on Xanax plus Ambien?"

On the freeway the Mexican guys are sitting on the shoulder with cops standing over them. A sergeant is searching the truck.

"You're reaching for something that isn't there," Mineo says.

The sergeant finds a small paper bag under the seat and holds it up triumphantly.

"Could be," Veasy says. "Could also be the biggest case since O. J. . . ."

ESTABLISH THE
UNSUSPECTING VICTIM

It's a call girl operation. They call it Hollywood Production Services so the clients can use it as a tax deduction. But it never fools the IRS and they collect interest and penalties from hundreds of men every year.

On Saturday, Lester Tarsis books Cassie for a thousand an hour. He takes her to the Ivy on Ocean Avenue for brunch. She wolfs down the shrimp and avocado salad with a couple of Diet Cokes. She's a skinny blonde with avid eyes. Watching her eat he remembers all the hungry young girls, day players, extras, wardrobe assistants, brushing their hair off their faces as they ate. Twenty, thirty years ago Cassie would have been one of them out on a legitimate date with the producer. It was called a "career hump" and there was no shame attached. If the girl was an extra, Lester would pay her off with a line of dialogue, which was an upgrade to day player and meant more money and a small residual. He'd give the day players a few more lines or even another scene, which meant they'd work an extra day and get a week's pay. It was a head start for some of them and they almost liked him for it. They'd wave to him in restaurants, introduce him as "the guy who gave me my big break." Promise to thank him when they got their Oscars.

Nobody dreams of stardom anymore. Cassie is just a whore in it for the cash. She talks about the ballplayers she dates. How they call her when they come into town or fly her out to Vegas. Watching her eat and listening to her prattle, the lust begins to rise in a warm wave. He ducks into the bathroom and pops a Viagra. Has a double espresso to ramp it up. By the time they've walked the few blocks back to his complex he's ready.

On Sunday, it's Jennifer, the star of the stable, two hours, two thousand per. She comes in the afternoon and sits by the pool in her string bikini as if she were his date. Lester rubs lotion onto her bare back and they play gin for an hour. She's a petite, sullen brunette, built like a Playboy cartoon. Her contempt turns him on.

He tells her Hollywood war stories. "You hate everybody," she says. "Did you ever work with anybody you liked?"

"Did you?" he asks.

She likes to smoke so he scores some weed from Zack, the assistant editor. Three tokes and it hits him like a ton of bricks. He tells her to take off the bikini and walk around.

"Want me to leave the heels on?" she asks.

"No, barefoot will be fine." He's so stoned he forgets to take the Viagra and has to book her for another hour while he's waiting for it to kick in.

"You should try Cialis," she says. "It's good for the whole weekend."

He wants to stick his nose between her legs and just smell her, but he knows that would be considered sicker than whips and chains.

"You do scenes with girls?" he asks.

"Sure, if that's what you want," she says.

"With Cassie?"

She makes a face. "If you don't mind, I'd rather bring somebody. Girl on girl is personal for me . . ."

Then, she's had enough socializing. She lays back on the couch and fingers herself. "C'mon baby, while I'm in the mood."

Fifteen minutes later she's gone. Lester calls for a pizza and falls asleep watching Sports Center.

He dreams that Jennifer is brandishing a big, black vibrator. "Bend over little boy," she says.

He wakes up. It's his phone vibrating in his pocket.

"You have two voice mails . . ."

One is his ex, Claire, in hysteria mode.

"Seth was arrested again, Lester. He was breaking into the Rite Aid on Wilshire to steal their drugs. They chased him with dogs and helicopters . . . The police say we have to send him to a lockup or they're going to put him in Juvie . . ." She sells it with a gulping sob. "I can't deal with this anymore, Lester. You have to take over . . ."

Lester does a quick calculation. Seth was conceived in a wardrobe trailer in Toronto eighteen years ago. He lived with Lester for less than a year and with support, alimony, private school, therapy, and now this drug thing, he has already cost close to a million bucks. Now, Lester will have to spring for a lawyer, a psychologist, and a rehab trap at twenty K a week and the little prick will get stoned as soon as he hits the street.

The other message is from David Owen, the New Zealand distributor of his syndicated show.

"Looks like we lost the Serbia, Croatia, and Bosnia territory, Lester," he says. "Kenya hasn't called to renew, either. Altogether we'll have to trim fifteen thousand off the production budget for the coming season just to break even. I've got a couple of ideas so give me a call when you wake up . . ."

Owen's idea is to find a tactful way of getting rid of him. Lester has seen that ax over his head for a year. He punches up the Charles Schwab account. Six mil and change . . . He'll be sixty-three in October. He'll have his Writer's Guild pension, early retirement, the munis, and the apartments in Northridge. His pressure is low, cholesterol under control. Prostate? "I've seen bigger," Doctor Pine says. He's got good genes. Dad keeled over at Aqueduct when he was fifty-six. Uncle Sid made the joke at the funeral. "Why do Jewish men die before their wives? They get tired of waiting." But Mom's in her eighties, doing needlepoint and folk dancing at the Amalgamated Home in West Palm.

Except for that little snot Seth, he's been smart with his money. When the gravy train comes to the last stop he'll be okay. He'll just have to cut down to one hooker a week.

FREEWAY TO REVENGE

It's ten-thirty. "Can't wait for the sun to burn off the marine layer," Jay says. "STEADICAM follow me out of the house."

Jay narrates as he walks:

"The screen door bangs and bounces behind Braffner. There are bricks missing from the narrow path. Branches from a scruffy, unpruned bush scrape his face. He walks through tendrils of sprinkler mist . . ."

("poetic.")

"Thank you," Jay says and continues:

"At the curb an '87 Mercedes 450 with a crumpled fender is parked over the red line, tickets fluttering like trapped birds in its wipers. The motor roars like an elderly lion . . ."

Jay switches on the jazz station. "Get an INSERT of Braffner's hands on the dial," he says. "We'll use it as a time cut."

("INSERT hands . . .")

He merges onto the 10 Freeway.

"Cool laybacked brushes," he says. "Lilting saxes. Jazz is the definitive California soundtrack. Coppola got it right in Godfather I. When the plane sets down in LA he put a cool jazz cue under it . . ."

(appreciative silence.)

"The networks hated jazz," Jay says. "So all the toadies fell into line. Jazz is the kiss of death on primetime, Mitch said. And Gary sat there shaking his head. Whaddya think this is, the '50s? I pleaded with them. Let's do something different for God's sake, I said. Let's be filmmakers. They laughed. Look at Federico fuckin' Fellini over here, Dave Kessel said. Next thing I know Lester hires Henry Mancini to write a jazz theme for *Babes in Blue*."

(murmurs of sympathy.)

"Their faces were bulging like out of a fisheye lens," Jay says. "Their laughter echoed like the reverb in a '50s horror flick. I started screaming at them: YOU FUCKIN' HACKS! YOU STOLE MY IDEA! Next thing I knew Lester had me by the arm in the parking lot. Stop scaring the staff, Jay, he said. Help me Lester, I said. I'm a man running down an endless

GREEN LIGHT FOR MURDER

corridor pursued by demonic laughter. I'm the star of the horror movie in my head. I don't know what's real anymore . . ."

("Riveting dialogue," someone whispers.)

"Go home and sleep it off, Lester said. But I've been clean for months, I said. Then go get loaded, Jay, he said. 'Cause you are out of your fuckin' mind."

A blonde in a red Testarossa convertible, hair flying, tan legs in a flesh-pink bikini bottom, whooshes by in the left lane.

"Look at that," Jay says. "Where else on the planet would you see a half-naked intergalactic piece of ass like that on a public thoroughfare?"

("only in LA.")

Jay speeds up. "PAN OFF me to the Ferrari," Jay shouts. "Drive abreast of the blonde, if you'll pardon the pun . . ."

(giggles.)

"It's taken twenty years to get this picture greenlighted," Jay says. "But now I'm on my way to kill Lester Tarsis and make cinema history at the same time. Fade up my credit."

It appears in blue letters, right over the diamond sparkling in her navel.

"A JAY BRAFFNER FILM . . ."

"Perfect!"

("we put your name above the title, chief.")

Jay is suddenly humble. "Thank you," he says.

BETTER SOLVING THROUGH TECHNOLOGY

"Have no fear, Angelina, Kate, or Paris,
 None of you I will ever harass.
 I just want to be alone
 With my iPhone."
Mineo tries to keep a straight face.

"Don't laugh, you'll just encourage me," Veasy says.

"Your iPhone gonna tell you who the serial killer is?" Mineo asks.

"If I use it right," Veasy says. He whips out the phone. "First, I punch up Internet Movie Database. In seconds I see every movie and TV show the three dead producers ever worked on. Now I make a file of the companies they all worked for together—cheap '70s horror movies at Galaxy Films, TV series in the '80s for Noah Reading Productions. Here's a show they all worked on—*Autocop*. The Executive Producer on that show was Lester Tarsis. Now what do I do?"

"You look up Lester Tarsis," Mineo says.

"Correct . . ." Veasy thumbs the keyboard . . . "Okay, so I find one movie credit for Lester Tarsis. *The Mad Bomber*. 1976. Cineart Films, Sig Shapiro, exec-producer. Screenplay Lester Tarsis. Directed by Jay Braffner. It's gotten 8.5 out of 10 on the viewer rating scale. Rave user review: The chilling true story that roiled the placid waters of the '50s. George Metesky, a meek, retiring bachelor who lived with his sisters, terrorized the city, planting bombs in public buildings and corporate offices for sixteen years. In an auspicious debut, young filmmaker Jay Braffner dares us to look into the horror of a man's soul and find redemption . . ."

"I'll have to Netflix it," Mineo says.

"No DVD or VHS listed," Veasy says. "It's barely a footnote in cinema history. Lester Tarsis never wrote another movie again." He thumbs the keyboard. "Lester Tarsis is now the producer of—*She, Queen of the Jungle*."

"That's the show with the blonde with the big ass who swings through the trees," Mineo says.

Veasy thumbs the keyboard. "Now I generate a cast and crew list for every episode in the show. Each of these guys was a producer in various seasons. I want to see if any other names keep coming up in the episodes they worked on. I do all this without using a second of department time . . ."

Mineo pulls off the Freeway at 20th street. "Okay, now let's work on this home invader . . ."

THE MADMAN PLANTS THE BOMB

"Driving from Santa Monica to Hollywood is like traveling into another dimension," Jay narrates.

"La Brea Boulevard . . . Black-coated, white-bearded, fur-hatted Hasidic Jews leading a column of side-locked boys . . . Orange Street . . . Transvestite hooker, head of a desperate housewife, body of a wide receiver, comatose in the doorway of a postproduction house . . ."

Jay pulls up to an old Hollywood building.

"Split-level '50s. Nondescript—you can use it for any kind of dilapidated noir setting."

There are plenty of Visitors spaces, but he drives to the far end of the parking lot and takes a long walk back to give the soundtrack a chance to build suspense.

"CAMERA is my eyes," Jay tells the crew.

("your POV, boss.")

"A rusty chainlink gate squeals onto a narrow walkway overgrown with California Wax Myrtle bushes," Jay narrates. "Braffner's hands open the door onto a shadowy corridor. DOLLY DOWN past photos of forgotten stars, Charles Boyer, Ida Lupino, Chuck Connors . . . Right up to a door with a sign reading: LESTER TARSIS PRODUCTIONS. There's a poster of Finola Newton, the star of *She, Queen of the Jungle*, in a leopard-skin bikini with co-star Charley the Chimp sitting at her feet . . ."

("co-star, that's hilarious.")

"Now Braffner walks into his close-up," Jay says.

("fluid camera move!")

"Thank you," Jay says. He takes a gleaming metallic pick out of his fanny pack . . . The sprung lock clicks and the door inches open.

"Braffner knows there are no alarms, no security systems in the production office. He was there when Lester bribed the insurance guy into letting him overvalue the office equipment so if there were a burglary he could collect for three times its worth . . ."

("what a conniver . . .")

"CAMERA follow Braffner as he moves stealthily into Lester's office," Jay says.

He goes behind the desk and unscrews the top of Lester's phone. Places the plastic explosive in the receiver and snaps the top back.

Places another piece on the underside of the desk and secures it with duct tape.

"The electric charge from Jay's phone will detonate the bomb in the phone," he says. "The heat and pressure from the first explosion will detonate the second."

("ingenious.")

"May I help you?"

("shit!")

A skinny redhead in a long skirt and a pleated white blouse is in the doorway.

(frantic rustling of pages.)

("she's not in the script.")

Jay ad-libs:

"I just wanted to drop a picture and resumé off for Mr. Tarsis."

"How'd you get in here?" the girl asks.

"Front door was open."

She has smooth white skin, pale blue eyes. Nice long legs under the skirt. Left nipple print on the blouse shows she's excited.

"We don't cast here," the girl says. "The show shoots in New Zealand . . ."

Jay puts his hands in his pockets to hide the latex gloves. "What's your name, dear?"

"Eloise Gruber."

"Can I just leave my resumé for future reference, Eloise?"

"Mr. Tarsis doesn't let me keep resumés or even talk to actors," she says. "He says it was an out-of-work actor who killed Abe Lincoln and destroyed America's chance for greatness. I never know if he's kidding or serious . . ."

"A little bit of both, probably, if you know Lester," Jay says.

"You know Lester?" she asks.

That was a slip. Now she has to die.

Jay pastes on a hopeful smile and comes around the desk.

"I have a niece in Auckland. I could work as a local hire."

The crew has gone dead quiet. Have to move quickly. He slips his hands out of his pockets . . .

"Am I interrupting something?"

("shit! shit!")

A kid is in the doorway. Snotty techie type . . . Stubbly shrimp in cargo shorts.

"He's just dropping off his resumé, Zack," the girl says.

"We don't hire American actors," the kid says. "Union thing . . ."·

"Are you a producer, Zack?" Jay asks.

The kid sniffs. "Assistant editor, but I know how the show is cast."

"He wasn't being snotty, Zack," the girl says. "He knows Lester . . ."

"Just leave your picture and resumé," the kid says, using his little thimble of power.

(now he's gotta die, too.)

Jay turns away so they don't see the gloves and pretends to look in the Halliburton. Then, with an "aw shucks" chuckle:

"Well, this is awkward. After all this drama I don't have a picture . . ."

"Just leave your name, we'll look you up in the Player's Guide," the kid says.

"No, no, it's okay . . . I'll go home and get a picture . . ."

"Good luck," Eloise says with a sad smile.

"New here," Jay tells the crew as he walks down the hall. "This town is tough on sweet girls. She'll go from one loser to another. End up nursing some failed druggie in a garden apartment in the Valley . . ."

("she'll be better off dead.")

"The kid is one of the invisibles as Lester used to call them. The assistants, the runners. The guys who bring in the menus . . . So he doesn't show up for work one day . . ."

("nobody will miss him.")

BACKSTORY OF AN INVISIBLE

Zack Toledano watches the big old dude, zigzagging down the hall, arms flailing, muttering to himself. Back in the cutting room he posts on his status page:

"Just saw another Hollywood casualty. Sixty-year-old bit actor trying to slip an 8×10 into the producer's desk. So much bizarre shit out here . . ."

Facebook is the only chance Zack has to do any serious writing. "Hollywood is a mirage," he posted this morning. "Even the weather is bogus. Mornings are puddle-colored. 'June gloom' the locals call it and say it'll 'burn off' by noon. Sunsets are beautiful because the light turns pink when it's refracted through brown clouds of pollution. Forget the women unless you have money. Even the bow wows who can't get into the clubs ask you what you're driving . . ."

He hardly had time to admire his prose when he got a reply from Beth, his college girlfriend.

"What, no adoring bow wow hanging on your every word . . . ?" It's like she was hovering over his page, waiting to pounce . . . "No supermodels swooning at your magic touch? Bet you thought that puddle-color line was so poetic."

Why is she so angry? The sex wasn't so great for him either, but he doesn't hold a grudge. And why are all his old film school friends rooting against him? Even his brother writes on his wall: "better watch out that sixty-year-old nobody isn't you in thirty-five years . . ."

It's because they're scrounging for square jobs and he's still chasing the dream. They're petrified that he'll make it. That they'll see his movies everywhere, read about him on Page Six, signing to do another big picture or hanging with another hot celeb, while they're sweating the rent.

A lot of negative energy coming at him. Maybe that's why he's having so much trouble. He's been out of NYU for a year. Can't get an agent, can't get anybody to read his scripts. Can't even get a job taking tickets at an art house. They don't hire people from East Coast film schools.

Actually, he had almost given up. Starbucks turned him down and he was applying at Coffee Bean when he saw an ad on Craigslist. "Assistant Editor wanted . . . Must know Final Cut Pro and be prepared to work long hours." Met Elliot, the editor, in the old Tower Records parking lot on Sunset like it was a dope deal.

"This is a nonunion job," Elliot said, looking around furtively. "Six hundred a week. No benefits . . ."

He immediately tweeted: "Editing *She, Queen of the Jungle*. Hours of Finola Newton in a leopard-skin bikini. Whoopee!"

Adam, his film school rival, tweeted back. "Congrats to Zack. A fatass, fortyish Australian ex-stripper will let him Photoshop her cellulite . . ."

"At least I'm not teaching second grade," he tweeted back.

Twitter silence told him he had scored big time.

But the thrill of "working in the business" didn't last beyond Zack's first day when he was given his duties—digitizing hours of footage, going on lunch and coffee runs, picking up Lester's dry cleaning, and telling Elliot's wife he's in a meeting. He's been on the show for eight months, working sixty-hour weeks and Lester Tarsis still calls him Josh.

"Josh was the last assistant," Elliot explains. "If it makes you feel any better he'll call the next guy Zack . . ."

Every Thursday, Lester asks: "Josh, can you get me something for the weekend?" Zack scores a twenty-dollar bag from the *vatos* on the Venice boardwalk, takes out a taste for himself, and charges Lester double.

Lester pays him in overtime. "Put in an extra fifteen hours," he says.

It's a cheap trick. Zack is putting in the time anyway. *She, Queen of the Jungle* is shot nonunion in New Zealand so they can work two crews all weekend at low rates without paying overtime or benefits. They courier the hard drives of thirty hours of raw footage to the editing room. Zack comes in Sunday afternoon just after the football games and starts to digitize. Elliot comes in after midnight and they make a rough cut. Lester comes in Monday morning at ten. He sits there popping Maalox and recuts everything they did. Elliot fumes, but Zack watches in amazement as he makes the film come alive. He knows every take of every scene they shot and remembers little moments here and there that can be stitched together to make a sequence. Finola Newton is barely phoning it in, but he can finesse the footage to cut her a performance.

"In his own way Lester Tarsis is kind of a genius," Zack posts on Facebook. Adam writes back: "Dude you have definitely pulled into the Hollywood Brainwash." But Zack has the pop culture high ground. "Dude, you don't get it," he replies. "I defy any pantheon *auteur* to create 198 watchable episodes about a bitch in a leopard-skin bikini. That's filmmaking, bra . . ."

Zack has watched every one of those 198 episodes and actually found a story they never did. He calls it "Ayeesha's Long-Lost Mother." A mysterious stranger appears in the jungle and promises to reunite *She* with the mother she never knew. But it turns out to be a trap concocted by evil white men who want her to lead them to the emerald mine deep in the jungle. He tried to sell it to Lester.

"Can't film a pitch," Lester said. "Write it."

Zack wrote and rewrote the script so many times the words lost their meaning. He finally dropped it on Lester's desk one afternoon. Lester took one look. "Never submit a script with coffee stains," he said. Zack reprinted it and dropped it off the next day. He also sent a copy to David Owen, the New Zealand distributor, with a note saying how much he'd like to work on the show. Hasn't heard back.

A TICKING CLOCK

Veasy and Mineo go from house to house on 21st Place. Nobody's home but the housekeepers.

"I don't think we're gonna need backup on this detail. Why don't you take 22nd Street."

"I feel rejected," Mineo says.

Veasy texts Tingley. "Need you . . ."

Tingley calls back.

"What now?"

"A producer named Lester Tarsis worked with the three victims at Galaxy Films."

"They're not officially victims yet."

"Okay, if you want to get technical. The three decedents worked as co-producers with Tarsis on a bunch of shows at Noah Reading Productions. And they worked for him on a show called *She, Queen of the Jungle*."

"Don't know it," Tingley says.

"Tarty blonde with a big booty. Mineo has every episode on his iPod . . ."

"Don't start that rumor," Mineo says.

"IMDB the cast and crew list and see if you can come up with more overlapping names . . . Then go back to the credits and see if these people worked on other shows with the dead guys."

Tingley drops her voice. "I've gotta get back to Jonas on this high school pot bust. He thinks it's gang related . . ."

"This won't take long. You can do it on your iPhone. I would handle it, but I'm on this home invasion."

"So, do it when you finish," Tingley says. "What's the hurry?"

"Call me crazy," Veasy says, "but I'd kinda like to stop this guy from killing again."

LOVE INTEREST

This is Eloise Gruber's second season with the show and she is, by her own admission, "desperately, tragically in love with Lester Tarsis."

"Lester doesn't look at me as a woman," she confides to her diary. "He goes for the girls from that escort service. I can smell their cheap perfume on him every Monday morning."

Eloise wants everything to be perfect for Lester. He likes the office cold, "like the frozen food aisle at Ralph's at three A.M.," he says. So she always comes in an hour early to get the AC started.

But this morning that desperate actor had distracted her. Then Zack, that little snot, had burst in and driven the AC right out of her mind. At five to ten she puts it on "High Cool." A minute later Lester strolls in. Everything on him is soft—the battered shirt and pleated slacks, the suede Adidas walking shoes, even the darling mound of belly over his belt. But he is all baggy-eyed and scowly and Eloise can tell he had one of those girls over the weekend. They always make him irritable.

Lester breathes "whew," and mimes mopping his face. "Hot as Hades in here. That's what you folks call it in Missourah, right?"

What a relief! He's kidding, which means he isn't really mad.

"We call it H. E. double hockey sticks, Lester," she says.

Eloise washes Lester's blue cup and pours fresh coffee, placing one Splenda and a soy creamer on the desk at his right hand. He is slouching in his special, ergonomic chair with that little head-tilting smirk he gets while he is reading a script. She loves to watch him slide his pen over the words, pausing to jot a note in the margin. Sometimes, for no apparent reason, he'll sigh as if a sad thought had just entered his mind.

This morning he seems distracted. He tilts his head and looks at her for such a long time she thinks her face is going to burst into flame.

"You went to a religious college, didn't you, Eloise?"

"Missouri Lutheran."

"A woman of valor, who can find?" he said. "Her worth is more than pearls . . . Where is that from?"

"Book of Proverbs, isn't it?"

"So it is," he said. "Turned into a hymn that religious Jews sing on Sabbath Eve in praise of their wives who have cooked the Sabbath meal, cleaned the house, raised the children to be pious and respectful . . ."

He has never made small talk with her before. How she would love to banter with him like the writers do. Even stupid old Zack can come up with a smarty pants remark. But she doesn't know how.

"I didn't know you had a religious upbringing, Lester," she says.

"I went to Hebrew school three days a week," he said. "Sat in the back and played with myself. Couldn't keep my hands out of my pants."

He likes to shock her. She tries to blush even deeper to please him.

"Are you a woman of valor?" he asks.

"That will be up to my future husband to decide," she says, hoping that doesn't sound too prim.

Lester puckers and blinks like a little boy who's had his feelings hurt and doesn't want to show it.

"This is my last season, Eloise," he says.

"Gosh, Lester," she says and thinks *omigod where did that stupid Gosh come from?* "Are they canceling the show?"

"They're canceling me," he says. "They won't renew my deal."

"It's your show. You created it."

"But I don't own it."

He nods, as if confirming it to himself. "I'm on wheels, Eloise. I'm just telling you so you can start looking for something else."

"Thanks, but I guess I'll stay to the bitter end," she says.

"If you think I'm gonna catch on somewhere else and take you with me, I won't."

"I'll stay anyway," Eloise says.

"Don't say I didn't warn you."

"I won't, Lester." She feels the tears welling. "And thank you so much for thinking of me. I really appreciate all that you've . . ."

He waves impatiently. She bites hard on her lip.

Hollywood rules. Feelings are phony. Everyone has an agenda.

"This is our secret," he says. "I don't want the rest of the rats leaving the sinking ship."

Eloise scootches a little closer. "It's our secret."

She could touch him now. Hug him real hard. Smooth the fine, silvery hairs over his mottled bald spot. Kiss his full lips with her mouth open so she could feel the bristle of his mustache and the soft brush of his beard. Rock him like a baby in her arms and tell him everything will be fine.

"After all," Lester says. "I still have a show to run."

CAUGHT IN THE ACT

It's so quiet Tingley can hear the cars whooshing by on the freeway. No one in the office. She punches up IMDB on her iPhone. Searches *She, Queen of the Jungle*. Clicks on "cast and crew." Nine years of shows. This will take forever.

"Checking your messages?"

It's Jonas looking over her shoulder.

Did he take his shoes off and tiptoe up?

"Just searching something," she says.

He takes her wrist and gently turns the phone.

"*She, Queen of the Jungle* . . . Wasn't David Kessel a producer on that show?"

"Kessel and Mitchell Helfand," she says. "And Gary London as well."

"Really. Quite a coincidence. But I guess he doesn't think so."

He hates Veasy so much he can't even say his name.

"He thinks all three were murdered."

"I guess."

He sits down and stares into her eyes with that searching look men get when they're hurt or jealous. Like they don't know whether to burst into tears or smack you in the face.

"Doing a little legwork for him?"

She tries to smile her way out of it. "Just researching the three guys. As a favor . . ."

"He shouldn't be presuming on your friendship like that."

Now she feels disloyal. "There is a thread. They all knew each other. All worked on the show for the same producer."

"You know what he's doing, don't you?" Jonas asks.

"He's trying to establish a link between the decedents . . ."

"There's no link and he knows it." Jonas leans forward and squeezes her knee.

One more second and I'll scream: WHAT THE FUCK DO YOU THINK YOU'RE DOING?

"Know how many homicides have been committed by Vicane?" Jonas asks. "None . . . How many homicides by drowning the victim in his own swimming pool? You'd think more, but there was only one in '94 and that was a deranged dad who drowned his kids . . . How many by knocking the victim unconscious and leaving him in a car to die of carbon monoxide poisoning? Three . . . In the last seventeen years . . ."

"I know it's a long shot," she says.

He squeezes harder. "Know how many suicides were committed by carbon monoxide poisoning? Eleven in LA county, this year alone . . ."

"You did your research."

"Veasy didn't."

I'm just a casual thing to Veasy so why am I defending him? Why am I endangering my own career?

"Veasy says there was no obvious suicide motive for London," she says.

· "No motive?" Jonas says. "His latest movie had been panned by the critics."

"Well, that's one verifiable homicide."

No smile? Okay, fuck him.

"If you're talking about statistics," she says, "no producer ever killed himself over a flop movie. Believe it or not, nobody has ever accidentally drowned in his own pool after a wild party, either. The last person who drowned in his pool was Brian Jones of the Rolling Stones and it turns out he was actually murdered. And certainly nobody ever died accidentally in a termite tented house, either. Got that from the president of the exterminating company."

Jonas jams his knees against hers.

"Do you know what he's doing?"

"He sincerely believes that there's a . . ."

Jonas puts his finger against her lips and repeats:

"Do you know what he's doing?"

Keep manhandling me, asshole, and I'll have a harassment lawsuit against you so fast . . .

"He doesn't care about the case," Jonas whispers. "He wants to turn you against me, that's all. He wants everybody to see that you've chosen him over me . . ."

Pointless to deny it. Would be nice if it were true.

"He sincerely believes that there's a serial killer out there planning to kill again," she says.

Jonas gets up.

"Right now I'm more concerned that gang members are selling marijuana on the campus of La Playita High School. You may think I'm being unreasonable . . ."

"I didn't say that," Tingley says. "I was going to suggest we put in an undercover . . ."

Jonas nods. "Good suggestion, Detective . . ." He pinches her cheek. "Quite the little multitasker, aren't you?"

WHERE THERE'S A WILL
THERE'S A RELATIVE

Veasy knocks at 468 21st Place. No answer, but he hears voices inside. He knocks again. A California blonde opens the door.

Just call her Dexatrim Slim.
Nose job, eye pop
Boobs are a hymn.
Hey, Miss Tummy Tuck,
If you run out of luck
Would you consider a cop?
Not on a whim, Jim.

"Detective Veasy, La Playita . . ."

"My mother told me you were here yesterday."

"And you are . . . ?"

"Lauren Finkelman . . ."

"Married name?"

"Of course," she says, as if no one who looks like her could ever have been born Finkelman. "My mother's name is Keene. You scared her to death."

"Didn't mean to."

"She was nervous enough with the Brownlee thing and the police saying someone was preying on senior citizens, but then to imply that the man was after her . . ."

"I just asked if she had a safe."

"A lot of people have safes."

"Could I take a look at your mother's, Mrs. Finkelman?" Veasy asks. "I don't want to upset her again . . ."

Veasy keeps it polite. "Could we let her decide?"

Mrs. Finkelman turns abruptly. Veasy follows her. There's no panty line under her white slacks . . .

Have to ask Tingley about that.

Heavy shades are drawn in the living room.

The native son

Shuns the sun
While the transplantee
Is all eggplantee . . .

A narrow hallway leads to the kitchen. Perfect place for family photos, but the walls are bare. Mrs. Keene is sitting stiffly at the kitchen table with a cup of coffee. She is wearing a print blouse, a white pleated skirt, and a diamond engagement/wedding ring combo, which she didn't have on the day before. Rouge blotches her wintry cheeks.

How sad to have been pretty
And now an object of pity.

"Afternoon, Mrs. Keene. Just wanted to ask you a few questions. Shouldn't take long."

Is that a silent plea in her eyes? Is this coldness strictly for the daughter's benefit?

"Could I see your safe?"

Mrs. Keene rises—*is that pretend weariness?*—and looks back at her daughter in the doorway. "I guess I have to show it to him."

She takes Veasy into the living room. More drawn shades and gloomy mahogany. A photo on the mantel: A young Marine lieutenant tries to keep a straight face, while a young Mrs. Keene looks up at him like he had just cracked a joke.

"That's a happy couple," Veasy says.

Mrs. Keene looks away, lips trembling. "Our wedding day."

She reaches into the fireplace. A latch clicks and a panel slides open revealing a safe embedded in the brick. "The original owners put this in," she says. "Coming out of the Depression no one believed in banks."

The daughter steps up, so avid for a better look that she brushes her concrete breasts against Veasy without realizing it.

"I didn't know you had a safe in there, Mom."

"Your father never wanted to tell anybody . . ."

"Not even Chap and me?"

"Especially not you . . ."

This is a moment we all can relate to,
When you discover your parents hate you.

"But what about the little safe in your bedroom?" the daughter asks.

"Dad called it our decoy. Kept some cash and the bankbooks and some of the deeds. Just enough to fool a burglar . . ."

"False brick," Veasy says. "No one would ever find this. Why are you showing it to me now?"

Mrs. Keene looks sidelong at her daughter. "Just in case something happens to me, I want someone to know it's there."

"What do you keep in here?" Veasy asks.

"Jewelry. The really valuable old coins—Roman, early European—that my husband inherited from his dad."

"How much are they worth?"

"He was offered $250,000 for the whole set years ago. Probably doubled since then . . ."

Her daughter steps back into the shadows.

"What else is in the safe?" Veasy asks.

"More deeds," Mrs. Keene says. "Every time my husband could scrape a few dollars together he bought land . . ." She looks past him at her daughter. "We lived within our means. Didn't need much . . . At first the idea was to build an inheritance for our children."

"At first?" the daughter asks.

"Yes. But then your father made a new plan for the coins. I was to keep them just in case I needed money and then when I passed, they would be returned to their countries of origin . . ."

"And the garden apartments in Northridge?"

"All the rental property would be put in a trust for the grandchildren," Mrs. Keene says. "Except the land in Ojai . . ." Mrs. Keene turns to Veasy: "We have seven hundred acres up there. It was my husband's hometown and he was very attached to it. Always wanted to retire and grow avocados, but that never worked out."

She is looking sidelong at her daughter again.

This is her revenge.

"We're going to leave it to the county to use as a park . . ."

She's loving this . . .

"Do you have a list of what's in the safe?" Veasy asks.

"Oh yes, it's at our attorney's office. I can give you a copy too, Detective . . ."

"That won't be necessary. But I would like to speak to your son . . ." Veasy gives her another card. "Have him call me and don't worry. We'll be patrolling the neighborhood until we catch this guy . . ."

"I hope so." No goodbye. She just turns and walks into the kitchen.

Outside, Mrs. Finkelman is sitting in a Lexus RX 350, talking on the Bluetooth. Veasy stands by the passenger window until she lowers it.

"Thanks for your trouble, Mrs. Finkelman," he says. He offers her a card. "If you speak to your brother, could you have him call me?"

She ignores the card. "I don't speak to my brother," she says.

Veasy flips the card onto the seat.

"Well if you think of anything I should know . . ."

"I won't." And rolls her window up.

Veasy crosses the street, hitting 1 in his speed dial.

Tingley answers. "Can't go fifteen minutes without talking to me."

"What do you think of a woman who doesn't put on underwear to visit her mother?"

"Did you get her pants off already?"

"No panty line."

"You wouldn't necessarily see a line . . ."

"In tight white jeans?"

"Okay, she was in a motel in Glendale with the UCLA basketball team when her mom called and she forgot to put her panties on . . . What's the rest of the package?"

"Eye job that gives her that look of permanent amazement like she just saw a huge erection."

"More like a diamond necklace . . ."

"Bleached blonde, pouty lips. All that stuff really works for five minutes . . ."

"Which is all you need, lover. Are you going to be thinking about her the next time we're together?"

"That'll be up to you. Talk about family secrets, the old lady's got a hidden safe, millions in rare coins and real estate, and a will cutting off the son and the daughter. Nice haul for the sibs if they can make it look like a home invasion."

"If you're right about this, I'll never speak to you again . . ."

"Which reminds me . . ."

"I couldn't check those names with the Owl breathing down my neck," Tingley says. "I'll get to it later . . ."

PRODUCTION MEETING

Jay stops off at Vons to shop for the meeting.

The crew apologizes.

("we should have had a production assistant do this.")

"Guerrilla filmmaking," Jay says. "Everybody pitches in." He has his list:

1. One pound of Starbucks Fair Trade coffee
2. Baker's dozen Einstein's bagels, four plain, two sesame, two poppy, two onion, two whole wheat, and one everything for Jay.
3. One Philadelphia cream cheese
4. Swiss and American slices
5. Three tomatoes
6. A fruit salad boat

No Winchell's donuts like in the old days. Muffins have too much sugar and will put the crew to sleep. No ashtrays or extra books of matches—the smoking days are gone forever.

"Havin' a brunch?" the checkout kid asks.

"Production meeting," Jay says.

"Need an extra? I do stunts, too . . . Also music . . ."

At ten minutes to eleven Jay is back at his kitchen table. He waits until the crew is settled with their bagels and coffee. Then he clears his throat to get their attention.

"Today we film a few words on the schedule," he says. "Braffner prepares to blow up the office of Lester Tarsis Productions."

(excited murmurs.)

"That's the bittersweet paradox of filmmaking. Those words don't reflect the years of careful preparation that have gone into the conception and execution of this simple, silent scene."

("how true.")

"We'll play the sequence on Braffner," Jay says. "We won't cut to Lester's outer office. Won't show the phone ringing, the assistant picking it up. Won't show the explosion in the office, blood spurting, heads and limbs flying around the room. Flames licking the blackened walls. Bodies sprawled in grotesque, mutilated poses . . ."

("no cheap tricks.")

"CAMERA follow me," Jay says.

He walks down the hall to the spare bedroom. "This is where Braffner slept it off in the old days. Out on the Hollywood trawl. Catch of the day, Lester called it. The darkest bars in the world . . . Washed out blondes in the headlights . . . Lipstick on the cigarette butts . . . Piles of blow, empty bottles, ashtrays . . . Smoke, stale, stench . . . Lust . . . Disgust . . ."

("Beckett meets David Lynch.")

"Thank you," Jay says.

The room is empty except for a tattered beach chair and a single bed. "I could portray Braffner as a loner brooding in a monastic room," Jay says, "but I don't see the character that way. To me he is Caliban. A monster perhaps, but we have to show his pathos. Make the audience understand, even sympathize . . ."

(murmurs of assent.)

Jay sets the blinds so the sunlight will fall on the bed.

("classic film noir lattice pattern.")

"Correct," Jay says. He lies back, hands behind his head.

("classic brooding position.")

"Introspective, not brooding," he says. "The allegory of an artist's life. The journey of Orpheus, Jason and the Golden Fleece, the Old Man and the Sea. The sirens and bandits and monsters who rise up to stop you from bringing your creation to the world."

("Prometheus.")

Jay checks the time on his cell phone. 11:15.

"The Monday morning staff meeting usually begins around 11:30," he says. "The writers and Lester will be in the room. The sweet girl will be outside in the office. That little punk assistant editor will come in with the lunch menus. Phone rings. Lester picks up. A deafening blast. Black smoke rises over Hollywood Boulevard."

Jay checks his phone again for effect.

"I'll make the call in twenty minutes . . ."

STRAGGLING WRITERS

Eloise's desk is outside Lester's office. Behind her are shelves lined with nine years of scripts. In the first year, Lester wrote every one of the thirteen episodes under a different pseudonym, but then the series took off. The distributors ordered twenty-two episodes so he hired staff writers. Now he has Noah Lippman, who has worked on tons of hit shows. And Sean O'Meara, an Academy Award nominee, who wrote some big movies in the '70s. But Lester's scripts are still the best.

More Hollywood rules. If you show enthusiasm you're an amateur. If you compliment someone you're just trying to score points. She made the mistake of raving about Lester's scripts one day. "The characters seem to jump off the page. You can see what they're doing, hear what they're saying."

"That's because they're wrestling with a woman in a leopard-skin bikini and screaming AIEE!" Lester said. "Maybe I'll apply for a retroactive Emmy."

"Why not make it posthumous?" Sean had yelled from his office.

They joke like that, trading insults. The kinds of things they say about wives and children and sexual problems would cause a shooting in her hometown, but here nobody cares.

Lester likes to start the script meetings late on Monday. "Give O'Meara's cocaine a chance to metabolize," he says.

At eleven-fifteen Sean saunters in, cool and relaxed in a Coachella Festival tee, khaki cargo shorts, and sandals, his leather envelope over his shoulder. Lester opens his office door. "Has Academy Award nominee Sean O'Meara brought an offering to our temple of the arts?"

"It's the best work I've ever done," Sean said. "It's so good it's almost mediocre." He flips the script toward Lester's desk, but it falls short, right into the trash can.

"Saves me the trouble," Lester says.

Then it gets quiet as Lester closes his door to read the script. Sean sits in his office, pretending to play with his iPhone, but Eloise knows he's anxiously awaiting the verdict.

At eleven-thirty she hears horns blasting and angry shouts in the parking lot.

Sean goes to his window.

"Noah is being chased by a Snapple delivery guy," he calls. "I'm not good enough to make this up."

In the editing room Zack and Elliot watch Noah Lippman run into the building with the Snapple guy in hot pursuit.

"We'd better go to lunch," Elliot says.

"But it's only eleven-thirty," says Zack.

"Yeah, but this is the kind of angry white dude who has a Glock in his glove compartment . . ."

In the production office Eloise hears Noah running down the hall, screaming:

"Help!"

"Close the door, Eloise," Lester shouts.

Noah sticks his arm through the door and squeezes through, gasping. "Let me in for God's sake. A Snapple guy is after me."

"Lock the door now, Eloise," Lester says.

Noah takes off his Lakers cap. Sweat has plastered his thinning hair to his head and sent his glasses sliding halfway down his nose. "I cut him off on the freeway. He followed me up La Brea blasting his horn. I saw you at the window, Sean . . ."

"Why didn't you rescue your union brother, Sean?" Lester calls.

"I didn't see the point in two sissy writers getting their asses kicked," Sean says.

"In my old neighborhood the Irish guys fought to the death."

"That was Brooklyn, Lester. I'm from Newport Beach."

Noah flops heavily on the broken swivel chair by the window, his XXX NBA tee dark with sweat. "He jumped out at me, screaming: I'll kill you, motherfucker . . . I'll cut off your head and shit down your neck . . ."

"Interesting image," Sean says. "Bloodthirsty Snapple guys dropping their pants and squatting over headless humans with hollow necks . . ."

Noah looks out of the window. "I think his truck is gone."

"Could be a trick," Sean says. "He could be in the hallway."

"Maybe he's hiding in the bathroom," Lester says. "You'd better piss in an Evian bottle today."

Line 1 is ringing. Eloise picks up.

"Lester Tarsis, please . . . Detective Veasy, La Playita Police Department."

Eloise freezes. What if one of those stupid girls is making some kind of a complaint against Lester? Like the time that girl kept calling to speak to him about the part he had promised her and ended up screaming, "Ask that motherfucker if he knows I'm seventeen!"

"He's in a meeting, you'll have to call back," she says and slams down the receiver.

A WARNING UNHEEDED

"She hung up on me!" Veasy says.

"She probably thinks it's a ruse to get to talk to her boss," Mineo says. "These guys get hundreds of calls a day from wannabes . . ."

"Maybe I'll just go to the guy's office."

"Not today," Mineo says. "You gotta show mug shots to the victim and those nannies who saw the dude. If they don't recognize anyone we'll get an artist in for a sketch . . . Gotta put in a progress report at the end of the day . . ."

They are in Inspiration Point, a picnic spot in Palisades Park on a bluff overlooking the Pacific. Mineo is pouring coffee from a thermos. Veasy gets up and raises his arms to the ocean.

"Balboa, you ruthless Castilian,
Godlike in sunset's vermillion . . .
Your sails unfurled,
Lost in this floating world . . ."

"You're getting worse, Tommy," Mineo says.

Veasy sits down. "Really? I thought that was a pretty good rhyme . . ."

"The Owl asked me if you were still smoking weed," Mineo says. "He's on your case, Tommy . . ."

"I've got a prescription . . ."

"You got it when you were a civilian. You know you can't smoke on the job."

"That's never been tested in court," Veasy says.

"He's an old bodysnatcher, Tommy. He's lookin' to set you up. Turn somebody . . ."

"Like who?"

Mineo offers Veasy a cup. "Roger Greenspun copping for you?"

"Coffee won't loosen my tongue, flatfoot," Veasy says, but then admits: "You sure know your turf . . ."

"Roger Greenspun . . . Aging hippie, super long, tie-dyed fingernails. Peddles New Age souvenirs on the Venice boardwalk . . ."

"I met him at the dispensary before I got back on the job. I was legal then."

"You're not legal now, but he's still sharing . . ."

"He is a bit of a marijuana missionary," Veasy says. "But he's got a prescription . . ."

"So he sells you half his scrip. That's still a felony. The Owl will lock him up in County on the Aryan Brotherhood tier. Think of him with his tie-dyed fingernails in a cell with two Nazi bikers . . . How long you think before he gives you up? The Owl will put a wire on him the next time he gets high with you . . ."

"You're right, I've gotta cut Roger loose," Veasy says.

"You oughta think twice about Tingley, too," Mineo says.

"Why? We're allowed . . ."

"By God maybe, but he don't run the department. The Owl was there first so he thinks he owns it. And thinks everybody is laughing at him because you moved in . . ."

"I'll try to keep it out of his face," Veasy says.

Mineo shakes his head. "Too late for that. He's a vindictive little shit and now he's after her as well. She's probationary. He can scare her with demotion or suspension or even worse if she conceals evidence of a felony . . ."

"I never smoke around her. Always take a walk to give her plausible deniability."

"Don't matter, she knows you're a head. She likes you—maybe a lot. If he tries to turn her, she'll refuse. Then, he'll threaten to charge her with abetting. She'll hate herself, but she'll have to give you up. He'll put a wire on her, too. After she helps him take you down she might feel so guilty she might have a breakdown or even hurt herself . . ."

"You're sellin' hard," Veasy says.

"Am I wrong?"

"I like her. I don't want to dump her."

"Then dump the weed," Mineo says.

Veasy's text bell clangs twice.

"This is her right here," Veasy says. And opens the text:

"Seven names linked more than three times to the victims . . ."

Veasy goes down the list. One of them is the guy who directed Lester Tarsis's only movie—Jay Braffner.

INTERCUT

"How did they show time passing in the old days?" Jay asks.

"Calendar pages turning, leaves fluttering, snow falling, second hand ticking on the old clock on the precinct wall," Jay says. "Cinema shorthand for time passing. Here's the updated version."

He holds his cell phone up to the light streaming through the window.

It says: 11:34.

Then the digital readout blinks . . .

11:35.

CUT TO ELOISE'S SCREENSAVER

A photo of her family's pasture in Missouri at sunset. The time is 11:35.

It's so quiet Eloise can hear Lester flipping script pages. The faster they flip the less Lester likes them. Sean and Noah are in their offices, but she can feel the tension behind their closed doors.

Lester comes out with that expression he gets after they have Mexican for lunch.

"Sean," he calls . . . "Noah . . ."

Sean is ready for a fight. He pushes his broken swivel chair, creaking and squeaking all the way across the room into Lester's office. Noah walks in, shoulders hunched, head down.

Lester gives them his quizzical look.

"Struck dumb by my genius, Lester?" Sean asks.

"Where is the show running now, Sean?" Lester asks.

"Don't play catechism with me."

"I have to since you still don't know the answers."

"Okay, we're running in the Balkans and Africa, Monsignor Tarsis."

"And who runs those countries?"

"Warlords, Lester, I know. But this episode is about a Burmese warlord who uses slave labor to harvest opium poppies . . . We're not running in Burma . . ."

Lester gives him the pitying stare. "Warlords stick together."

"The Warlord Benevolent Association?"

"They'll kill the show. You'll be unemployed and unable to afford the crop they so diligently cultivate . . ."

"How about a Burmese warlord who adopts orphan elephants whose mothers have been killed by poachers?" Sean says.

"Now you're talking," says Lester.

Line 1 lights up again.

"Lester Tarsis, there?" It's a familiar voice.

"He's in a meeting right now," Eloise says. "Can he call back . . . ?"

"I'm on the set . . . It'll only take a second . . ."

Now she remembers. "Aren't you the gentleman who was in the office this morning?"

An embarrassed laugh. "You're very perceptive, young lady . . . I'm an old friend and associate. Name's Jay Braffner . . ."

"I'm sure he will want to speak with you as soon as the meeting is over, Mr. Braffner. If you leave your . . ."

Too late, he hangs up without giving his number. Now the poor man is going to sit by the phone waiting for the call that will never come.

In the office Lester fans himself with Noah's script.

"Makes a nice breeze, at least," he says. "How long are our scripts supposed to be, Noah?"

Noah blurts his answer like he's been anticipating the question. "Forty-seven pages. I know I'm short at forty, but I wrote in a lot of action."

"Action I get from director schmucks," Lester says. "From writer schmucks I get dialogue . . ."

"Well, this tribe I invented doesn't speak . . ."

"I know, they come silently out of the jungle spritzing into their blowguns," Lester says. "Are we intruding on their burial grounds? Trampling their ancient shrines? Have we offended their tree gods?"

Noah looks hopeful. "All of the above?"

Zack comes in with a pile of DVDs. "Here's what they shot this weekend." And then whispers to Eloise: "Do you know if he read my script?"

Line 1 lights up again. That same shy voice.

"Hi, this is Jay Braffner. I called before."

Eloise tries to sound encouraging. "Oh sure, Mr. Braffner. I'm sorry, but he's still in a staff meeting . . ."

"Please," Braffner pleads. "All I ask is that he pick up the phone for a second and say hello . . ."

The man's desperation is heartbreaking. "Alright I'll try." Eloise puts him on hold and steps into the office.

"Lester, Jay Braffner on Line 1 . . ."

Everybody turns and stares.

"You're kidding," Lester says.

Noah looks at Eloise in astonishment. "Jay Braffner? He still alive?"

"He's really desperate to speak to you, Lester," she says. "I found him in the office this morning . . ."

"He was in my office?" Lester says.

"I saw him, too," Zack says. "He was driving an old Mercedes 450."

"Maybe it's someone posing as Jay Braffner," Sean says.

"Posing as a junkie has-been?" Lester says. "Interesting career choice. What did he look like, Eloise?"

"Kinda tall and beaky with frizzy hair and a bushy mustache. Wearing a khaki jacket with lots of pockets and one of those lens thingies . . ."

"View finder," Lester says. "He always had one around his neck. Take his number."

"Jay Braffner," Zack whispers. "I know that name . . ."

"I thought Jay Braffner committed suicide in rehab," Noah says.

"That was Jon Pfeffer," says Sean. "Lester drove him to it."

"I have not lived in vain," Lester says.

Eloise goes back to Line 1. "Mr. Braffner, if you leave a number, Lester will be sure to call you back as soon as the meeting is over . . ."

"No way of getting him to come to the phone?"

"He promises he'll call you right back . . ."

"My phone is off. I'm on the set."

This is excruciating. Eloise goes back to the office. "He says he's on the set, Lester."

"On the set? Jay Braffner is working?"

"Ask him if he needs a rewrite," Sean says.

"If you tell him I'm torturing writers, he'll understand," Lester says.

Eloise goes back and tries to reassure the poor man. "Believe me, Mr. Braffner, Lester will call back. He is very reliable."

"In this business reliable means I'll call you back if I need you," Braffner says. And he's gone.

VICTIM EX MACHINA

A cloud has passed in front of the sun. The beautiful lattice pattern on the bedspread breaks into a hundred smudges.

(anxious whispers behind the camera.)

Everybody was primed for a big bang. It didn't come and now they're deflated. Jay has to be positive, energetic, brimming with ideas. If he shows doubt he'll lose them.

He tries a little black humor. "They were all in one room—Lester, Sean O'Meara, Noah Lippman. We could have struck a major blow for the cinema if he had only picked up that phone."

(half-hearted chuckles.)

Then, he tries to reassure them. "This is not a setback, it's the breakthrough we strive for in every film. The moment when we stop telling the story and the story starts telling us . . ."

("we're just the medium for the message.")

"Right. Now I'm going to call Lester back in an hour. How do I indicate time passing?"

Silence. They're waiting for him to answer.

"Backstory," Jay says. "Bio-montage . . . The Rise and Fall of Jay Braffner in quick cuts. Flashback in the style of *Citizen Kane*."

("go for it.")

Jay dictates his shot list.

1. "Jay at the peak of his career. Assistants knock softly at the trailer door.
2. The crew respects his expertise.
3. The actors trust his guidance.
4. INSERTS . . . The bottle on the table. The 'unwinder' at the end of a long day. The baggie full of white powder.
5. The cute little extra, naked and crazed and sprinkling cocaine in his navel . . ."

("that's hot!")

"This is how we lived in those days," Jay says. "Remember, this was precorporate Hollywood. A world unto itself."

He goes back to his list.

6. "Slow descent to the bottom. Hundreds of thousands up his nose.
7. Sleazy dealers rob him blind.
8. Whores and sycophants.
9. Agents who don't return calls.
10. Years in and out of rehab."

("bio-montage . . . very cool . . .")

But Jay's not sure. "Explains a lot and creates sympathy, but doesn't move the story forward. As Lester used to say, don't give me a time step when I need a pirouette."

Then, he hears that stupid *Mission Impossible* theme that came with his cell phone.

"Nobody ever calls me," he says. "Even telemarketers have deleted my number . . ."

It's an anxious voice, nasal, vaguely familiar. "Mr. Braffner, this is Roy Farkas . . ."

It takes a second. But then Jay remembers and covers the phone to tell the crew:

"This is the geek I found on Craigslist. The one who sold me the RDX. Taught me how to make the explosive, wire it up, booby-trap the phone, the whole deal . . . A very cryptic guy. Code words for everything . . ." He goes back to the phone. "Nice to hear from you, Roy."

"Remember I told you I had some script ideas and you said you'd love to hear them?"

"Sure I remember."

"Well, I'm in town. I think I've got some dynamite projects, if you'll excuse the pun . . ."

"Funny, Roy. Lunch tomorrow?"

"How about coffee now?"

"I'm a little short on time . . ."

"Won't take long. I'm right outside your door . . ."

Jay looks out the window. A skinny black kid with a mountainous Afro is peering in with a tentative smile.

The crew is alarmed.

("what do we do . . . ?")

Jay stays calm. "Don't you see? The movie gods have sent us a second act. With all due respect to *Citizen Kane* this is a lot better than a flashback . . ."

He opens the door with his famous charming smile. "Well Roy, nice to finally meet you . . ."

The kid is suddenly shy as if he expected to be turned away.

"If I'm interrupting . . ."

"Not at all . . ."

Jay puts a bearlike arm around Roy's shoulders. "C'mon in, let's hear some of those killer ideas."

AN UNHAPPY FAMILY

In the squad room, the detectives are putting together a photo display of possible suspects in the home invasion. They find the mug shots of people arrested for "home invasion," "burglary," "robbery," and "robbery of a senior . . ." Following the victim's description they remove all blacks, Asians, and obvious Hispanics. They delete everyone under thirty and over sixty . . .

Veasy sends around a text message:

Bored beyond comprehension,
Your ass begins to throb,
But don't slacken your attention
You're doing a good job.

Mineo texts him back. "Stop clowning. Jonas has a mole."

They separate out all the people who are dead or in jail. That leaves a database of hundreds of photos to show to Mrs. Brownlee.

"The old lady won't be able to sit in front of a computer that long," Mineo says. "We'll have to put the photos in a book with a three hole punch and take them to her house."

While they're printing out the photos, Veasy looks up the Keene house on the tax rolls. Built in 1947 on five-eighths of an acre, its original assessment was three thousand dollars. It was purchased by Mr. and Mrs. Steven Keene in 1963 for twenty-eight K and now is assessed at a million-six.

Veasy checks the address on the police logs. Officers were called to the house seventeen times from '82 to '89. Noise complaints, teenagers in the street, property damage, domestic dispute . . . "Complainant Steven Keene claims that his son Chapman Keene, a minor child residing at the address, attacked him with a baseball bat . . ." An ambulance responded three times. Once in '86 for "Chapman Keene, minor child, possible drug overdose." Another time in '87 for "Lauren Keene, minor female resident . . . Deep cuts in arms and wrists, possible self-mutilation or suicide attempt . . ." And finally in '03 for . . . "Steven Keene, male resident, 79, unconscious, possible cardiac arrest . . ."

Veasy sends Mineo a text:
My name is Veasy
And I'm in a rage.
Police work's too easy
In the computer age.
Mineo waves him over.

"What?"

"We got a serious dysfunctional family here," Veasy says.

He shows him the Keene file. Mineo is not impressed. "This is normal for Southern California . . ."

"What do you wanna bet Chapman Keene's got a record?"

"He could be the Hillside Strangler, it doesn't matter."

Veasy looks up court records. A Chapman Keene from the same address appeared four times in the '80s and '90s on misdemeanor drug charges, each time sentenced to counseling and community service. He has arrests for menacing a traffic officer, for drunk and disorderly, forging his father's name on checks and credit applications. He ducked jail for all that, but got six months in LA County for attempted sale of methamphetamine to an undercover officer.

"Chapman Keene is a classic sociopath," Veasy says.

"You oughta know," Mineo says. But he looks at the rap sheet and admits: "Jail time does make him a little more than a rebellious teen."

"Six months in LA County, ninety days in Baker County jail in Oregon for shoplifting . . . And another ninety for forgery . . . He's getting an MO . . . Steals girlfriends' checks and forges himself a little walking-around money . . ."

"Chickenshit stuff," Mineo says.

"It's pretty chickenshit to put out a burglary contract on your parents' house."

"You keep overlooking one minor detail. The burglary took place at the Brownlee house . . ."

"Don't confuse me with the facts," Veasy says.

Mineo gives him a weary look. "Let's ID our home invader first. Then, we can get cute with the theories . . ."

Veasy brandishes his phone. "While you're plodding along, I'll check back with my serial killer . . ."

He finds Tingley's text . . . *"The guy who directed Lester Tarsis's only movie—Jay Braffner."*

He goes back to IMDB and types in Braffner's name.

"Tommy," Mineo calls. "Mr. Brownlee just died in the hospital."

Veasy bookmarks Jay Braffner's IMDB entry for future reference.

THE PLOT SICKENS

"C4 explosive is harmless until it's detonated," Roy Farkas says. "Then, it's mushroom cloud city . . ."

He's pitching his masterpiece. It's his only child—he's been gently nurturing it for years.

Jay wants to warn him:

"This isn't Finished Basement, South Dakota, kid. The guy outside blowing leaves has a script about a guy who blows leaves. Every story you can think of has been pitched and repitched since 1904 . . ."

But false hope is kinder than no hope. Jay nods and looks interested. Encouraged, Roy talks faster. "You drop the charge in a storm drain on a busy street like Santa Monica Boulevard. Late at night when the street is deserted . . ."

The kid doesn't know he's being filmed.

"Drop some more in a drain down the street. Another package in the next drain . . . The heat from the first explosion will set the next one off and the next one after that."

Jay gives him that phony intense look he always used on actors to make them think he was paying attention.

"Set off one charge with your phone to start the chain reaction and watch the others go off down the street . . ." The kid's eyes shine. "We're gonna wreak havoc, dude . . ."

"Great," Jay says. "But who are the bad guys? Muslim terrorists?"

"That's kind of played out, don't you think?" the kid says.

"A priest defrocked for molesting altar boys?"

"Too sleazy."

"A disgraced cop, forced to take the heat for something he didn't do . . ."

"It's kinda been done," the kid says, tactfully.

He sits back like he's thinking, but Jay knows he has it all planned.

"How about a blackballed director," the kid says like it just occurred to him. "A big talent who fought to keep his integrity. Got into drugs, wouldn't toe the line. Bankrupted by divorce suits. In and out of rehab, nobody would hire him."

"Sounds familiar," Jay says.

Kid gives him a sly look. "Committed to a state hospital after a DUI with cocaine and heroin found in his car . . ."

"A little close to home. What does our hero do next?"

"Pretends to be cured. They let him out. He's got this plan. He contacts an explosives expert. This dude is the product of a multiracial marriage. Worst of two worlds. He's got grudges of his own . . ." Another sly look. "That ring a bell?"

"Rings Big Ben, baby," Jay says. "Let me take it from here. The two of them team up to get even with LA. An odd couple buddy movie with a big bang at the end . . . It's fresh . . ."

The kid looks relieved. "You're not mad that I stole your life."

"I'm flattered that somebody would want it. But how did you catch on to me?"

"I Google everybody who contacts me. You were all over the Internet. All those stories when you totaled your car on the PCH. The trials. The judge who committed you . . ."

"Bad timing," Jay says. "A lot of Hollywood drug busts and fatal accidents had happened. He made an example of me." He gives the kid that deeply interested look again. "You knew what I was up to all along."

"It was easy," the kid says. "I get at least ten queries a month. People say they are researching a book or a movie, but I know they really want to blow the shit out of something or somebody and I'm cool with helping them . . ."

He leans forward, earnestly. "You don't want to make a movie, Mr. Braffner. You wanna blow the shit out of this stupid town for real . . ."

"Busted," Jay says with what a script would call "a hearty laugh." Then he gives the sincere look. "Will you help me?"

The kid's voice cracks with excitement. "Let's do it, Mr. Braffner. Let's shake these fuckers up."

He's a bruised soul just like me.

"If we're gonna be partners, you should call me Jay."

"I'd be honored to . . . Jay."

Jay rises slowly, giving the camera time to TILT UP with him.

"I should be popping a bottle of Dom Pérignon to celebrate this historical alliance, but I've been sober for years . . ."

"Coffee will be fine," the kid says.

"I'll make it." Jay crosses to the bookcase. "Meanwhile, if you want to read about your new partner . . ." He finds the book *'70s Noir* . . . "There's a nice bit about my first feature in here."

"I'd love to read it," the kid says eagerly.

Jay finds another book, *Coke, Cuervo, and Crazy Bitches: Cinema of the '70s*. "I'm in this, too . . ."

"Cool . . ."

In the kitchen Jay gets out the coffee filters.

"You like it strong, Roy?" he calls.

"Stronger the better," Roy calls back from the living room.

"We should be swapping life stories," Jay says, filling the filter to the top. "That's always a good scene."

"Mine's not as interesting as yours," Roy says. "Every other house in Culver City had an abusive father. The only difference was that mine was black, which made me even more of an outcast . . ."

"Good line," Jay says.

"This is amazing," Roy says. "I'm reading here that you did a movie about George Metesky, *The Mad Bomber*. He's a hero in certain circles, you know . . ."

Jay hears the couch creak as the kid gets up and walks down the hall.

"Metesky was the first bomber. He had to develop his own technology," the kid says. "Pipe bombs loaded with gunpowder . . ." The kid comes into the kitchen, still talking . . . "A timer made out of an old stopwatch . . ." Then, he sees Alison Sobel.

"Jeez, Jay," the kid says.

Jay whips around. One giant step gets him to the doorway. He cracks the kid in the head with the coffee pot. The handle breaks off in his hand and he hits the kid with its jagged edge.

The kid tries to shield his face. Jay twists his wrist and cracks him again. He wobbles. A bloody gash opens in his forehead. Jay body slams him face-down onto the kitchen floor. Puts his knees on his shoulders.

"PUSH IN, HANDHELD," he yells.

He reaches behind him for a dishtowel. Pulls the kid's head back and knots the towel around his neck.

"I once owned a script by the same guy who wrote *Mad Bomber*, Roy," Jay says. "Lester Tarsis . . ."

The kid gurgles. Blood dribbles out of his mouth, rolling down the grouts in the tile.

"It's about a con man who uses accomplices for complicated scores, then kills them so they can't talk," Jay says.

He slides a salad spoon into the knot and turns it clockwise, tightening the towel like a garrote.

"Lester called it *No Partners in Crime*," Jay says. "Good title, right? It needed work, but what script doesn't? Lester was off on a series and wouldn't do the rewrite. The work didn't mean anything to him anyway. It was all about money and pussy for him . . ."

The towel squeaks. Jay can't get another turn out of it.

"Anyway, Roy, the point is: no partners in crime. So thanks but no thanks."

The kid doesn't respond. Jay watches him for a while.

"No actor can ever sell the total stillness of death as well as a real corpse," Jay says. He gets up off the body and tries to catch his breath.

"Let's get a noir low angle of Jay in the kitchen with the two bodies."

He stumbles and bumps into Alison Sobel. She falls forward, banging her head on the kitchen table.

"It's getting a little crowded in here," Jay says.

SURPRISED WITNESS

"They always get a lucid moment near the end," the nurse says. "All of a sudden the old man was like: hey nurse, did they catch that guy who tried to rob us? Then he lay back and closed his eyes and moved on . . ."

"Too bad we couldn't have shown him a few photos before he went," Veasy says. He looks down at Mrs. Brownlee, her head propped on pillows.

"You wouldn't think her hair could get any whiter, but it did."

"She buckled when we told her," the nurse says. "They gave her chlorpromazine."

"When can I talk to her?"

"She'll be out for a few hours. And after that she'll be disoriented and may never come back . . ."

"You mean she'll wake up senile?"

The nurse looks down at Mrs. Brownlee. "A lot of these old couples base their lives on the strong one taking care of the sick one. When the sick one dies the spouses have no reason to live, but we keep them breathing anyway . . ."

Veasy watches her plump the pillows with practiced hands.

A veteran, squat and strong
Could lift a gurney over her head
Doesn't bother with right or wrong
Why waste sympathy on the dead?

"She's the only one who saw this guy," Veasy says. "Without her we may never get him."

The nurse picks a crust of dried tear out from under Mrs. Brownlee's eye.

"Try her tomorrow morning," she says.

The detectives have brought three of the housekeepers back for the photo show. The women huddle together, care lines grooved into their brown skin, wispy strings of gray in their black hair. They've been reassured that nobody will ask their immigration status. Nobody will check IDs or Socials. But still they look around anxiously, afraid they won't be allowed to leave.

"There was a young one," Veasy says. "*Dónde está su amiga?*" he asks. "*La señorita que habla inglés . . .*"

"Listen to Placido Domingo over here," Walsh says. He's one of those old-timers who make a virtue out of not speaking Spanish. "Can you say the pen of my aunt is up the ass of my uncle?"

The women look at hundreds of photos, shrugging and shaking their heads.

"*Puede describe la camioneta?*" Veasy asks.

The women look at each other and agree . . . "*Roja . . . Vieja . . .*" And smile . . . "*Cacharro . . .*"

Veasy clicks his translation app. "An old wreck." Then types in "California license plates . . ." and gets:

"*Matrículas de California?*"

Shrugs, puzzled looks. But then one woman pipes up.

"No California," she says. "*Porque había un árbol verde en el centro.*"

Veasy gets that. "There was a green tree in the middle of the plate," he says.

"Oregon," Walsh says.

"Okay," Veasy says. "So we got a beat-up red van with Oregon plates." He turns back to the woman who remembered the tree. "*Recuerda una carta o un número?*"

She shakes her head.

"*Cierre los ojos,*" Veasy says. "*Ve la matrícula.*"

All the women close their eyes.

"Did you tell them to make a wish?" Walsh asks.

The woman who saw the tree opens her eyes in astonishment.

"*Creo que veo un L y quizás un tres . . . Pero no estoy seguro . . .*"

"Thinks she sees an L and a three, but she's not sure," Veasy says. "Does that sound a klaxon / To one of you Anglo-Saxons?"

Walsh gets up. "I'll run a registration check."

Veasy smiles at the women. "*Término,*" he says. "*Muchas gracias . . .*"

They exchange looks of relief.

Veasy calls Lester Tarsis's office again. Again that stupid secretary picks up.

"This is urgent police business, Miss," he says.

"Mr. Tarsis is out to lunch and can't be reached," she says. "If you leave a number, he'll call when he returns . . ."

DOING LUNCH

At noon sharp the phone rings in the editing room. It's Eloise . . . "Lester wants California Chicken today."

Zack leaves Elliot moaning over a sequence—"uncuttable, un-fucking-cuttable." He'd been hoping for the burrito wagon. It's right around the corner, walking distance. He can sneak a few tokes on a roach as he goes. The line of Mexican laborers moves fast. The food is salty, juicy, messy, "scrumptious," as Zack's grandpa used to say. He hates going to California Chicken. Has to drive all the way to Melrose and Lester never reimburses him for gas. The side streets are reserved for permit parking so he has to find a meter, which is another buck or two out of his pocket. There's always a long line. The cashiers are illegals who only know "California Chicken" English. If you stick to the menu you're okay, but any variation stops the whole process cold. You find yourself trying to explain "a chicken wrap with no lettuce or mayo," or "California Chicken Salad with no chicken" to a stone-faced Mayan while the people behind you mutter and glare.

California Chicken doesn't sell canned drinks so he has to put lids over the cups and carry them on a drink tray. While he's waiting in the line he looks up "Jay Braffner" on IMDB. He's the director of cult masterpiece *The Mad Bomber* for fuck's sake, which they watched in every directing class he had at NYU. Also, he's an NYU grad and he directed all the cool TV shows in the '70s and '80s.

Aaron Sklar, a kid from Zack's documentary group at NYU, has a website called "Hollywood Train Wrecks," which runs gossip and where-are-they-now features about scandal victims. He pays in screening passes and concert comps.

Zack calls. "Jay Braffner, two Fs, one of the iconic TV directors of the '70s snuck into our production office this morning begging for a day player job."

Silence as Aaron IMDBs. "Jay Braffner, director of cult classic *The Mad Bomber* plus tons of tacky TV credits," he says. "The dude directed *Knight Rider*, David Hasselhoff's breakout role. Cool, he's got a Wikipedia, too. Means somebody was interested enough . . . Oh glee, he's a drug casualty, tragic hero, headline of the future, when he's found dead."

"We could set up a screening of *Mad Bomber*," Zack says. "Have him intro the movie and do a Q&A after . . ."

"Is there a print?"

"I don't know." Zack scrolls down to the screenplay credit. "Holy shit! My boss Lester Tarsis wrote the script."

Aaron looks Lester up. "How much do we love Lester Tarsis? Winner of the Rotten Tomato for worst TV producer three years running."

"We'll have them both there for an intro and Q&A," Zack says. "Lester will come if we tell him there's a lot of young pussy . . ."

"Which there never is, but he won't know that until he gets here. We go partners, rent the print for two-fifty, and buy the theater for the night for fifteen hundred. Nine-seventy-five a piece, let's make it an even G. We'll pack the place at twelve-fifty a seat plus a piece of the concessions. Six hundred seats, we walk away with a cool five, six Gs . . ."

"Pack the place?" Zack says. "Jay Braffner is not exactly a household word."

"A coupla lines in the LA Weekly. Every nerd who's been couchin' it with Nick at Nite will have an excuse to leave the house. Give mom a chance to air out the room. People show up for these events . . ."

"I'm glad you think so," Zack says. "Just front me a coupla tickets to Seinfeld at the Ford and I'll call it even."

"Jerry is sold out," says Aaron. "I can hook you up with front row Christina Aguilera and backstage passes."

"Not a fan," Zack says.

"She's got four smokin' bitties dancin' backup. Bring some blow, you never know . . ."

On the way back to the studio, Zack calls Eloise. "Did that crazoid leave a number this morning?"

She is immediately suspicious. "Are you going to prank call the poor man?"

"Braffner is a cult director from the '70s," Zack says. "I want to do an homage to him for my friend's website. Maybe even help him reinvent himself . . ."

He hears Eloise tapping on her computer.

"Okay," she says. "This is his cell number. You'd better not do anything sneaky . . ."

GENRE CONFUSION

"If this were 1948 there would be a steamer trunk plastered with stickers from far-off places," Jay tells the crew. "The corpse would fit with room to spare. The trunk would go easily into the roomy back seat of a '40s sedan. We'd be in San Francisco, noir city, USA. Dissolve to an isolated spot under the Golden Gate Bridge . . . Gray of dawn . . . Soft splash as the trunk goes into the bay . . . Film noir reality . . ."

("how we miss it.")

"But this is a world of backpacks and gym bags. Of hatchbacks with no trunk space. Surveillance cameras everywhere. Helicopters. Security patrols. Can't do a classy disposal. Have to chop up the body in little pieces. Switch genres . . . Slasher reality . . ."

("welcome to our world . . .")

Jay finds a rusty hacksaw in the garage. Must have belonged to the old guy who sold him the house thirty-three years ago. He hears the gasps and the whispers as he lays Alison Sobel on the garbage bags he has spread on the kitchen floor. "Warning," he says. "There's no way to make mutilation pretty."

Jay raises Alison's skirt and saws into her hipbone. There's a gasp from the crew.

("oh God!")

"Take that person off the set," Jay orders. He pulls out the bloody hacksaw and moves to the other leg.

("oh God, no.")

. Angry whispers . . .

("shut up.")

Shadows mill behind the light.

"Here's the irony," Jay says. "The decapitation won't be as shocking. You've all watched the YouTubes of terrorist beheadings."

("tragically true.")

"Strange how the facial expression doesn't change when you cut off the head," Jay says. "But then why should it?"

He puts Alison's head and limbs in one garbage bag, her torso in another. Earlier, he had backed her Civic up the driveway into the garage.

Now he knots the bags and takes them out the back door. A flagstone path overgrown with weeds leads to the side door of the garage. A fat old tomcat crouches under a dusty bush, watching.

Jay's cell goes off in the kitchen. "This is it people," he says. "This is the climactic moment."

, The crew whispers, excitedly.

("Lester Tarsis is calling back . . .")

The tomcat inches out of the bush, staring fixedly at the garbage bags.

"Follow me into the kitchen," Jay orders. Is that the cameraman panting behind him or his own excited breaths? "Tight, tight," he urges. "Right up my back . . . Let it go out of focus . . ."

Jay trips over Roy's body getting to the phone on the kitchen table. It's an 818 area code . . . Lester's office.

("they're returning the call.")

"Mr. Braffner?"

"Yes . . ."

Jay has his thumb poised over the phone, ready to tap out the detonator code.

"This is Zack Toledano, the assistant editor on *She* . . . I met you this morning?"

The snotty kid. He's talking fast as if he's afraid Jay will hang up on him.

"I didn't realize it was you this morning, Mr. Braffner. I'm a big fan of yours."

"Are you in Lester's office?" Jay asks.

"Actually, I'm in the editing room."

("It's the wrong extension!")

"I'd like to do a short interview with you," the kid says. "It's for this website about underrated filmmakers . . . People are just discovering the TV of the '70s and you're considered a major auteur of the genre . . . It's a popular site. Global exposure. We can do it any time or any place you want."

("shit! another false start.")

(groans of disappointment.)

Jay has to reassure the crew. "Excuse me, Zack," Jay says. He puts the kid on hold and addresses the milling shadows.

"Cheer up people, we've switched genres again. Gone from noir to slasher and now we're in black comedy. Bodies multiplying . . ."

("black comedy of errors.")
("post modern.")
Jay goes back to the call.
"Still there, Zack?"
"Sure am, Mr. Braffner."
"Appreciate the offer but who'd wanna read about an old hack like me?"

"I think a lot of people would be very interested in learning about the life and times of the director of *The Mad Bomber*, Mr. Braffner."

Jay covers the phone. "Kid knows my credits," he tells the crew. "Tellya what, Zack," he says. "You come over here tomorrow night. You'll supply the pizza. I'll supply the war stories . . ."

CLOSE-UP OF A PRINTOUT

You can't hide the painful truth
It's there on the computer's page
Can't lie about your reckless youth
Or conceal the sins of your middle age.
Some bozo in an Arizona mall
Has a computer that knows it all.

Veasy tries to call Chapman Keene in Portland, but the number is unlisted. Can't call the Portland PD without official permission. He texts Mineo.

"Chapman Keene, Portland Ore. Tel.?"

A minute later Mineo calls. "Never trust a man with two last names. No listing for Chapman Keene."

"So he's buying prepaid phone cards. He has no Facebook, no e-mail account, no bank. Probably uses the Capital One prepaid cards, $500 a pop."

"His street address is the best I can do . . ."

"Think Jonas will let me go up to Portland?"

"If you promise to stay."

"Our invader could be a middle-aged white alcoholic who was in jail with Chapman Keene."

"That's a call to Oregon Corrections," Mineo says. "Find out about Keene's cellies. Get prison intel about him if there is any . . . Ass time for a clerk. Jonas has to clear it at the highest level."

"Okay so I'll call Oregon DMV to trace the owner of a red van with an L and a three in the plate number?"

"They won't release that information to an out-of-state agency without an official request. That means Jonas again."

"I'll bet you have a friend in the Portland PD," Veasy says. "Some Cali cop who got tired of duckin' and dukin'."

Silence.

"C'mon, you're a popular guy. You gotta know somebody up there who can make a call for us."

Another silence. "Ashland Sheriff's Department," Mineo says. "This better pan out."

SCROLLING DOWN
MEMORY LANE

Tingley looks up Jay Braffner and is overcome by a wave of nostalgia. The man directed every '70s TV show she watched with her dad.

As the baby in a family of three brawling brothers, cop shows were her only special time with Dad. After dinner they would bring their desserts into the family room—her chocolate pudding, his coffee cup. They'd snuggle on the battered leather couch and watch reruns of *Kojack* or *McCloud*; *Macmillan and Wife* and *Magnum PI*; *Simon and Simon, Jake and the Fat Man . . . Colombo*. She remembers the warmth of his body, the crumpled pack of Marlboros in his shirt pocket, the mingling scent of Old Spice and Coors. When she was in middle school, he would let her watch *Miami Vice* over the protests of her mom:

"Every girl on that show is a prostitute or a drug addict, Ron . . ."

At that age the male closeness was beginning to perturb her so she sank into the armchair across the room and watched *The Equalizer* and *TJ Hooker*.

Later, when she was home from college and the house was full of the cries of grandchildren, the whispered bickerings of her brothers, the closed-door arguments about money, they would watch the familiar episodes, quoting the wisecracks, predicting the plot turns. "Isn't this the one where . . . ?"

And at the end when he was wasting with cancer she found the shows on TV Land. And sat on the couch, holding his suddenly frail hand . . .

She must have seen "Directed by Jay Braffner" flashing across the screen a hundred times. Didn't remember the name.

But she did remember almost every episode. A crime, a problem, some danger, and it all came to happy closure an hour later. Those shows had inspired her to major in criminal justice in college. To apply to scores of departments against the pleadings of her mom—"this isn't a job for a woman, honey." To push her body through the grind of training, taking and retaking the PT tests until she passed. To spend hours on the firing range, even though she was jumpy around guns.

On TV, the good guys always won and justice was done. The cops were always smarter, tougher, and nicer than the bad guys. They hadn't portrayed the petty humiliations of a policewoman's life. The patronizing bosses, the snide remarks, the harassers and outright molesters who you couldn't report for fear of violating the code. The hyper-competitive women, who wanted to be Alpha-Bitch.

The TV cops were never afraid. They never doubted. They hadn't prepared her for the terror she would feel when confronting a deranged, drug-addled, three-time loser in an alley with the male cops watching to see how she would do. When a TV cop solved a case, order was restored to the universe. In the real world the predator did his time, but the victims didn't recover. Raped women carried the stigma. Abused children never regained their innocence. Families who had lost a loved one mourned forever.

Tingley YouTubes Braffner and finds a scene in a documentary. In the shadows he talks about "battling his demons." How he struggled with drugs and booze. Collided with a tree, killing the "promising" young actress next to him. The trips in and out of rehab. The six months in prison.

Then, an ominous narrator's voice:

"Three months after this interview was filmed, Jay Braffner was pulled, stoned and raving, out of his burning 1967 Mustang in a ravine off Topanga Canyon. He was committed to the Psychological Ward of Harbor Medical Center where he remains to this day, still battling his demons."

Tingley looks around to make sure Jonas isn't lurking and calls Veasy.

"Jay Braffner directed all my favorite shows. He's the reason I'm a cop."

"Then he has a lot to answer for," Veasy says. "Think he's still around?"

"Doubtful from his bio. Rehab was his last address."

"Any facility will want a court order before they give out any information," Veasy says. "Maybe the reclusive Lester Tarsis can tell us if he's still alive. I'll beard him in his den."

"Speak English."

"I'll go to his office."

THIS ONE IS THE KEEPER

"We called it the Martini," Jay says. "It was the last shot of the day . . ."

("the martini . . . cool movie trivia . . .")

"It was when we did our best work," Jay says. "The ADs were watching the clock to make sure we didn't go into overtime so they drove the crew hard. The cameraman wanted to beat the traffic on the freeway so he set up quickly and didn't fuss with the lights. The actors all had drinks or dinner dates. They spoke their lines quickly without acting, which is what you always want."

In the respectful hush Jay hears a laptop clacking. Someone is taking notes. iPhones glow in the dark. They are taping him, recording everything he says. He is a fount of wisdom for these young filmmakers.

"Lester's routine hasn't changed in thirty years," Jay says. "At five he's in his office watching the weekend footage with the editors. He gives his notes and they go back for another few hours of work. Then he returns the calls he blew off during the day. He'll have plenty of time to talk to me. I planted that hint about being on set . . ."

("brilliant tease.")

"Thank you."

Late afternoon and it's dark in the back bedroom. The sun has moved to the front of the house and is glaring like a Ten K through the living room window. Can't shoot there, Jay decides. Too harsh, no nuance. The kitchen won't work. It's the most boring room in the house.

"Never play a big scene in the kitchen," Jay says. "A kitchen sucks the drama out of any moment."

("good to know.")

"We'll set up outside in the garden," Jay says. "It's weedy and untended. I'll sit on the chipped stone bench by the rusty, nonworking fountain. Wheel the old grill out from under the dusty hedge . . ."

("resonant metaphor.")

"The writers are just coming into the office, hoping to get Lester's approval on their changes . . . That sweet little girl is in the doorway. She can't leave before Lester. I'm really sorry about her."

("she won't feel a thing.")

"The phone rings," Jay says. "Jay Braffner on the line. Lester gets that quizzical look. Wonder what schmuck hired Jay Braffner, he says. He picks up the phone. Never says hello, just goes right into it like we just had coffee this morning. So Jay, good news. Where'd you land? I dial the detonator code. Nowhere Lester, I answer, but you're gonna land on Hollywood Boulevard . . ."

("BABOOM!")

"Push the decibels," Jay says. "Smoke and flames fill the frame."

("awesome . . .")

"Thank you."

LESTER'S LAST WORDS

Lester usually leaves his office door open so he can shout out orders to Eloise, but after lunch he shuts it tight as a signal that he doesn't want to be disturbed.

Maybe he's hiring prostitutes for one of the foreign distributors who had come to town and doesn't want her to know.

He usually speaks so quietly that people have to strain to hear him. But this time his voice comes through the wall. "I'm on wheels, Stewie. You gotta gimme a hammer on this guy."

It's Hollywood English, still an encrypted language to Eloise.

Line 1 blinks.

"This is Detective Veasy, La Playita Police . . . Is Mr. Tarsis available now?"

The closed door means Do Not Disturb . . . For anybody . . .

"Can I tell Mr. Tarsis what this call is in reference to?" she asks.

There is a deep breath like the caller is trying to keep his temper.

"Tell him I want to talk about Gary London, Mitch Helfand, and Dave Kessel . . . Oh yes and I'm looking for Jay Braffner . . ."

"Mr. Tarsis is in a meeting . . ."

"Tell him it's a police emergency . . ."

Eloise's e-mail dings: "Come in here . . ."

Lester wants her.

"Mr. Tarsis will call you as soon as his meeting is over, Detective Veasy . . ."

"Hey lady, did you hear what I just said?"

"Yes I did, sir. You'll be his first call back, I promise . . ."

She hangs up and hurries into the office. Lester is rummaging in his desk with the phone in his ear.

"Print up the statements I've been getting from New Zealand . . ."

She leaves the door open as she goes back to her computer. Lester's voice has a panicky edge she's never heard before.

"Next to Fiona I'm the biggest above-the-line number in the budget, Stewie," he says. "Thirty-five hundred creator royalty and fifteen

120

thousand producer's fee. Comes to eighteen-five a week, not to mention the twenty Gs I pay myself for the scripts I write . . ."

He jumps up from his desk and switches on the speaker. "Owen makes one call—hello Lester, time to get on with your life, which is Hollywoodese for schmuck, you still here?—and he saves himself seven hundred and fifty Gs . . . If I were him I would have gotten rid of me three years ago."

"He needs you to run the show," says a familiar voice.

It's Stewart, the lawyer. He's an old friend from New York who always says, "The boss dere, doll?"

"He needed me while we were big in the domestic market," Lester says. "Now most of the audience doesn't speak English. He can get some Aussie hack for two Gs . . ."

"Don't sell yourself short. He won't find somebody like you . . ."

"Nobody needs somebody like me. Owen's got a year or two left to make hay before the show dies. He dumps me, he's good for a million pure net. I just wanna know where my leverage is and how much I can settle for."

"Well, he's on the hook for the residuals," Stewart says.

"He won't pay 'em."

"He'll be in breach . . ."

Lester's voice cracks. "Jesus Stewie, the guy's a *goniff*, he don't care about contracts. He's been cheatin' me on the distribution, pushin' the goal posts back every time I get close to profit . . ."

"We can request the court to freeze his U.S. assets, pending disposition of our case," Stewart says. "It's a long shot. Lemme look at the statements."

They disconnect—they never say "goodbye"—and Lester goes to the window. "Can't remember my ex's number," he says. "Think I should talk to my therapist about that?"

Eloise blurts: "I know the number by heart. Think I should go into therapy?"

Lester turns. "Eloise goes Hollywood. Throwing lines like a regular *tummuleh*."

Eloise gets warm all over. She doesn't want to break the mood by asking what a *tummuleh* is. Probably some kind of Jewish expression. She keys in Claire's number. It rings forever.

"She's sitting there watching *Access Hollywood* and letting it ring so I'll think she's busy," Lester says.

Claire picks up as the message begins. She never dropped her married name, but Eloise can't call her "Mrs. Tarsis." Instead, she just puts on her best officious secretary voice. "Lester Tarsis calling . . ."

Lester stands at the window, leaving it on speaker.

"What now, Claire?"

"Nice of you to find time for your son in your busy schedule," Claire says.

"Is Seth in the house?" he asks.

"Doug got him a new lawyer, who specializes in these drug cases. He's in a meeting with him."

"Hollywood rules," Lester says. "Everybody's gotta be in a meeting after lunch, even kids. So what happened this time?"

Eloise gets up to leave, but Lester shakes his head and points to his ear like he wants her to listen.

"They broke into the back door of the pharmacy. Kenny Shuster put a bag over the surveillance camera . . ."

"Bobby Shuster's son?"

"Yes . . . Doug says they must have got the idea from that movie *Drugstore Cowboys*. Doug says Bobby produced it?"

"He didn't. Your pool guy got it wrong . . ."

"So he made a mistake. Anyway, he's a contractor and he has a lot of clients in the business . . ."

"Yeah and he's pitched a series about a pool guy to every one of them . . ."

"Well, it is a good idea."

"It's a fifteen-minute porno spot on Spectravision," Lester says. "Who else was with Seth on this caper?"

"Holly Spitzer was driving the car. And Justin Levin . . ."

"A regular Who's Who of teenage losers."

"And your son is the biggest loser of them all," Claire says. "Doug's lawyer says he can get a spot for Seth at Pathways in Malibu. He says the judge will put him on probation pending results of the treatment . . ."

"How much is it, minus the judge's bribe and Doug's referral fee?"

"Fifteen a week. It's usually twenty-two, but the lawyer says they'll lower it if all the kids register . . ."

"A package deal for parasites," Lester says. "And next week or month when one of these kids ODs . . ."

"It's the only way to keep Seth out of jail, Lester . . ."

"It's blackmail and I won't pay it."

There is a silence. "You have to," Claire says.

"Read your agreement," Lester says. "Seth's eighteenth birthday is coming up next month. He's legally an adult and I'm no longer responsible for his support . . ."

"You mean you're not gonna pay . . . ?"

"No more support, Claire. Just alimony . . ."

"I can't live on ten thousand a month, Lester . . ."

"Once Doug sells his pool man show you'll be rolling in dough. Of course if he does sell it, first thing he'll do is dump you for some young chippy . . ."

"You'd let your son go to jail . . . ?"

"Don't worry, he won't. Bobby Shuster will build a gym for the La Playita PD and the case will miraculously disappear. Go to Bobby. Tell him your mean ex-husband won't cough up. He's Mr. Hollywood Benevolent, Mr. Ethiopian War Orphan, Mr. Testimonial Dinner. He'll cover Seth, and you too, if Doug won't mind sharing . . ."

"I'll go to court, Lester," Claire says. "You have to maintain me in my standard of living . . ."

"Talk to your lawyer, honey," Lester says. "You've been living with Doug for a few years and before that there was Arthur, who you bankrupted and threw out. In other words I haven't been your sole source of support . . ."

"This is low, Lester, even for a cheap bastard like you . . ."

"I've been keeping records for the last seventeen years, Claire," Lester says. "The twelve Gs a month support. The loan for the down payment—the cars I bought you—the insurance, the doctor bills—private school, summer camps, tutors, therapists, not to mention the lawyers, court-ordered shrinks, detoxers, locker-uppers, medications . . ."

"He's your son for God's sake . . ."

"My mother said he didn't look like me at all, Claire . . . Was I just the best candidate?"

"I was faithful to you . . ."

"By default, babe. You were a banged-up Canadian lap dancer with nothing going for you. I was your ticket out . . ."

"I paid for that ticket, putting up with your bad jokes, letting you slobber all over me . . ."

"Comes to about a million bucks I spent over and above the agreement, Claire," Lester says. "You weren't worth it . . ."

"Fuck you, Lester!"

"Hang up, Eloise," Lester says.

Eloise pushes the extension button, cutting Claire off.

"It's the only way to shut her up," Lester says.

He looks out of the window, shaking his head slightly as if listening to a sad story.

"Actually, my mother said Seth could have been my twin," he says. "I took him to visit her in the assisted living in West Palm. She showed him to all the old *bubbes* in the card room. 'This is my beautiful grandson,' she said. Then they sat in her room and ate Fig Newtons and watched *The Lucy Show* . . . In the car back to the hotel, he said, 'Thanks Dad, I had a real nice time with Grandma.'"

Is that a catch in his voice? "See that brown mist rising over the mountains?" he says. "Inversion . . . Pollution. The air is unhealthy for the elderly and for young children with respiratory ailments, they say. Seth has asthma. He has to carry an inhaler. The kids made fun of him, of course. He was a lousy ball player. Couldn't even hit the ball off a tee. Had to quit AYSO because the coaches wouldn't play him. If you can't play ball in LA they treat you like a leper . . . Marijuana is about the worst thing for him, not to mention whatever else he does . . ."

The office phone rings.

"That'll be Claire with a few more choice words," Lester says.

Eloise runs back to her desk and picks up. "Lester Tarsis's office . . ."

"Hi, this is Jay Braffner calling. Lester available?"

That poor man again.

"Lester, it's Jay Braffner . . ."

Lester sighs. "Another lost soul on the highway of life . . ."

Eloise has to say it. "You make up the best lines, Lester."

"I stole that one from a song, honey," Lester says. "Only psychos can make things up . . ." He thinks for a moment. "One lost soul is enough for the day. Tell Jay I'll call him tomorrow."

FROM NOIR TO GORE

It's the laughter of a lunatic. Karloff, the body snatcher, Rathbone, the mad scientist. The inmates are shrieking in the asylum. Lightning crackles in the secret laboratory. Insane, vein-busting, unnerving . . .

"Mirth and frank incest . . ."

("great pun.")

"Lester had it on his Christmas cards," Jay says. "Jon Pfeffer, his resident groveler, wrote it for him."

His chest is aching. He has to catch his breath, he's laughing so hard.

"I mean IT'S FUCKING HILARIOUS."

He knows they're confused. They expected frustration.

"For me of all people not to know that nobody in this town takes a call from a bum, which is what I am, Charley," he says.

("Brando, On the Waterfront.")

"For me who called around for eight years—agents who had kissed my ass, producers who had pleaded with me to attach myself to their projects—and never got one call back . . . For me, who made money for people, got them high and laid and then couldn't even get a coffee meeting in return . . . For me to be stupid enough to think that Lester Tarsis, who unapologetically does not give a shit about anything but his dick . . ."

Jay stops. Is the speech going on too long?

"Lester used to say: 'First line got the point, second line *forgot* the point.'"

("best script note ever.")

"He liked to say, 'It's not a pretzel without a twist.' So here's the twist that keeps the Second Act alive. Lester won't pick up the phone unless I find someone he wants to talk to. I have to get that person to call Lester and hand me the phone so I can detonate the explosive when he picks up." Jay goes into the kitchen. "It's the best kind of plot, beautifully complex, but crystal clear at the same time . . ."

("Hitchcockian.")

Jay almost trips over Roy's body. "And then there's the comic element. Two bodies to dispose of . . ."

("gallows humor.")

He grabs the kitchen towel wound around Roy's neck and drags him out the kitchen door into the backyard.

("oh God, not again.")

"What did Todd Browning say about gory scenes? First time gasping, second time giggling . . . Let's put that theory to the test."

He stops. "Weird sound off screen."

The fat, gray tomcat is tearing at the garbage bags, trying to get to the remains of Alison Sobel. Jay kicks him in the heaving flank. Sends him flying across the backyard.

"I left Alison out here when the phone rang," Jay says. "Sorry Alison and sorry Mr. Cat . . ."

The cat watches, green eyes gleaming in the rustling bushes.

"Can't have you trotting around the neighborhood with a foot in your mouth. Might alarm the neighbors."

(giggles.)

Jay throws the Hefty bags into the trunk of Alison's car and slams it shut.

"Naked is good, but not for exposition, Lester used to say. He's nothing if not quotable."

He drags Roy into the garage.

"So while I'm figuring out who Lester will pick up the phone for"— he lays Roy on a garbage bag on the bloody floor—"I'll deconstruct the late Mr. Farkas . . ."

GOOD CALL

The traffic imps lie in wait
  For someone with an important date.
  They empty the road of gridlock's sludge,
  Then ooze it back as he starts to budge.
  It's a little after two. The 101 Freeway looks clear. Veasy makes the turn and finds himself in gridlock on the ramp.

Can't move. He'll have to crawl five agonizing miles to the next exit.

He calls Mineo at Headquarters. "How we doin' with the little red van?"

"Working on it," Mineo says and hangs up.

Veasy fishes a roach out of the heel of his sock. The size of a thumbnail. Good for a hit, but it will stay in his blood for thirty days.

Marooned drivers use the time,
Texting, thinking,
Coffee drinking,
Searching for a rhyme.
  The phone interrupts.

"Got a trace on that van," Mineo says.

"Reported stolen, right?"

"Yeah. But today the owner, a Mr. Olin Sandusky, who is also the complainant, called Portland PD and said the car was back in front of his house."

The answer pops into Veasy's head so quickly he is tempted to credit the weed.

"Like the dog."

"What dog?"

"The old Lab that was taken from in front of the Vons and mysteriously reappeared. Sometimes cases form themselves into a mysterious symmetry. As if the gods were sending an all-purpose clue . . ."

"And what do the weed gods tell you?"

"That Sandusky stole his own car."

"Does that mean the man stole his own dog?"

"He reported the car stolen so he'd be off the hook in case it was spotted. Then, he said it had shown up so it would look like he'd been home all the time. It's the kind of scheme that passes for clever in the recreation areas of our major correction facilities."

"Hold it, the Owl's calling . . ."

Veasy's on hold . . .

You can see at a glance
Why detectives have shiny pants.
Standing on your feet
Is strictly for rooks on the beat
Or workers of the street
Or chimps in heat.
Detective work is done
Shifting from bun to bun.

Mineo pops back on. "The Owl wants a 20 on you."

"Tell him I'm stuck on the 101. But don't tell him about our Portland guy."

"I won't. We gotta decide if he's our man, first. Then, figure a way to get him down here because the Owl won't let us go to Portland unless we have DNA, three eyewitnesses, and a letter from the Pope."

"Do we like Sandusky for this?" Veasy asks.

"Love him. He's got eleven arrests. Check kiting. Possession of stolen credit card. Two residential burglary convictions . . ."

"Sounds like Chapman Keene's secret sharer. Get a picture?"

"Mug shot. Droopy white dude. He could fit the description, but so could a million other guys."

"Where did he do his time?"

"LA County . . ."

"Where the birds of a feather might have flocked together."

"Only Keene was there in '02. Sandusky in '06."

"Don't confuse me with the facts," Veasy says. "I'm into the big philosophical question."

"Which is?"

Nature's wonders abounding,
Its logic astounding
But what is the reason for Olin Sandusky?
A purposeful field mouse
A task for the head louse

But a thief in the wrong house?
With booze on his breath
Scares an old man to death
Was that God's plan for Olin Sandusky?

ZACK PANICS

Elliot is hunched over his laptop, screaming at someone in New Zealand.

"How you can shoot thirty hours of tape and not produce one cuttable minute? A fuckin' chimpanzee could do it by the law of averages . . ."

The phone . . . Eloise . . .

"Lester wants Elliot in for edit notes."

Elliot shakes his head.

"You go, Zack."

"He doesn't want me."

Elliot's shake gets spastic.

"I don't care, I'm not putting up with that abuse today. Tell him I'm trying to get a fine cut on this week's episode . . . Fine cut, what a joke . . ."

A tall guy in a dark suit is going into the office. From down the hall, under the gloomy old fixtures, he looks familiar. Probably an episodic actor.

But as Zack comes closer he gets a better look. The guy is standing at Eloise's desk.

"Detective Veasy, La Playita Police Department."

Zack flattens against the wall. A cop? He's seen this guy scoring weed from Roger, the senile hippie who hangs out in front of Dwayne's. The guy has seen him copping, too. And smoking under the tree by the beach.

Zack runs down the hall back to the cutting room where Elliot is getting apoplectic on the phone.

"You give me three hours of Fiona climbing up a palm tree. Had a good time shooting up her ass, did you? Lotsa laughs? Well, guess what, none of it is usable . . . You can see pube stubble, that's why. Did I say stubble, I mean beard. She looks like fuckin' ZZ Top . . ." He blinks like he doesn't recognize Zack. "What's up? Did he send you back to get me?"

"I can't go in, Elliot. There's a cop in the office."

Elliot screams into the phone: "Don't hang up!"

"An undercover cop. I know him from buying weed on the boardwalk. He must be here to arrest me . . ."

"He came all the way from La Playita to arrest you for weed? I don't think so."

"Why else would he be here?"

"Maybe he wants to arrest Lester for indecent exposure. He's probably peddling a script . . ."

"Please Elliot, I can't go in there."

"Marijuana is a summons in La Playita, Zack, okay? Don't ask me how I know."

Zack has to confess. "It's more than weed. I have a record . . ."

"If it's a second offense it doesn't matter, believe me . . ."

"It's not about weed, Elliot. I have a restraining order against me."

Elliot puts down the phone. "What did you do, stalk your ex-girlfriend?"

"No . . . Well, she said I did. The girl I came out here with from the city. We were supposed to move in together, share expenses. Then she dumped me for this beach bum."

"Surfer dude, right? East Coast chicks go crazy over them. Middle-school dropouts. They find them exotic . . ."

"I just wanted to get my stuff out of the apartment. I was outside waiting for her to leave, that's all, but she got paranoid and called the cops. They told me the second time it would be ninety days . . ."

Elliot nods. "Guys who look like us don't do very well out here unless we run a studio and even then we gotta watch the tennis pro." He goes back to the phone. "Hello . . ." Then reddens. "Jerk hung up on me." And picks up a legal pad. "I'll cover you, but no overtime this week. Lester's been bugging me about the postproduction budget."

No overtime means no Cosmos for the babes at the clubs, which means the sex odds have gone from slim to none. But he has no choice.

"Okay, no overtime."

"Go hide in the office," Elliot says. "I'll call you when he leaves."

JUST THE FACTS, MA'AM

Veasy is sitting across from Eloise. He jumps up as Elliot rushes into the office. "Back of the line, pal."

"This gentleman is part of Mr. Tarsis's meeting," Eloise says.

Veasy takes out his phone. "Do I have to call for backup or should I just use him as a human shield?"

Elliot steps aside. "After you, I'm in no hurry . . ." He follows Veasy into the office. The three look up in surprise. "Is one of you Mr. Tarsis?" Veasy asks.

Two men point to the guy behind the desk. "He is."

Squirrelly, chewing on a gray mustache, sour look like he just ate a bad clam.

"Traveling with a bodyguard, Elliot?" Tarsis asks.

"Mr. Tarsis, I'm Detective Veasy, La Playita PD," Veasy says. "Can I get the rest of the cast members?"

Veasy pretends to be writing their names in his notebook, but jots a couplet:

Can I match wits
With these Hollywood shits?

"Noah Lippman," says the little fat guy with the Lakers cap on backwards.

"Sean O'Meara," the tall guy in cargo shorts says as if Veasy should know who he is.

"If it's about my son, you should speak to his mother," Tarsis says.

"It's about Dave Kessel."

The three men look at each other in puzzlement.

"What did Dave Kessel do?"

"He died," Veasy says.

The three look surprised.

"When was this?" Lester asks.

"Day and a half ago. They were fumigating his house for termites. He fell and hit his head in his wine cellar and died of Vicane gas poisoning."

"Was he drunk?" Lippman asks.

"Maybe he wanted to try Vicane," says O'Meara. "Thought it might help him get an erection . . ."

"That's Viagra."

"Then he was misinformed."

"Dave Kessel, the Canarsie connoisseur," Tarsis muses. "World's foremost authority on vintage Armagnac . . ."

"Victor Hugo's favorite beverage," O'Meara says.

"You mean Victor Hugo, the haircutter on Rodeo Drive . . . ?" says Lippman.

Tarsis shrugs. "Usable, but uninspired."

"Story of my life," says Lippman.

"I guess you didn't hear about Mitch Helfand either," Veasy says.

"Mitch Helfand, half man half party animal?"

"A Yentaur?" Lippman tries.

Tarsis shakes his head. "Only works if you know Yiddish."

"A dead language," says O'Meara.

"Unlike Gaelic which is spoken all over the civilized world," Tarsis says. "What happened to Mitch, Detective?"

"Drowned in his swimming pool."

"Probably the first time he was ever in it," Tarsis says.

"I heard he did laps every day," O'Meara offers.

"Laps with skirts over them," Lippman counters.

"Too complicated," Tarsis says. "Audiences hate it when you make them think."

"Okay," Lippman emends. "Laps with slits in them."

"Why don't you say hairy laps?" says O'Meara.

"Vulgar," Tarsis says. "How would you phrase it, Detective?"

"He does laps lapping laps," Veasy says.

"Positively Shakespearean," O'Meara says. "But can you fix a speeding ticket?"

"Mr. Helfand is survived by a Bosley hair tech and two pole dancers," says Lippman.

"A Leno outtake," says Tarsis.

"Let's see what you can do with Gary London," Veasy says, writing "London" in his notebook.

"The luckiest Jew in Hollywood," says Lippman.

"That was the quarter final," O'Meara adds. "Now he's up for luckiest in the solar system."

"Are there Jews in the solar system?" Veasy asks.

"Ever hear of Jew . . . piter . . . ?"

At least Tarsis has the good manners to look almost surprised.

"Are you saying that Gary London is no longer with us, either?"

"Died of carbon monoxide poisoning in his Panamera early yesterday morning."

"Could that be suicide?" Sean asks.

"Could be."

"Gary London falls on his sword?" Lippman says.

"'Tis a far, far better thing I do than I have ever done before?" adds O'Meara.

Lester's e-mail dings. "May I interrupt this roll call of the honored dead?"

It's from Eloise. "Jay Braffner from his car . . ."

Lester types "call back." And turns to Veasy. "I thought nothing could shock me."

"Are you shocked?"

"No."

"You know why I'm here?"

"Because I knew the three of them, I guess."

"And they worked for you."

"They did, among many others."

Veasy starts a new page and asks: "Three men, late middle-age, relatively healthy, all of whom knew and worked with each other, die unnatural deaths in a two-day period . . . Any reaction?"

Lester shrugs. "It's the end of an era."

"An incalculable loss," says Sean.

Noah pipes up: "How have the mighty fallen."

Veasy stands over Lippman with the patented cop glare of disbelief.

"Kessel's death was in the paper," he says.

Noah cringes. "I only read the sports page."

Veasy tries the glare on Sean.

"In Europe they wipe their asses with yesterday's paper," Sean says. "Then they read it."

Now Tarsis.

"I live in a newsless void," he says.

"Nobody called to tell you about any of these deaths?" Veasy asks.

The three shake their heads. "We're out of the loop," Tarsis says.

"The phone doesn't ring when you're doing a show that only runs in Botswana and Montenegro," says Lippman.

O'Meara nods. "People probably think we're dead, too. I haven't gotten junk mail for months."

The three stare impassively at Veasy.

The funniest man
Has the deadest pan.
When the humor gets delirious
He keeps his expression serious.

"So you don't anticipate a big Hollywood-style memorial service for any of the three of them," he says.

"They could have it in the back seat of Gary's Porsche," Lippman says.

"They weren't well-liked?"

Lester sits back. "Neither liked nor hated, Detective Veasy. Just guys you work with, get to know pretty well, and then never see again after the show is canceled."

Veasy checks his notes. "The name Jay Braffner keeps coming up. Is he dead?"

"Not if he passed away in the last fifteen minutes," Lester says. "He just called." He taps out a message to Eloise. "Jay is a tragic figure . . ." His e-mail dings. "My assistant says it came up 'no number.' But he's been calling about something so I should hear from him again."

Lippman takes off his Lakers cap and wipes his sweaty strands. "Do you suspect foul play, Detective Veasy?"

"Noah's been watching Charlie Chan movies again," O'Meara says. "Since the unsolved murder of William Desmond Taylor, no producer has ever met that well-deserved fate."

"I get suspicious when deaths come in clusters," Veasy says.

"Deaths come in clusters," Tarsis says. "I like that line."

"Watch for it in an upcoming episode of *She, Queen of the Jungle,*" O'Meara says.

"I'd be flattered," says Veasy.

Tarsis regards him with interest. "Most cops have a script in the glove compartment of the black and white."

"I'm a detective. I travel in a Crown Victoria and write poetry."

"A homicide detective who writes poetry." Tarsis looks around the room. "Whaddya say geniuses? Sound like a series?"

"If it is, you're just the man to get it canceled," Lippman says.

"You're the anti-Spielberg," says O'Meara.

Veasy gives Tarsis his card. "When you speak to Mr. Braffner could you ask him to call me?"

"Mr. Braffner is probably certifiable."

"All the more reason," Veasy says. "If you get him to call me I'll give you two free tickets to the Policeman's Ball."

"They don't have a Policeman's Ball anymore," O'Meara says.

"Okay then . . . Three tickets."

Tarsis makes a sour face. "Chico Marx, 1935," he says. "But still funny."

THE INSANITY CLAUSE

Jay cruises down the Pacific Coast Highway in Alison Sobel's charcoal Honda Civic.

"In Brooklyn you went to the beach if it wasn't raining," he says. "But out here, one cloud in the morning and everybody stays home."

("spoiled, entitled . . .")

Jay dallies in the right lane. "How to be invisible in Hollywood," he says. "Drive five miles under the speed limit in an unwashed, tastefully dinged Japanese economy car on the PCH, the freeway of the stars. You will transcend nobodiness—you will literally disappear."

A La Playita police cruiser speeds by, siren screaming, lights flashing, and pulls over a Lexus RX 350 full of teenage girls in bikinis.

"Here's where experience comes in," Jay says. "Most directors would shoot a sequence in which the killer turns off at Topanga Canyon, drives to a wooded area, takes the corpses out of the trunk, covers them with leaves, and drives away."

While the cops cautiously approach the teenage bikini car from both sides, hands on their Glocks, a "Missing Person" alert for Alison Sobel with her plate number GEU479Z appears on their computer screen.

"It's a perfectly good sequence, but I'm not going to shoot it," Jay says. "Know why?"

(baffled silence.)

Jay smiles in gentle reproach. "Because the stash-the-bodies-in-the-woods sequence pops up in every cheap thriller ever made."

("of course, why didn't we think of that?")

"Predictable is the kiss of death in a thriller," Jay says. "As soon as I turn off onto a country road the audience knows I'm getting rid of the bodies. Attention flags, heart rate slows, alpha waves flatten . . ."

("you've lost them.")

"But now," Jay says, "I'm going to freak them out. There'll be screams in the screening room."

He turns hard right. Alison's Civic swerves across three lanes of traffic. Brakes screech, horns blast. A guy in a rusty pickup speeds by with a Doppler curse—"Stu . . . pid . . . mother . . . fucker . . . !"

La Playita's finest is busy checking IDs on the girls in the bikinis and doesn't notice.

Jay drives into a parking lot by the Santa Monica Pier.

"A little moment of jeopardy. An anxious shiver for the audience. What if I'm blindsided or rearended—or both? The tailgate flies open, hefty bags come bouncing out, two severed heads roll down the road like psychedelic bowling balls. Brakes screech. Fenders crash. News flash: A torso, penis attached, was found on the PCH this afternoon, film at eleven . . ."

(helpless hilarity.)

"I could have been followed into the lot by a red-faced, road-raging prole," Jay says. "Screaming threats he runs up to the window with a twelve gauge and blows me away. Happens every day. Or in a more mundane version I am pulled over by the cops. As soon as they see that my license was revoked in 1994 it's: could you open the tailgate, sir? What's in those garbage bags, sir? Would you mind explaining that foul odor . . . sir?"

There are always plenty of parking spaces on a bad beach day. But Jay drives right at two vans full of surfers, unloading their gear. They step back glaring as he noses into a space between them.

"I've made it harder for these surfer dudes to get their boards off the roofs," Jay confides. He gets out and gives them the what-are-you-gonna-do-about-it smirk.

"They're blonde, strong, dumb, and stoned," he says. "In the real world they beat me unconscious with their boards and drive away. But here they step aside and let me pass. Anybody know why?"

(silence.)

Jay tries to stifle his impatience. He knows they're so awed by him they don't want to look foolish.

"Because this is a movie, people, that's why. I'm scripting reality. These surfers have been turned into characters. The real world has become a virtual universe of my own creating . . ."

("the real is imaginary.")

"And the imaginary is real," Jay says. "The real world is having its usual humdrum day. But in my universe a few more scenes of horrible death will be followed by the incineration of Lester Tarsis in a fiery inferno."

("the imaginary is the real.")

"An artist can hold two conflicting ideas in his mind at the same time," Jay says. "This is a paraphrase of . . ."

("Fitzgerald?")

"A genius can transform the imagined into the actual."

("the movie is the reality.")

Jay walks away from the befuddled surfers. "The surfer dudes think I'm a maniac talking to myself. I'm really a hyper-rational filmmaker, who just dumped two bodies right under their noses. I'm a crazed killer, but I am also forging a new cinema in the smithy of my psyche."

("transformative.")

("Joycean.")

"Thank you," Jay says.

SCENT OF A PERP

A lion growling under a tree
  Wondering where he should go pee
  Suddenly a breeze across the Serengeti
  Brings the scent of recent parolee.
Veasy calls Tingley.
"I need you to find Olin Sandusky's lawyer."
"Mineo is working this with you, isn't he?"
"How'd you guess?"
"He's crouching under his desk like he just dropped something and whispering into his phone, which is how people usually talk to you around here."
"You can find Sandusky on the DMV database. Get his DOB and look up his record . . ."
"You too busy checking panty lines?"
"This is gonna be a good grab," Veasy says. "I want you to get a piece of it."
"And what do you get out of this selfless act?"
"The fun of hearing the Owl's teeth grind as he gives us a commendation. Plus one hour of degrading sex with you at a venue of my choosing."
"I'm putting you on hold," says Tingley.
Veasy burns his cuticle and his lower lip finishing another roach. Then Tingley is back.
"Sixty-five Sanduskys, but only one Olin. Paroled last year after doing three of a four to seven for breaking and entering."
"He's in violation, living out of state," Veasy says.
"Oregon's his place of birth. He got a waiver to be close to his family. Said it would help in the rehabilitation process . . . He was represented by Jared Finkelman Esquire . . ."
Veasy sings a falsetto note.
"Was that a celestial chord I just heard?" Tingley asks.
"You hope your perp is the smartest
So you can enjoy your work.

You want to feel like an artist,
Instead of a plodding clerk."
"Case closed already?" Tingley asks.
"But I can say with authority,
Sandusky's no Professor Moriarty."
"Who?"

"Here's the scenario," Veasy says. "Olin Sandusky is a career criminal, caught twice so you know he got away with it a coupla hundred times. But he's fresh out of jail, hasn't got his land legs. He's broke and he gets careless. Takes a burglary contract from Chapman Keene, a punk check kiter he met in County, a guy who would definitely roll over on him as soon as a cop made a fist. He drives his banged-up van into an upscale neighborhood and sits on the street until every housekeeper north of Guadalajara wonders what he's doing. Doesn't double-check the address. Hits the wrong house and when he realizes he's made a mistake, he panics and assaults an old lady, thus adding another charge to the sheet. Now he's sitting in Portland shitting a brick because he's a two-time loser with no money and no place to run."

Tingley swoons like an infatuated student. "Oh Professor Veasy, you're so wise. I could just sit at your feet forever."

"My feet are a good place to start. How about tonight?"

"Sorry, PTA meeting. Where will you find solace?"

"I'll try the lady with no panty line," Veasy says. "But I'll be thinking of you."

A MADMAN'S MEMORY

("hey dude, the boss just dumped two bodies on the beach in broad daylight and got away with it . . . Dude.")

The crew's footsteps crunch the sand behind him. They are awestruck. Their pantheon is being rapidly revised. Ford, Welles, Hitchcock are dropping a notch to make room for Braffner, who is bursting forth from obscurity.

"Now for a pop quiz," Jay says. "How do you turn a commercial thriller into an art film?"

Their puzzlement is palpable.

"One-word answer, people," Jay says. "Digress."

(furious whispers.)

Jay raises his hand to quiet the consternation.

"When you digress you are telling the audience: there's more to this film than cheesy suspense and cheap thrills. You take a Godard moment. Do a monologue in a handheld close-up with the sound of cars whooshing by on the PCH. Relate an anecdote that might or might not illuminate the story. Stops the picture dead, but gives cachet. You see, if you're too entertaining they mark you a hack. You have to bore the bourgeois into thinking you're an artist."

("bore the bourgeois . . . love it . . .")

Jay trudges to a beach house. Picture windows floor to ceiling. Pebbled stone terrace, ocean view.

"In 1977 I spent six very happy months in this house with Marie Page," Jay says.

("Marie Page, the blaxploitation star?")

"The first and only black female series star in the history of '70s TV," Jay says. "I directed her pilot and we fell in lust . . ."

("witty but pithy.")

"She was my tigress," Jay says. "We'd spend the weekends alone. No barbecues, no business parties. Just the two of us, consumed with each other. Tigress, tigress, burning bright. She was rangy and strong, one of the few women I ever met who could match my intensity. She told me I was the only white man she'd ever had great sex with."

("talk about a compliment!")

"I was bigtime bankable in the '70s. You could attach my name to a project and get a deal. So I was getting maybe ten, twenty offers a week. Pilots, features, minis, commercials, even plays. Marie and I would smoke Thai stick and lay in bed, reading them aloud and getting hysterical at how bad they were. Every month I would stick about a hundred in a Hefty bag and put them out for recycling."

They are shooting in front of the house, the Palisades Bluffs looming behind him. Beachgoers see a large man orating to an imaginary crowd and veer off the path onto the sand.

"Get those tourists in the shot," Jay orders. "Pan off me and get those frightened people avoiding the wild-haired prophet of a man ranting on the beach . . ."

He waits until the crew gets the shot and pans back to him and then picks up his story. "So one Sunday I'm out there and the bag is so full that it opens as I throw it on the street and scripts come tumbling out. Just at that moment a homeless guy comes walking by. In those days we had a lot of them hanging out on the beach. Viet vets and hippie burnouts. In New York they look like scarecrows, but out here they're always in the sun so they get bronzed like agents or golf pros. This guy is schlepping around in a pair of torn-up slacks that look like they might have come from the dumpster behind a men's store like Jack Taylor's in Beverly Hills . . . He squints like he thinks he knows me and says: I see you're throwing away all these scripts. You must be a big shot. Who are you?"

"I keep a straight face. I'm George Lucas, I tell him. No you're not, he says. George Lucas lives up north. Next time try Ridley Scott. He's in Malibu and gets so many scripts he has to shred them."

"Now the guy bends down and picks up a script called *Double Deal* . . ." Jay stops. "Can anyone guess what he says?"

(quizzical murmurs.)

"I wrote this, he says."

("the homeless guy wrote the script???")

"Too crazy, right? You could never put this in a movie. The guy points to the *screenplay by* credit. Dennis Kornbluth, that's me. Did you read it? I hem and haw, tell him I'm booked pretty solid into next year. You don't have to make excuses, he says. I was an unknown and my agent was a scumsucking pig. There was no reason for anyone to read my script except that it just happens to be fucking great. He walks away. You want it back? I ask. What am I gonna do with it? he says. He sticks his finger through his pants pocket like it's his dick. I don't jerk myself off about my career anymore, he says . . . Enjoy . . .

"Living in LA is like walking past a river after a flood. You see all the debris floating by. Dennis Kornbluth must have done something to be homeless—like have no talent. That won't happen to me. I'm gonna be hot forever. But I'm curious and take a look.

"After the first few pages I'm thinking, okay this is moving pretty fast. Script's about a cardsharp who gets caught cheating and has his hands broken by a Mafia boss. He trains a kid in crooked dealing to get revenge for him in a big game. The kid wins big, get chased by the same guy who broke Svengali's hand, hooks up with a tarnished angel— hooker with a back story—and steps over a bunch of bodies into the sunset. It's *The Hustler* meets *Godfather II* with a little *Love Story* thrown in. The audience has seen so many movies like this they know every plot turn, but that's good. Audiences like to know the ending. They get irritated when you surprise them . . ."

("have to remember that.")

"I send the script around, but can't sell it. Poker stories aren't happening this year, I'm told. I give it to Lester. Too dark for TV, he says. Then I jump on the C and C express—Cocaine and Cuervo for the uninitiated. Three years goes by like a minute and a half. When I'm ready to restart my life, I find out I don't exist anymore."

(pained silence.)

"I stumble out of Betty Ford into temporary lucidity and see a headline in Variety: TARSIS PAIRS ACES FOR DOUBLE DEAL. Story says Lester Tarsis has signed Robert Culp and Doug McClure to star in a 'dark, twisty melodrama' for the CBS Movie of the Week. It's been 'penned' by Jon Pfeffer and will be 'helmed' by producer David Kessel in his directorial debut."

"Pfeffer is a gelded, strung-out desperado, Lester's pet hack. The late Dave Kessel couldn't direct traffic."

"Lester doesn't return my call so I go to his office. He's at Universal and the guards won't let me on the lot without a pass. I wait outside his house, but he drives by me into the garage and the gate swings closed while I'm trying to get in."

"I follow him to a Hama Sushi on Venice. Slide in next to him at the counter. You're slippery as this eel, Lester, I say. He shakes his head. Stop trying to write dialogue, Jay."

"I thought you didn't like the script, I say. I didn't, he says, but Culp did and Culp's got a three-picture deal with CBS. I ask why he didn't get the real author to do the production rewrite. I'm not gonna comb the town for a homeless guy, he says. If he's still alive he'll pop up with his hand out."

"Why'd you hire Dave Kessel? I say."

"To help him get pussy. Kind of a bonus that doesn't cost me anything. That brandy collection isn't much of a pimp with the cheerleaders he likes. Script's so good he can't hurt it and he gets to say he's a director."

"I tell him: I brought you the script. You could have at least offered it to me."

"He gives me that long look like he just drank an Alka-Seltzer and he's waiting for a belch. Schmuck, here's your mantra, he says. I'm Jay Braffner and I'm unemployable. Say it a thousand times a day until it sinks in . . ."

("cold.")

("motherfucker deserves to die.")

"Wait, it gets better," Jay says. "Flash forward a year. Pfeffer wins an Emmy for best MOW script. No-talent Dave Kessel is nominated for directing. He's hot for a minute and a half. Gets one more shot, bombs abysmally, and never directs again."

("what happened to the homeless author?")

"Never came forward so we're free to imagine."

Jay puts his hand together, framing a shot.

"FADE UP on a homeless shelter. Because it's LA everybody's watching the Emmys. Pfeffer collects his award, thanks Lester and his mother. A guy in tattered slacks jumps up, screaming: This guy's an imposter, I wrote that movie. Then, an old man on the next cot pipes up: Big deal. I was Steve McQueen's stunt double on *Bullitt*. I did all his driving and then they blacklisted me so nobody would know. Not to be undone, a wino yells from across the room: I banged Jane Fonda's maid in the guest house while she and Tom Hayden were having a party for Ramsey Clark and Abbie Hoffman . . . You mean Dick Clark and Dustin Hoffman, you asshole, somebody yells back . . ."

(helpless hilarity.)
"Then the paramedics come and shoot them all full of thorazine."
("powerful scene.")
"Thank you," Jay says.
("what about Marie Page?")
"Show was canceled," Jay says. "She blamed me."

VEASY TAKES A STAB

Veasy calls Mineo.

"Need a number. Finkelman, first name Lauren . . . Thousand Oaks . . ."

"Try 411?"

"She's definitely unlisted."

"How do you know?"

"She's not wearing panties."

"So, you're saying all women who don't wear panties are not in the phone book."

"If they're also under forty, skinny, tennis-tan blondes with large breasts . . ."

"Can you furnish photos to support your claim?"

"Front and back views . . . Plus a keyhole shot of her on the crapper. Available to collectors only, of course . . ."

"I'll get right back to you."

While he's waiting Veasy calls Tingley's cell and leaves a voice mail.

"Things to do in a traffic jam,

Open your e-mail and delete some spam.

Ogle a blonde in the adjacent beemer,

Pick at a corn,

Check out some porn,

Suck on a package of nondairy creamer."

He gets a text from Tingley:

"Owl is all over me."

And texts back:

"Bragging or complaining?"

Mineo calls back. "Where are you?"

"Ten feet further down the 405."

"Mizz Lauren Finkelman in Thousand Oaks is unlisted. Can I interest you in a Jared Finkelman, Attorney at Wachtel, Krantz, et al?"

"I think Jared is Lauren's hubby, unless there's more than one Finkelman in Thousand Oaks."

"Maybe the Finkelmans have a compound like the Kennedys."

"Think I'm getting a hunch-on," Veasy says.

"Which is . . . ?"

"When an idea actually makes me horny . . ."

"TMI."

"Try this: Jared does cheap criminal work and Olin is his client," Veasy says. "Olin gets out on parole and is immediately recruited by Lauren and check-kiting brother Chapman to burgle mama's house, take the rare coin collection, and make it look like a home invasion."

"I'm checking out Jared Finkleman, Esquire, as we speak," Mineo says.

"Good, I don't want to have a premature speculation . . ."

"He's got a Google Ad," Mineo says. "Got a DUI? Facing loss of license, heavy fine, possible imprisonment? Call Jared Finkleman, California's foremost vehicular law specialist . . ."

Veasy is inspired.

"Jared Finkleman is my name,
Bilking alkies is my game.
I'll take your bucks
But you're shit outta luck.
You're going to jail all the same."

"I'll text you the home number," Mineo says.

"Give me the office, too. I wanna try something."

Veasy calls the law firm. Gets Finkleman's paralegal.

"Jared there?"

"Who's calling?"

"Olin Sandusky . . ."

He's on hold for a second. The phone is quickly picked up, but then there's a silence with a few shallow breaths as if the person on the other hand is reluctant to talk.

Finally, a cautious . . . "Yes . . . ?"

"I got a problem, Jared . . ."

Another silence. Then a suspicious . . . "Who is this?"

"Ha ha, LOL. Just a little prank, Mr. Finkleman. This is Detective Tommy Veasy, La Playita PD . . . That's capital V followed by easy, in case you're writing it down for the complaint . . ."

"I'm sure you know it's a felony for a police officer to impersonate an attorney's client," Finkleman says.

"In the universe of felonies, conspiracy to commit a burglary ranks a lot higher, sir."

"What's that supposed to mean?"

"Just an observation."

Another silence.

He's scared and trying to keep it together.

"What can I do for you, Detective?"

"I'm investigating a home invasion and would like to speak with a Lauren Finkelman. Any relation?"

A rustling sound as if Finkelman is holding a mini recorder to the phone. "She's my wife. What do you want with her?"

"I met her yesterday in La Playita."

"She told me. Said the police were harassing her mother."

"A home invasion took place around the corner. Based on information we've received we think Mrs. Keene was the real target."

"What information?"

"I can't divulge that at the moment, sir."

"And I can't let you speak to my wife until I know what you want to ask her."

"I thought she would be concerned to protect her mother."

Finkelman's voice cracks like a teenage boy's. "Her mother is not in danger."

He's caving already.

"Well, could you ask your wife to have her brother call me?" Veasy asks.

"My wife doesn't speak to her brother."

"By choice or because she doesn't know where he is?"

"By choice."

"The suspect is described as a seedy-looking male Caucasian, early forties, pale and blotchy, bloodshot eyes like he'd been drinking. Sound familiar?"

"Sounds like most of my clients."

"Well this guy roughed up a senile old man. The man died in the hospital this morning so it's manslaughter . . ."

Finkelman interrupts:

"I told you, this has nothing to do with us . . ."

"Take it easy. I just want Lauren to tell me . . ."

"Don't call my wife by her first name . . ."

"Is Madame Finkelman acceptable?"

"I'm going to call your commander right now . . ."
"Can't you take a joke, Jared . . ."
The line goes dead.
They get nervous when you first-name them.
Means you're getting ready to arraign them.

LESTER TAKES A CALL

At five everyone goes into Lester's office to watch dailies.

"What, no Doritos, no Mrs. Fields?" O'Meara says.

"They said I could either cut the snacks or fire a writer," Lester says.

Zack stops at Eloise's desk.

"Do you know if Lester read my script?"

She turns away, red-eyed and distraught. "No I don't. Why would I?"

He whispers to Elliot. "Is she crying?"

"Allergies," Elliot says. "Pollen count's off the charts."

They watch an hour of close-ups of Finola Newton shinnying up a tree.

"Finola's still got it," Lippman says.

"And I hope it's not catching," says O'Meara.

"Somebody should have shaved her pussy," Lester says.

"Can I volunteer?" says O'Meara. "I'll pay my own per diem."

"What kind of tree is that anyway?" asks Lippman.

"It's not a tree, it's Finola's Maori driver," says Lester.

"You know what they say about Maoris," says O'Meara.

"Why are we watching this?" Elliot grumbles. "None of this stuff is usable."

"What's a little pubic hair between friends," Lester says. "They'll eat it up in Botswana."

Elliot shoots Lester an aggrieved look. "Of course if I said it was good footage you'd probably say we should cut it."

"Sure I would because you're always wrong."

Lester's e-mail dings. "My son, I'd better take this . . ."

"Lester Tarsis embraces fatherhood?" O'Meara says. "This is a major paradigm shift."

"Or the first symptom of dementia," Lester says.

As they shuffle out, Elliot whispers to Zack: "First time I've ever seen him take a call . . ."

"Hold on for a second, Seth," Lester says and calls: "Close the door, Josh."

Zack keeps walking.

"I knew editors were blind," Lester says. "Didn't know they were deaf as well."

"Name's Zack, Lester. I thought you were talking to someone else."

"Maybe I will be, tomorrow."

The door closes.

Lester goes back to the phone. "Your mom tell you to call, Seth?"

"I told her it wouldn't do any good, Dad." In the few months since they last spoke, Seth's voice has deepened. Lester senses an older man's resigned weariness in his tone. "She told me what you said about the million bucks you said you'd spent on me."

"I'm sorry she's upset, but I can't support her lifestyle and your life of crime anymore."

A sniff. Lester remembers how quick he was to cry at the smallest hurt. "I know I've been a major pain in the ass to you, Dad. I'm almost glad you're pulling her money. Even Juvie will be better than being in this house with her and Doug. They're drunk and fighting all the time. They were throwing pots at each other in the kitchen the other night. He must have hit her because she was screaming about calling the cops and getting a restraining order. Then she locked herself in the maid's room. He was banging on the door, cursing. I almost went down there . . ."

Lester feels a pang of fear in his chest.

"Stay out of it, Seth. Your mother can take care of herself . . ."

"I fuckin' hate him, Dad. The next time he calls me a little rat-faced bitch I'm gonna fuckin' brain him with my Little League bat . . ."

Lester's heart flutters. A montage is strobing . . . Crime scene tape and police vehicles. Doug's sheeted body wheeled on a gurney. Seth in orange overalls cuffed and shackled and dwarfed by two fat detectives.

"Why don't you come stay with me for a while," he says.

"Mom won't let me. She says you have hookers over on the weekend. Her friend Sienna saw you in the Ivy with a slutty blonde. I mean that's what she called her. I'm sorry . . ."

"I don't care what your mother thinks, Seth, and after the seventeenth you won't have to either. You'll officially be an adult . . ."

"You mean Mom can't tell me what to do?"

"You'll be responsible for your own life."

"If you're sure I won't cramp your style, Dad. If you wanna keep having the hookers . . ."

"Don't worry about me, Seth. Let's just get you out of that house ASAP."

"Might as well wait until I get out of Juvie," Seth says. "Actually, they'll probably put me in County because I'll be over eighteen, although I was arrested when I was seventeen . . ."

Another montage. Seth in a circle of gang kids, Mexican and black. Pushing him from one kid to another. Leering . . .

"Let me talk to Bobby Shuster's lawyer, Seth," Lester says. "See if we can get you in that program with your friends. How's that sound?"

"Great, Dad. Can I move my stuff in tomorrow?"

"Sure. Tell your mother to call me if she wants to talk about it."

Lester hangs up and opens the door.

"Who wants to watch Finola Newton hump a gnarled palm tree?"

O'Meara rises from his squeaky chair. "Me and a million Botswanans." He stops and points. "Is that plague rictus or are you smiling?"

"I'm beaming," Lester says.

"What's the occasion?" Lippman asks. "Your son just get a scholarship to Stanford?"

"Better," Lester says. "He just guilted me out of twenty Gs. And he wants me to fix him up with a hooker."

"Congratulations, he's a sleazy hornball like his old man," O'Meara says. "High-five."

Lester slaps his hand. "I think the boy's gonna be alright."

A MADMAN'S DOCUMENTARY

"There's a shot I always wanted to make," Jay says as he trudges along the Pacific Coast Highway.

("we're here for you, boss.")

Jay squints through his viewfinder. "FADE UP on a long lens—a three-sixty—of Malibu jutting into the Pacific at Dana Point . . ."

("putting up a three-sixty . . .")

"Definitive California day. Heat waves shimmer, sunlight dances along the waves. PAN across the Santa Monica Mountains, getting the blur of speeding traffic in the bottom of the frame and sweeping past the mansions on the Bluffs. Bright yellow California light blasts like a 10K spot. Hockney sun—shows everything, tells nothing. ZOOM IN—I know zooms are so '70s, but that's the point, it's a visual flashback, a paradigm of the past . . ."

("the ultimate in cinema semiotics.")

"Now ZOOM to a TIGHT SHOT," Jay says. "Reveal fast food wrappers, cheap wine bottles, rolling papers, torn, bloody clothing. Eyes peer out of dusty bushes on the hill. Homeless people live and die in the tangled thickets over the highway . . ."

("the splendor and the squalor.")

"I always wanted to do a documentary about the California Incline. It's an iconic location, featured in a thousand movies. Also the perfect spot for begging. Cars turn off and climb up the hill to go into Santa Monica, or they go down the hill to head out to Malibu. Panhandlers wait at the bottom. It's a three-minute light and they have a captive audience. It's a legal mugging. They scream and plead and drool on the windshields until the drivers slip them hush money."

("what a social comment.")

"In the '80s a pregnant girl worked the Incline," Jay says. "Big girl, so banged up you couldn't tell her age. Autistic gape. Flushed from sun and drugs. Belly protruding under a short sleeveless tee, rising like a boulder over a pair of baggy warmups. Inverted navel, deep as an open ditch. She would scream at the drivers trapped at that three-minute light. *Help my baby. Puleeeze.* Run up to a Jag or a Rover and wail like a wounded dog through the tinted window. *Puleeeze, help my baby.* Diamond fingers and Rolex wrists reached out of windows to drop bills in her Lakers cap."

("a visual metaphor that says it all.")

"Nine or ten years straight that girl was always pregnant," Jay says. "I wanted to make a film to show how she did it."

("great character.")

("a human statement.")

"I was going to give her a coupla hundred just to let me follow her with a small crew. See how she lived. How she stayed pregnant. What happened to her kids. Was there one father who sold them for adoption or trained them *a la* Fagin for other begging gigs? Was she carrying babies for other women?"

("a homeless surrogate.")

"I pitched the idea to the public station. They were blown away. Offered me a grant. Said they would put it on their fall schedule . . . Assigned one of their execs to follow up . . ."

("perfect for public TV.")

"Better than perfect," Jays says. "But it never happened."

("why?")

"Why is a question that is never answered in Hollywood. All I know is the same guy who had been bird-dogging the project suddenly sounded lukewarm. Then, he stopped returning my calls."

("what happened?")

"The cone of silence descended," Jay says.

("but why?")

"My agent said they were worried about dealing with me. You know, the busts and all. But Lester said they were jealous. Schmuck, he said, these are guys who couldn't get jobs on the networks and now they have to pretend that public broadcasting is a sacred calling. To them you're an episodic hack who makes ten times more money and gets all the good-looking women. All they have is their public TV prestige and they're not gonna share it with you . . ."

As they approach the Incline, Jay steps out onto the road, buffeted by the draft of the passing traffic. "Here's the shocker," he says, pointing.

At the bottom of the hill a pregnant woman, belly rising like a mottled boulder over baggy warmups, is waving her arms and screaming as cars drive around her.

"Puleeze help my babeee . . ."

(confusion.)

("can't be the girl Jay was talking about.")

Jay knew she was there all along. "Maddening, isn't it? It's the same place, same hustle. Looks like the same girl, but it's thirty years later."

("not possible.")

"Now come the questions," Jay says. "Is this the daughter of the original beggar? Is this a family business passed on over the generations from mother to daughter? Like circus acrobats?"

Jay can tell he is screaming by the pressure in his head.

"THERE IS NO END TO THE QUESTIONS. AND NO ANSWER FOR ANY OF THEM . . ."

Brakes squeal. A horn blasts.

"Get off the road, asshole!"

He hops back onto the narrow path.

"Somewhere in this vast, unknowable city there is a family of large, incredibly hearty women who can stay pregnant for years and beg at the California Incline. If they had let me do that documentary I would have been able to follow these women through the changing Hollywood scene."

There's that pressure again.

"I WOULD HAVE HAD A FUCKING HUMAN DOCUMENT!"

The phone goes off.

"Mr. Braffner, it's Zack Toledano from *She*? I spoke to you about an interview?"

"Oh sure, Zack . . ."

"Everybody's real excited about this. I'd like to do it tonight, if possible."

("uh oh . . .")

Jay motions for quiet.

"CLOSE UP so tight that you don't know where I am," he whispers. "Turn off the sound, we'll loop my dialogue later."

He waits for the CAMERA to poke in close to his face.

"A little early, isn't it, Zack?"

"Lester's gonna let me off after editing notes. In lieu of overtime."

"Sounds like Lester."

"Won't take long, Mr. Braffner. You can cut me off whenever you like."

A broad wink.

"And wherever?"

(giggles.)

"Excuse me . . . ?"

"I said c'mon over, Roy."

"It's Zack, Mr. Braffner . . ."

Jay has to fight off a giggle himself. "Sorry, Zack," he says. "Just gave another interview to a young filmmaker named Roy. C'mon over, we'll pick up where he left off."

ENTRAPMENT

Six o'clock. Jonas sits in his office watching the day tour go home.

Cops are supposed to love their work. My guys run out like the building is on fire.

Tingley's Corolla bounces over the traffic bump and squeals away down Olympic Boulevard. He's been moderating her e-mails so he knows where she's going. Still . . .

She's in an awful hurry to get to a PTA meeting.

After lunch he had checked in with Romero at the DEA. "Did you find my guy?"

"Found him, but you can't have him for a while. He's associating with one of our targets."

"Who?"

"Roger Greenspun. Hippie son of Leonard Greenspun, who owns half the real estate in La Playita. Roger's been using his marijuana prescription to buy weight from Dr. Klinger's dispensary on the boardwalk. He resells it at twice the price and kicks back to Klinger."

"Where's my guy fit in?"

"He's in photos and surveillance video, copping and smoking under a tree."

Jonas starts blinking uncontrollably.

"You've got him smoking?"

"We thought he was just another stoner, didn't know he was a cop."

Jonas reaches in the drawer for the haloperidol, but decides he doesn't need it.

I'm alone, I can twitch up a storm.

"These dispensaries are all in violation of federal statutes," Romero says. "The city of La Playita is defying us by allowing them to operate. We're gonna raid Klinger's dispensary in a couple of weeks. Just want to keep everybody happy until then."

Can't wait a coupla weeks.

"Greenspun can't be Klinger's only peddler," Jonas says.

"He's the most photogenic. Ponytail, long fingernails, boardwalk icon. Billionaire dad, politically connected. It'll play the news cycle bigtime. Anyway, if we bust him the word will go out and Klinger might shut down the operation . . ."

"I'm gonna grab my guy now," Jonas says.

Romero gets low and ugly. "Better not throw a rock in my pool . . ."

"I'll protect your operation."

Jonas hangs up and calls Walsh into his office.

"This didn't come from me. Call Narcotics. Get an undercover on Roger Greenspun. Deals weed in front of Dwayne's . . . Splits his scrip with Veasy."

Walsh shakes his head. "You have to go out of the department to get Veasy. Our guys will warn him off."

"He'll be hard to sucker," Jonas says.

"Honey pot's the way to go," says Walsh. "LA Narcotics has a couple of hotties who work the clubs . . ."

"Will they lend us one?"

"To bust a La Playita cop? Absolutely."

THIRD TIME'S THE CHARM

Jay jogs, breathing easily, up the California Incline. "Steep, huh?" he calls to the crew. "Sixty degree grade . . ."

The crew labors to keep pace.

("the man's unstoppable.")

"You get a surge of energy when you're directing," Jay says. "For that moment in time you're stronger, smarter, and sexier than anyone else in the world. People want to stand in your glow. Talk to you, get a picture taken, sleep with you . . ."

Jay stops at the top. "Quick digression?"

("always.")

"CAMERA PUSH IN to CLOSE-UP," Jay says. "Keep the ocean in the background."

("rolling . . .")

"After *Mad Bomber*, I had serious heat in New York," Jay says. "I was determined to build a body of work, making films in every borough. Critics would call it Jay Braffner's New York Cycle. I saw myself written up in Film Quarterly and *Cahiers du Cinéma*. Honored at Cannes. Showered with every award but one—the Oscar—which I would famously turn down at an international press conference . . ."

("it could have happened.")

"Instead I came out here. You know why?"

("why?")

"Because Lester Tarsis told me to come, that's why."

("you two go back a long way.")

"Lester had parlayed his *Mad Bomber* credit into a job working on horror scripts for Corman. He wrote me: You have to come out here. You can get a place on the beach for nothing. Pick up a used car . . . Ever have Mexican food? It's fantastic and cheap. The women are like baby Eves, gorgeous, innocent, unashamed . . . I was against it. My work is here, Lester, I said . . . Can't do serious work in the city, Lester said. All you can do is journalism . . ."

("the difference between Scorsese and Coppola.")

"It's like being in a crowded subway car, Lester said. You're nose to nose with your characters. You react instinctively without understanding. Out here you have time . . . And distance. There is physical and conceptual space between you and the subject . . ."

("Lester was into the gaze.")

("totally postmodern . . .")

"They love young filmmakers out here, Lester said. There are hundreds of low-budget production companies."

"So I said okay, I'll give it a try. Broke my lease, sold my shit, and drove a loaner across the country."

("fun trip.")

"It was Valentine's Day, 1976, but the sun was shining like July Fourth. People in convertibles heading for the beach. Girls in bikinis sitting on top of the seats, waving, hair blowing . . . Passersby smiling . . . 'Good morning' . . . Beats the shit out of Avenue B, don't it? Lester said."

("another day in paradise.")

"Next day I realize Lester has totally sold out. He's up for a staff job on *Perry Mason*. Won't fix our script *No Partners in Crime*."

("the little gem about the con man serial killer?")

"Says it's too dark, there's no one to root for. If we show it around they'll type us as pretentious New Yorkers. He has a seventeen-year-old beach blonde living in his house. A natural-born sex machine, he says, and she doesn't know who Robert McNamara is . . ."

("sad . . .")

"I had a Motor Becane racing bike, which I had brought out from the city. Every morning I coasted down the Incline, sea breeze in my face, crossed the PCH, and rode the path all the way to Malibu. Had coffee in a little place and rode back. I was black from the sun. I had never felt this good in my life."

("the Golden State.")

"A month later I was directing *Jake and the Fat Man*. Making more money than I ever thought I'd make. Screwing girls who looked like movie stars . . ."

("all that potential wasted.")

"If you ask Lester he'll say he did me a favor getting me out here. He'll say I never would have made another picture after *Mad Bomber* flopped."

("a Faustian bargain.")

(*"now Lester will die a forgotten man."*)

"Forgotten he won't be," says Jay. He takes out his phone. "Lester Tarsis is about to go out with a bang that will be heard around this town."

THE END BEGINS

Eloise makes a fresh pot of coffee. She brings cups for Lester and O'Meara.

"What am I, chopped liver?" Lippman says.

"Eloise didn't want to wake you," Lester says.

"You know what coffee does to your acid reflux, dear," says O'Meara.

Eloise covers her face. "I'm sorry, Noah, I'm having a bad day," she sobs, between her fingers. And rushes out, head down.

"What's her problem?" O'Meara says.

"She's mad because our guys killed the baby Jesus," says Lester. "You Gentiles can really hold a grudge."

Eloise comes back with a cup for Lippman and a couple of extra creamers.

"I'm sorry, Noah. You were sitting in the corner and I didn't see you," she says.

"Now I'm the Invisible Man?"

Eloise blinks back the tears.

"I'm only joking, Eloise. You know me, JK all day."

"What's JK?" Lester asks.

"Means 'just kidding.' In my kids' teenage textese."

"Textese . . . Aren't you Mr. Au Courant."

"Having young sons keeps me relevant in the business."

"Now if you could only write." Lester points to the door. "Think you can find something constructive to do in the outer office, young lady?"

Eloise tries a brave smile. "Guess I've caused enough trouble for one day." And closes the door gently behind her.

"I've never seen her like this," O'Meara says. "She's usually all Midwest cheery like she's got gingerbread cookies warm from the oven in her apron . . ."

"Why don't you put your face in her apron and get a good whiff of those cookies?" Lester says.

"I caught her doodling little faces of you yesterday, Lester," Lippman says.

"Bet she made my nose too big."

"Act One, Lester takes advantage of Eloise's schoolgirl crush," O'Meara says.

"I never sleep with women who like me. Too much pressure . . ."

"Act Two, she's pregnant," Lippman says. "Lester insists on killing the fetus."

"Sell it to Lifetime," Lester says. "And find another culprit. I had my tubes tied after Seth."

"Should have done it before," says O'Meara.

Lester rips open a Splenda. "Sean O'Meara, dialogue slut. Never met a cheap joke he didn't like."

O'Meara looks at Lester in surprise. "After seven years of trying, I think I finally hurt your feelings."

Lester's computer dings. He stirs his coffee and goes on:

"Sean never did thank Dennis Hopper for rewriting his Academy Award–winning script. Would have been smart politics. The whole town knew he had done it. Hurt him in the business."

O'Meara winces. "You've had your finger on that button for quite a while."

Lester stirs his coffee.

"Not a dad myself so I don't know the pain of parenthood," O'Meara says.

"Can I take that as an apology?" Lester says.

"Take it or leave it."

Lippman takes a quavery breath. "Guys can we get serious for a second? There's something I have to talk about."

"Tweet it first and we'll decide," O'Meara says.

"No really, I have to get this off my chest." He walks to the window. "Arlene is fucking the guy who runs the soccer camp."

Lester's computer dings. He types out a response.

O'Meara sits back, arms behind his head.

"Can I get a new chair? This one squeaks when I'm trying to create."

Lippman turns. "No one is surprised by this?"

"Personally, I'm too stunned to speak," says Lester.

"Adultery in LA," says O'Meara. "What is this world coming to?"

"He's a Scottish guy, blonde, buff, looks like David Beckham's stunt double . . ."

"And she prefers him to a bald, overweight, neurotic klutz with prickly heat? I find that hard to believe."

"How'd you find out?" O'Meara asks. "She yell GOAL! in her sleep?"

"Give you a red card and throw you out of the bedroom?" says Lester.

"Parents' day was last Thursday," Lippman says. "He and his coaches got the dads out on the field."

"You mean the pitch," O'Meara says.

"Ran us ragged. Made us look pathetic in front of the wives and kids."

"Good tactic," O'Meara says.

"How to lop off twenty dicks at once," says Lester.

"After, they had a little party."

"And the dads paid for the pizza, of course."

"At the end the instructors were hugging the moms. Quick hug and peck, but when it came to Arlene the peck lasted a little too long."

"How much longer?"

"At least a second."

O'Meara nods. "He's fucking her."

Eloise opens the door.

"Sorry to bother you, but Jay Braffner is on the phone again."

"I saw the message," Lester says. "Call back."

She closes the door.

"How's the sex?" O'Meara asks.

"By appointment only. She's asleep by the time I brush my teeth. Sometimes if she's still awake she sends me back to floss."

"How long you been married?" O'Meara asks.

Lippman dabs at his sweaty forehead. "Seventeen years."

"And you still want to shtup your wife," Lester says. "Consider that a bonus . . ."

"She was a stripper, right?" O'Meara says.

"Backup dancer at the Golden Nugget. I met her when I was doing *Vegas*."

"That show ran the town in the '80s," O'Meara says. "You could have had anybody you wanted, but you decided to fall in love."

"So correct me if I'm wrong," Lester says. "Arlene's on the dark side of thirty and getting desperate. Suddenly there's a bigtime TV guy making goo-goo eyes. She has you in the palm of her hand."

"In more ways than one," O'Meara says.

"From the start she doesn't respect you."

"Why not?" Lippman asks.

"After ten years in Las Vegas she has no self-esteem. How many guys you figure?"

"Coupla hundred for low," O'Meara says.

"Bust-out gamblers, low-level wiseguys. They abused her. Made her mule drugs, maybe even turn a few tricks. So now this pudgy Jewish kid shows up . . ."

"Her natural prey," says O'Meara.

"Like the panther and the bush pig. She's been feasting on guys like you for years. And here you are with candy and flowers and a diamond as big as the Ritz, asking her to marry you. The way she feels about herself at that moment, anybody who loves her has got to be a moron . . ."

"She loved me once," Lippman says.

"Look at yourself, Noah," Lester says. "Is there one part of your entire anatomy that a woman could find attractive?"

"This is a body not even a mother could love," says O'Meara.

"Not to mention your effervescent personality."

"I told you not to mention that," O'Meara says.

"Women don't fall in love with guys like us, Bobby. Best we can get is a heavy like . . ."

"If we buy them a lot of stuff," O'Meara says.

"Arlene let you flop around on top of her like a dying flounder how many times in seventeen years? Four, five thousand?"

"Not to mention the obligatory birthday blowjob," O'Meara says.

"She held up her end of the deal. Gave you three handsome kids. Good athletes, right? Better than they would have been with your genes."

"Mind if I use that dying flounder line?" O'Meara says.

Eloise sticks her head back in.

"It's Jay Braffner again . . ."

"I saw the message, Eloise," Lester says. "Call back."

"He says he only has a few minutes until they set up the next shot."

"Aren't you curious to know what schmuck hired him?" O'Meara says.

"He's not working. It's just a trick to get me on the phone."

Eloise looks at Lippman twisting his Lakers cap in the corner. "Can I get you more coffee, Noah?"

"Go bake Sean some gingerbread cookies, Eloise," Lester says.

She sticks out her tongue and closes the door.

"My therapist says we should go for counseling," Lippman says.

"To cure Arlene from shtupping other guys?" Lester says.

"Or cure you from caring," says O'Meara.

"He says she's having a mid-life crisis . . ."

"C'mon Noah, Arlene's been fooling around for years," Lester says.

"You can't say that," Lippman says. "You hardly know her."

"I specialize in self-loathing women," Lester says.

"If you knew floozies / Like Lester knows floozies," O'Meara sings. But then he gets thoughtful. "I don't like the sudden carelessness. Means she doesn't care if she gets caught because she knows the marriage is about to end . . ."

Lippman jumps up. "Jesus, Sean . . ."

"Wives are the best career barometers. Sharisse left me when I was fired off the Eastwood picture. I went downhill like the Jamaican luge team after that."

"Dumping you is the right move for Arlene right now," Lester says. "You're at the bottom of the greasy pole. What do you do after this show shuts down?"

Lester's computer dings.

"You sit around the house waiting for the phone to ring. Depleting your capital until there's nothing left. Arlene knows if she leaves now she gets a bigger settlement."

Lippman rises in protest. "Arlene's not that cold-blooded."

"Leave reptiles out of this," O'Meara says. "They don't cheat on each other."

Lester shakes his head. "Too complicated. Requires a knowledge of herpetology."

"Arlene remembers the glory days," O'Meara says. "When her husband was the producer of the hottest show on TV."

"I *was* big," Lippman says. "The phone was ringing, offers pouring in . . ."

"Noah is voted most popular for the first time in his life. Everybody wants Noah and Arlene at their party."

Lippman gets a faraway look. "We used to spend New Years going from house to house. The big question was where do we end up at midnight?"

"But the invites slowed down when you came on *She*, didn't they?" Lester says.

"Immediate expulsion from the A-list," says O'Meara. "Like Dreyfus. They rip off your epaulets, break your sword, and march you off the parade ground . . ."

"We were the top syndicated show in the world. But we were softcore, low-budget, cheap date, no prestige . . ."

"Don't upstage Noah's story, Lester . . ."

"Then, we lost our U.S.-Canada distributor. We're still the biggest show in Africa . . ."

"A million spear chuckers can't be wrong," says O'Meara.

"But Arlene sees the future and goes into panic mode," Lester says.

"The flounder is starting to stink," says O'Meara.

"You're lucky she's not plotting to kill you."

"Who says she's not? A little *Double Indemnity* with that soccer bum?"

Eloise peeks in again. "Don't get mad, Lester. It's Jay Braffner again."

"I saw the message, Eloise . . ."

"He sounds so lost. He might do something to himself . . ."

"He's done everything he can do, short of dying . . ."

Eloise steps in, hands clasped. "Please Lester, just say hello . . ."

O'Meara waggles his cup at Eloise. "Another cup for me and an empty glass for the Invisible Man over here."

"Maybe you should tell him that detective was looking for him," Lippman says.

"I should do that, I guess." Lester picks up the phone, but changes his mind. "That'll just give him another five minutes to bullshit me and he'll never call the cop anyway." He hangs up. "Tell him I'm in a production meeting."

Eloise's clasps her hands. "The man is crying for help, Lester. It's a sin to turn him away."

And slams the door.

"No fear of divine retribution?" says O'Meara.

"I've already shtupped a thousand underage hookers," Lester says. "Making nice to one burnt-out director won't get me back in the book of life."

Lippman complains: "Braffner is the B story. We're talking about my domestic tragedy . . ."

"Best thing that ever happened," says Lester. "Gives you an excuse to cheat on Arlene."

"Get the dumbest, blondest bimbo you can find," O'Meara says. "And take her to Arlene's favorite restaurants so all her friends can see. Then shtup her in the Irene Dunne suite of the Beverly Wilshire. You'll be embarrassing Arlene, spending her settlement, and getting your rocks off at the same time."

"What about my kids?"

"They'll be better off," Lester says. "All their friends come from broken homes, they were the oddballs. Now they'll have two houses to go to. Competing birthday presents and vacations, stepsisters to shtup . . ."

"What if I want to save the marriage?"

"Get a show on the air."

"Which will never happen," O'Meara says. "But if it does, do you need a staff writer?"

Lippman erupts with sudden vehemence. "I hate this rotten business."

"If it wasn't for TV, you would never have gotten any pussy at all," says O'Meara.

"You would have married a woman who looks like you," Lester says.

O'Meara pats Lippman on the shoulder. "Look at this way, Noah," he says. "At least you're not Jay Braffner."

Lippman nods and sips his coffee. "Thanks guys, I feel a lot better now."

HONEYED PORTAL

Check out that sunset
  Said Romeo to Juliet.
  Old Sol oozing like a broken yolk,
  Sky all bloodshot like an ancient stoner.
  Juliet said shut up bro,
  This hackneyed verse has gotta go.
  Your poetic license I now revoke.
  All you do is talk of tokes.
  I should have listened to my folks,
  And married that dude from Verona . . .
Veasy walks home past the pier. The beach is changing shifts. Anglo day trippers pushing strollers with squalling toddlers give way to the *cholo* night crowd, hoochies and coolers, tats and swaggers . . .

He gets home at seven. Opens the door and the walls start closing in. It's going to be a long night alone on an unmade bed in that messy room with only the street noise and the voices in the hall for company. He never keeps more than a day's supply, but there's always a taste around somewhere . . . He picks up old newspapers, looks under the computer, on the bathroom sink . . .

I'm getting desperate . . .
There's a matchbook on the floor by the trashcan. A roach behind the matches. Just enough to burn his lip.

He puts on his bike shorts, Dos XX T-shirt and Raiders cap. Laces up his blades. Skates down the block past the homeless guys in the alley and hits the boardwalk looking for Roger Greenspun.

The bars are filling,
At the end of the day
The surfers are chilling,
The bands start to play,
The tourists are willing
To overpay.
To them it's just thrilling,
Hooray, Hooray.

Volleyballers, chess players, hard bods swinging on the rings, tumblers on a turf sward—the night show is about to begin.

But no Roger.

Veasy puts on his shades. Pulls the cap over his eyes. Best to avoid Dwayne's—too many locals, somebody will know him. Skates low with his head down.

Roger likes to stand behind an old dusty tree by the bike store. He's not there.

Darkness oozing through the smog,
Streetlight beacons in the fog,
Breeze smoothes my cheek like a lover's caress . . .

A shadow whirls in his path. An Amazon on blades is doing circle turns in the hazy beach lights under the pier. Tall and rangy in volleyball shorts and a cutoff tee. Faster and faster. Arms out, one long leg extended like a ballerina, blonde hair flying. Raggedy beach ghost cheering her on . . .

"Yeah . . . Girl . . . Whoo whoo . . ."

Her skate comes off the ground. She falters and flails—"Ahh, shit . . ."

He lunges and grabs her. Long arms wrap around his neck. Warm breath in his face. He has to hold on to keep his balance.

"Oh, sorry . . ."

Hard belly. Baby down bristling in the hollow of her spine . . .

"That was close."

They turn and turn. With her skates she's as tall as he is. Blue eyes glitter in the tangle of blonde.

I wish they all could be
California girls . . .

"Nick of time, Tommy . . ."

Roger Greenspun comes out of another dimension. Stringy gray hippie hair, long nails, painted DayGlo green.

"Almost had a nasty fall," Veasy says.

She's in no hurry. Stays in the clinch.

"I'm too stoned to do stunts."

"You're not stoned enough if you know you're stoned," he says.

"Words of wisdom from a man who always knows he's stoned," Roger says. "Tommy, this is Bree . . ."

"Sexy name."

"If you like cheese," she says.

They slow to a stop. Veasy steps back and frames his hands. "Ready for your close-up?"

She laughs and flips her hair back off her face.

Love how they do that.

"How come girls who look like you are never named Gertrude?" he asks.

"Maybe we were once . . ."

Roger slips a joint into his hand. "For the trip." And a baggie into his pocket.

"Special blend. They call it Love Colors . . . $1200 an ounce."

Veasy offers his hand. "Shall we?"

Her grasp is warm. "Roger is the world's oldest love child," he says.

"He's sweet," she says.

She pulls him along. "C'mon . . ."

"Through the jaundiced haze we go / Into the pure moon glow."

"Excuse me?"

"Just mumbling. Got a match?"

She takes a Bic lighter out of her fanny pack.

"Ready for anything," he says. "What else do you have in there?"

"Car keys, credit cards, pepper spray . . ."

"Thanks for the warning."

He offers the joint.

"Not yet."

"Too whacked? / Close to a panic attack?"

"I have a head start," she says. "Catch up, I'll join you later."

"Promise . . . ?"

She flips her hair back again.

"Promise . . ."

OUTTAKES

Film the trudge down Ocean Avenue to Pacific Street across Venice to Lincoln to my house. We'll cut it later.

("done.")

Film the kid waiting outside, saying, "I know you're from Brooklyn, Mr. Braffner, so I thought a pizza with sausage, pepperoni, and meatballs would be appropriate . . ." Great shot, but it has to go.

("every director cuts the scene he loves.")

Good character stuff but doesn't move the story forward. Besides, you can see the pizza box on the coffee table and the kid's manner will show how desperate he is to please. There was a nice moment when he showed Jay the little phone camera and said: "I'll shoot the whole interview on this, Mr. Braffner . . ." But that can be cut too, because he's sitting on the couch pointing that absurd little gadget right now and the audience will get that he's filming.

"I'd like to talk about *The Mad Bomber*," the kid says.

Jay can't speak his instructions because the kid is sitting right there across from him. But it's okay because the crew is so tuned in they can read his mind.

Ready?

("rolling.")

"That kind of Indie film was very rare in those days," the kid says. "How did you raise the money?"

Jay slides over a bit so they can get a better angle.

"It was our senior project in film school," Jay says.

"You and Lester Tarsis were students together?" the kid says.

"The star students. We collaborated on . . ."

The kid interrupts:

"Could you just say: Lester Tarsis and I were star students at NYU Film School. We collaborated on *Mad Bomber* as our senior project in film school. I need it in one continuous take."

"Sure . . . Good filmmaking . . ."

"Coming from you that's high praise, Mr. Braffner."

"Jay . . ."

"Jay . . . Now, ready? Action . . ."

Jay begins. "Lester and I collaborated on *Mad Bomber* as our senior project at NYU Film School. The idea was I would direct his script and he would direct mine . . ." And takes a beat. "I didn't want to say star students. Brian DePalma was in that class as well . . . Was it okay?"

"It was great." The kid turns the camera off. "Now I'm going to change the angle." He crouches on the floor and points the camera up at Jay.

"Back in the day the networks didn't allow low angle shots," Jay says.

Jay sees the little red light blinking. "Could you just say: the networks didn't allow low angle shots . . . ?"

"It doesn't fit with what I've been talking about . . ."

"It's a tasty sidebar. I'll use it later."

All of a sudden he's directing me. Think I don't know that patronizing tone? Think I never had to explain scenes to dumb actors?

("he'll be sorry.")

The red light is blinking again. The camera is up under Jay's chin. "Action . . ."

Jay repeats: "The camera never let us make low angle shots . . ."

"Networks," the kid corrects.

("little runt, where does he come off?")

"The networks never let us make low angle shots," Jay says. "Said they were too artsy-fartsy, their favorite word."

Ah, why not tell the whole story?

"Of course the actors didn't like them either," Jay says. "Selleck said low angles made him look jowly . . ."

The kid gets to his feet and moves around for an eye-level angle.

"You won't be able to cut out of the shot if you move," Jay warns.

The kid keeps moving. "I'll jump cut it. It's a documentary, I can break the rules."

("what a jerk.")

("amateur night in Dixie . . .")

The kid sits on the couch next to Jay and points the camera right at him in a profile shot.

"Where am I looking?" Jay asks.

"Straight ahead, don't talk to the camera."

("pretentious asshole.")

"Getting back to the question," the kid says. "Tarsis wrote *Mad Bomber*. What was your script about?"

"About my dad. He was the unofficial handball champ of Coney Island. People would come from all the over the city to challenge. The bookies gave odds . . ."

"Cool," the kid says. "How did the movie turn out?"

"We never made it," Jay says.

The kid moves in closer. "Tarsis couldn't direct, right?"

"Actually, I never finished the script," Jay says.

"You got writer's block," the kid says.

("kill him now!")

"I couldn't sit still long enough to finish," Jay says. "A writer's talent is in his ass, Lester used to say. I had to be on the move . . ."

"So you failed the course."

"Didn't matter. By then Lester had shown *Mad Bomber* to Sig Shapiro at Cineart. Sig promised us fifty grand to expand it to a feature if we got the right casting."

The kid moves into a full face close-up.

("you're smiling, Chief.")

It's a happy memory.

"Lester's uncle was the actor Mike Kellin's accountant," Jay says. "Mike committed to play the bomber, George Metesky. Deferred his salary for 20%. Sig gave us ten Gs to go into prep. We put casting notices in *Backstage* and *Show Business* . . ."

The kid doesn't even look away from the screen. "Say: we put casting notices in *Backstage* and *Show Business*, the theatrical newspapers . . ."

("how rude.")

Jay plays along.

"We put casting calls in the show business papers."

"Say *Backstage* and *Show Business*," the kid insists. "Just for the record . . ."

("one more remark like that and he's toast . . .")

But Jay stays calm.

This is what a director does. If we begrudge him his vision, we have no right to ours.

("you are so giving.")

"We put casting notices in *Backstage* and *Show Business*, the theatrical newspapers," he says. "Advertised for middle-aged spinster types, cops, white collar guys, phone company workers. Every out-of-work actor in town showed up. It was a mob scene. Chorus boys, black revolutionaries, little kids with their moms . . ." Jay laughs . . . "And all these hot women, strippers and dancers, showing a lot of skin . . . Lester gave me the wink and told the babes our next picture was a musical . . ."

Jay smiles, remembering.

"Lester had a pimp for the first time in his life," he says.

The kid moves in even closer. "What do you mean?"

"He had something he could use to get women."

"You had it, too."

"I didn't need it," Jay says. "I was a lifeguard . . ."

The red light stops blinking. The kid sounds impatient.

"Could you say: I didn't need to use the movie to attract women, I was a lifeguard? And then go on . . ."

("the fucking gall . . .")

Jay says: "I didn't need a movie to attract women. I was a lifeguard, a high school jock. I'd been screwing since I was fourteen. But Lester was a mousy little dude, couldn't get a sniff. Even as a kid he went to the hookers in Brownsville. All of a sudden he's living his fantasy. He spent the whole day collecting eight-by-tens. Went out with a different girl every night. I couldn't get him to look at locations or cast the small parts. You do it, he said, you're the director. All he cared about was the pussy."

The kid is gloating. "That is so Lester."

He climbs on a chair and shoots down.

"So Lester didn't have much to do with the actual filming," he says.

"He hated the process," Jay says. "Hated the crew. They're just a bunch of lazy thieves, he said. Said the actors were pretentious phonies. After a rehearsal one day he said, why are you wasting so much time explaining things? They always do it the same way no matter what you say. Lester didn't believe in nuance."

The kid laughs. "Still doesn't."

"The Hollywood defense mechanism," Jay says. "They stop trying to be artists and after a while they deny that art exists . . ."

The kid shakes his head in total awe. "That is so profoundly true, Mr. Braffner . . ."

"Jay . . ."

"Jay . . ." The kid turns the camera off. "Take a little break, okay? Then we'll come back and talk about the making of *Mad Bomber*, distribution, reviews . . ."

"Sounds good," Jay says. He gets up and stands over the kid.

("you're dead, asshole.")

"Actually, I have one more question for this scene," the kid says.

Jay sits down. The red light goes on.

"Did you and Lester stay friends throughout the filming?" the kid asks. "Please answer in a complete sentence."

"I know the drill, Roy," Jay says.

"Zack . . ."

"Lester and I got along great during the filming," Jay says. "It was probably the last time that I could get him on the phone."

"Don't feel bad," the kid says. "Lester never takes calls. The only person he's ever picked up for is his son Seth."

Seth! That's it. Try to keep the excitement out of your voice.

"Oh yeah, Seth. He must be seventeen by now."

Spiteful smile. "He's a disaster. Drug problems, in and out of rehab, lockup, the whole deal."

"Sounds like somebody I know," Jay says.

"He called yesterday and Lester actually spoke to him. Actually had that worried dad look."

Seth . . . He'll get Lester to the phone . . . Seth is the key . . .

("can little Zacky go bye-bye now?")

Jay flashes his charming smile. "How about some coffee, Zack?"

"In a minute, Jay. I'd like to try one more thing."

"Sure," Jay says.

("twerp just bought himself a few more minutes.")

COP ON THE BEACH

Veasy and Bree skate hand in hand along the beach path to Washington Street.

"Magic time's about to end," Veasy says.

"But we just met."

"It's getting to the point where we'll have to tell our life stories."

"So soon?"

"It's required, like filling out a questionnaire at the doctor's office. We tell each other all about our ordinary lives. Dull jobs, any illness or incapacity, broken marriages or relationships—don't you hate that word. With every detail we lose a little bit of our mystique until we see each other's nakedness and hide our eyes. Like Adam and Eve *ex post serpento* . . ."

"Like an old married couple," she says.

"Sex won't be as exciting."

"I must be seriously faded. Have we had sex already?"

"In our minds. We wondered what it would be like. Were curious enough to skate away with each other. But when we finally get it on . . ."

"You think we will?"

"It will be a big anticlimax."

Bree flips her hair. "I've got the cure for that."

She steers Veasy past a homeless guy nodding on a bench into a clump of stunted palms on the beach. Takes a white pill out of her fanny pack.

"Viagra?" he says.

"Ecstasy, EX-primo . . . Made in Amsterdam. Guaranteed for mind-blowing sex."

Veasy pushes it away. "Won't work for me. I'm the most boring lay in the world."

"I've known guys who could give you some pretty stiff competition."

"If they're stiff they're already ahead of me."

More laughter and a brush of the hand.

When they like you they want to touch you . . .

"I'm sure you've heard the macho pitcho a thousand times," he says. "I'm hung like Sea Biscuit, got a tongue like a cobra, and can go all night like the train to Seattle . . ."

"Two thousand times," she says.

"I'm the anti-stud," he says. "I'm limp and quick . . ."

"You must be very secure to be able to joke about it," she says. "*After a night with me*
You'll get thee to a nunnery."

She is laughing so hard she has to lean on him to keep from falling.

"Let's trip on it," she says.

"I don't like to hallucinate on an empty stomach. There's a place on the boardwalk that has the best corn dogs in the world. And fresh squeezed lemonade . . ."

"Not hungry."

She feels around in his pocket.

"Keep that up and the evening will end even sooner than you think." She finds the bag Roger gave him. "This'll give me the munchies . . ."

Veasy takes out a trumpet mouthpiece.

"Cool bong," she says.

"If anybody stops me I can say I'm on my way to a gig and got so whacked I forgot my trumpet."

She holds the bag up to the light. "Such a pretty red . . ."

"Love colors," Veasy says.

"At twelve hundred an ounce, I should chip in."

"My treat . . ."

"No, no . . ." She zips open her fanny pack. Slips a few crumpled bills into his hand.

"Hundreds," Veasy says. "You in the business?"

"In a small way." She takes out a small envelope. "Put a couple of buds in there and we're even."

He tries to stuff the money back in her fanny pack. "I told you, my treat."

She pushes him away.

"I pay my way or I don't go."

"Matter of principle? Okay . . . Deal . . ."

"Sealed with a kiss," she says.

Electric lips. She slides her nails down the nape of his neck.

"I want to know you better," he says.

She drops the pills one by one into his hand. "These'll help."

"I want to be inside you," he says.

She pushes him away. "No kidding."

He reaches for her. "Not the way you think. I want to be inside your mind. See the world through your eyes. Feel what you feel, know what you know . . ."

She steps back with a wary look.

"Am I too intense?" he asks. "I get that note once in a while."

"Time to fill out that questionnaire," she says. "I'm a hostess at Maderos Steak House in Beverly Hills. What's your day job?"

"I'm a cop," Veasy says. He flashes his ID card. "And you're under arrest for attempted sale of narcotics . . ."

She freezes for a moment. "What?"

"On your knees, hands behind your head," Veasy says.

She tries to spin away. Veasy grabs her hand. Squeezes the pressure point under her thumb. Forces her to her knees. He yells at the pile of rags on the bench. "Hey rookie . . . Lend me your cuffs . . ."

She tries to get up. "Wait a second.".

Veasy pushes her down by the top of her head and warns the rags: "If I don't get those cuffs, I'll have to secure the suspect with an article of her clothing. Her top or maybe her cute little shorts . . ."

"Okay, okay . . ."

Bree shrieks. "No . . ."

The rags are a young cop with a helpless shrug. He hands Veasy the cuffs. "How'd you know?"

Veasy cuffs one of Bree's wrists. "Maybe it was your two hundred dollar New Balance shoes . . ."

Bree writhes and arches her back like a trapped cat. "You asshole!"

Veasy cuffs the other wrist. "Some of the old pros wear something that marks them as a cop so the bad guy will take off and they won't have to fight a two-time loser with a coupla hundred jailhouse brawls under his belt."

"This is my first undercover," the kid says. "They pulled me off Auto. I never worked backup before."

"Who you backin' up?" Veasy asks.

Bree flips her hair. This time to get it out of her eyes so she can look at Veasy with pure hatred.

"You know fuckin' well who he's backin' up."

BEST IDEA WINS

So the kid pitched a pretty good scene.

"I'll follow you down the hall, Jay. Just keep talking about your life while you're making coffee and moving around the kitchen."

("it kept him alive a la Scheherazade.")

"What'll I talk about?" Jay asked.

"Free associate. How you got started in the business, what it was like working in TV in the '70s and '80s, the sex and drug scene. Do you have any quirky movie star stories?"

"Plenty."

The kid points the camera and calls:

"Action."

"Should I walk slower?" Jay asks.

"Normal pace."

"How about a Claude Rains story?"

"We love Claude Rains. Make sure you mention his name . . ."

("we know the drill.")

"We had Claude Rains on *McMillan and Wife*," Jay says. "Wanted his own trailer. We gave it to him. Hated the dialogue. We rewrote it. But then he couldn't remember his lines. Ran off the set in tears . . ."

The kid interrupts. "That's more pathetic than quirky, Jay. Also, it's a tad ageist. Rains must have been close to ninety . . ."

("that's the point, putz.")

The kid backs up into the living room, pointing the camera. "We're still rolling. Let's start the walk again and tell me a quirkier story . . ."

Jay searches his memory.

"We had a pretty weird experience with Olivia de Havilland on *Burke's Law*," he says.

"Don't look back at me, Jay," the kid says. "Remember Lot's wife."

("you believe the attitude?")

"Things were pretty loose back then," Jay says. "The old actors would ask for a girl or a boy sometimes and the ADs would make a call. The actresses usually just wanted some kind of a gift—a scarf or a bottle of their favorite perfume—and the prop man would take care of it."

181

"De Havilland was flying in from Scottsdale. Her agent called and said she wanted to be taken to a cheap motel by the airport. Wanted a dark room, blinds drawn. Then she wanted a girl sent up. Didn't want the girl to know who she was. No talking, she was very specific about that. When it was over she wanted the girl to leave and the car to bring her to the studio."

The kid whoops. "That's what I'm talkin' about, Jay . . . Olivia de Havilland has a lesbo interlude to put her in a working mood . . ."

("great story, boss.")

But Jay has a sudden doubt. "At least I think it was Olivia de Havilland . . ."

"You have to be sure or we can't use it, Jay," the kid says.

"Well we had a lot of lady guest stars that season. Nina Foch, Marjorie Reynolds, Eve Arden—could have been any one of them. Agnes Moorehead, it could have been Agnes Moorehead . . ."

"It could have been Sandra Dee," the kid says. He turns off the camera. "That's a wrap . . ."

("kill him now!")

Little runt. Jay could grab him by the neck—von Sternberg Expressionistic shot of struggling silhouettes playing along the hallway wall. Drag him into the kitchen . . .

But now he feels he has to sell the kid.

"Orson Welles took me to lunch once," he says.

The kid doesn't even answer so Jay pitches harder.

"This is a great Hollywood story, Zack, believe me."

The kid sounds skeptical. "Okay . . . Go back to first position. And . . . Action . . ."

Jay starts his walk. "I was prepping *Baretta* on the Universal lot. Robert Blake, the star, liked me. We'd arm wrestle and I'd drag it out to make him think he was really beating me . . ."

"Slow the walk, Jay," the kid says.

"Every morning they would put up the list of birthdays in the commissary. Wasserman wanted us all to be one happy family. I was so busy I didn't know what day it was until a PA came into my office all wide-eyed and said, Orson Welles is on the phone. He wants to wish you happy birthday."

"I figured Blake was pulling a gag. Like all good actors he was an incredible mimic. It was probably him doing Welles in the production office with me on the speaker and everybody giggling."

"I grab the phone. Who the fuck is this? A big basso laugh on the other end. You think some prankster is impersonating me, don't you Mr. Braffner? The prankster is me. I still do the best impersonation of the character known as Orson Welles."

"I'm still not convinced. To what do I owe the honor of this call? I ask. To your work, Mr. Braffner, he says. I'm a great admirer of *Mad Bomber* . . ."

"I'm stunned. You know my work? I ask."

"You're one of the great artists laboring anonymously in this *kitsch* factory, he says. I don't want to let the auspicious anniversary of your birth go unnoticed. I'm going to buy you lunch . . ."

"I run out. Can't talk now, Orson Welles is taking me to lunch for my birthday. People in the office gaping at me . . . Whaaat . . . ?"

"This huge black stretch rolls up. Welles is in the back seat with a foot-long Cuban and a bottle of Dom Pérignon in an ice bucket. "Happy Birthday, Mr. Braffner. May I call you Jay . . . ?"

"We drive to Ma Maison in Santa Monica. Famous place, he eats there every day. A-list faces waiting at the bar, but we get the round table in the middle of the room. Agents and producers do double takes. What's this TV hack doing with Orson Welles?"

"I'm blitzed out of my gourd from the champagne. Waiters appear with special appetizers, everything off the menu. The chef and the owner come to the table and Welles gives precise instructions for the meal. He's tasting wines and sending them back. Telling me great stories about Harry Cohn, Rita Hayworth, William Randolph Hearst. You know what FDR said to him? You and I are the two best actors in the world . . ."

"Stop here in the hall, Jay, this is great," the kid says.

Jay stops just outside the kitchen.

"Welles says he wants to work with me," he says. "With his prestige and my clout . . . I don't know about clout, I say. Don't be modest, dear boy. He pats my hand. You don't know how respected you are . . ."

"We have Chablis with the sand dabs *à la française*, Burgundy with the tournedos *Béarnaise*. The wine is making me droopy. I need a powder pick-me-up. I ask Welles: Do you indulge? Overindulgently, he answers. We go into the bathroom, two big guys nose to nose in a stall. Welles grabs the vial like a club slut and hoovers a gram up each nostril. Then he booms: Let the games begin!"

"He's doing the room with coin tricks. People laughing, applauding, calling to him. He snaps his fingers and the waiters wheel out a cart with a cake and a bottle of champagne. They put glasses on the tables of the big shots, compliments of Mr. Welles . . ."

"A toast, Welles says. He pops the champagne, pours drinks all around, and raises his glass. Happy Birthday to the new head of TV development at Universal, Jay Braffner . . ."

"All these heavy hitters—Diller, Ronnie Meyer, Ray Stark—raising their glasses to me . . . Happy Birthday, Jay . . ."

"I go cold. The inside of my mouth feels like Welles's dead cigar butt. I think there's a little mistake here, Orson, I say."

"He scowls down at me like the sheriff in *Touch of Evil*. You're not Jay Braffner?"

"I am Jay Braffner. But I'm not the new head of dramatic development. That's Jon Pfeffer. I guess it's his birthday, too."

"You think he'd laugh. The famous Wellesian sense of irony. Instead, he puts his glass down, turns without a word, and walks out. I hear him saying: Michel, could you get my car . . ."

The camera shakes as the kid moves in for a close-up.

"This is the most definitive Hollywood story ever told . . ."

"And you haven't heard the punch line yet."

Jay pauses for effect.

"Orson Welles has stuck me with the check." ·

The kid explodes. "Holy shit, Jay! This is too good to be true."

"No it's too true to be good, as our friend Lester used to say. The check is four hundred and thirty bucks, which was a fortune in the '70s. I pay it and leave a huge tip. Back at the office they ask, how was your lunch? Great, I say . . ."

Jay goes into the kitchen.

"Never saw Welles again. Never told anybody the story until now . . ."

The kid follows. "This is more than a story, Jay. This is a parable, a fuckin' allegory. It's a . . ." He stops with a frightened look and points screen left. "Is that blood?"

A crimson blotch, going brown around edges, is on the floor where Roy went down.

("frying pan time.")

Jay covers quickly. "Killed a rat there. They live in the palm trees, you know."

The kid looks back at Jay. Sees something that makes his face change.

("smell the fear?")

He backs out of the kitchen, eyes darting toward that blood spot. "Let me get this off right away so they can post it tomorrow morning." *("keep him here.")*

Jay takes a step toward him. "You might need B-roll of me just walking around the place. Bookshelves, posters . . ."

The kid backpedals. "Nah. We got it in the walk and talk."

("make him shake hands and pull him back.")

Jay extends his hand. "Thanks for coming by, Roy . . ."

The kid's voice cracks. "Zack . . ."

Running for his life. Not even trying to nonchalant it. Reaching behind him for the knob. The screen door flies open and he runs out.

"Bye, Jay . . ."

There's a shriek of feline rage in the darkness.

"Oops . . . My bad . . ."

("the schmuck tripped over the cat.")

NOBODY LIKES A SMARTASS

Yes it's me and I'm in love again.
Had no lovin' since you know when.
"Let's just forget this ever happened," Veasy says. "Undercovers get their wires crossed all the time. Nobody has to know."

She's rubbing her wrist from the cuffs and won't look at him.
Never try to flirt
With a woman whose pride you've hurt.
"Why do you want to bail us out?" she asks.

"Cops have to stick together."

"But we tried to bust you."

"It was your detail. I don't take it personally."

The rookie comes over with a guilty look. "What should I tell the bosses?"

"Say the target hit on Miss Bait, but only offered his body—no narcotics—so you decided to string him along until another day."

"They'll never buy that story."

"A cop who can't sell a lie has no future on the job, son."

"Tell them the target got suspicious when he saw your stupid two hundred dollar shoes," she says.

Veasy puts a hand on her arm. "Don't blame him. You were blown before then."

Bree flips her hair.
I could do a PhD
On tress-toss choreography
On the hidden meanings in flying locks
From lover's glee to hater's mocks.
"How'd I tip it?" she asks.

"Shall I count the ways?" Veasy says. "First and foremost, you're way too beautiful to be a piece of beach ass. Too beautiful to be a cop at all. Guess you became one because you like to lock people up."

"I suppose you did it to protect and serve . . ."

"It was the best offer I got. Cop is the top of the blue collar pyramid. It's either lock people up or install their entertainment systems . . ."

"Let's get back to my tells," she says.

"Not amused by my witty asides?"

"Are they witty?"

"Okay, more tells . . . Beach ass ain't fine diners. The only cheese they know is Kraft slices . . ."

She's making mental notes. "So you were onto me after the Brie joke."

"Right from the jump."

"Anything else?"

"You played it straight-up sexy. Beach ass is teasey—crotch stares, finger sucks, tarty porn moves. The look was wrong. You're gym tight. Even young beach ass droops and sags. You're tan all over. Beach ass sleeps during the day. You're clean, no ink. Beach ass is covered with tats. Your breath is fresh. Beach ass blows a gust of nicotine and tequila . . . College girl sticks out all over you. Beach ass is DNA dumb . . ."

She's had enough. "I've pulled Crips and Mexican Mafia and Israeli ecstasy dealers with this act . . ."

"Thugs are easy. They think they're irresistible."

"You don't?"

"I'm not."

"You just think you're the smartest guy in the room."

"I am."

"Not even close. In fact, you're clueless."

She skates a little circle around him, taunting:

"You've got the LA County Narcotics Task Force on your ass and don't know it."

Veasy lunges at her. "Are you on the Task Force?"

She skates out of reach. "We know where you are, where you're gonna be, and what time you'll be there . . ."

"All you have to do is ask . . ."

She stops for a moment, hands on hips.

"Don't you care?"

"If I call the Task Force and ask for Bree, will you come to the phone or will they send me to Whole Foods?"

She skates away, calling over her shoulder:

"Somebody is setting you up, smartass."

She crouches like a speed skater and takes off down Washington Avenue.

He starts after her. "Don't go away mad."
But stops . . .
Women go by pheromone
That's the attraction.
If they don't like your aroma,
They'll go right homa
And you won't get no satisfaction.
His phone rings. Tingley's number.
Thank God for a wench
Who digs my stench.

THE MISSING LINK

"I just had a Eureka moment," Tingley says.

"In the bathtub?"

"In the PTA meeting."

Veasy skates down the boardwalk looking for Roger Greenspun.

Have to warn him not to get caught in the net they're spreading for me.

"They were droning on and on about taking soda out of the vending machines," Tingley says. "I could feel myself starting to lose consciousness so I got out my phone and Googled Lester Tarsis. In 1995 he had a show called *Wheelies* about Santa Monica bike cops. Guess what? The three dead producers, Kessel, Helfand, and London, were on staff. And Jay Braffner directed three episodes . . ."

"That's not news. We've already established that they worked together."

"Here's the Eureka part," Tingley says. "I go on the Encyclopedia of Episodic TV. Can you imagine the nerds who put that together? Has story summaries of all the TV shows since 1950. I look up *Wheelies*. Find an episode about a guy who is knocked out and left to die as they fumigate his house for termites. Another one in which the victim is drowned in his swimming pool. Another where a guy is locked in his car. The murderer turns on the motor with the remote. Then drops a forged suicide note on his wife's night table . . . Sound familiar?"

Two obvious undercovers are walking onto the beach with Roger.

They'll try to flip him. To set me up.

"Guess who wrote all three episodes?" Tingley says.

The undercovers high-five Roger and walk off the beach. He waves goodbye, the tip of his blunt glowing red.

It was a buy. Nothing to do with me . . . Weird . . .

"Veasy, you still there?" Tingley says.

"I give up," Veasy says. "Who wrote the episodes?"

"Lester Tarsis."

Tarsis? That doesn't seem right.

"I saw Tarsis today. Told him how the three guys had died. He didn't react."

"Maybe he already knew. Maybe he's using his scripts as scenarios for murder . . ."

"Are there any photos of Tarsis online?" Veasy asks.

"There's one on his IMDB page."

"Let's scan it and show it to the exterminators tomorrow. Show it around Helfand's neighborhood and Gary London's . . ."

He can feel her heart beating. She's waiting for the bouquet.

"Good detective work, Detective," he says.

He feels her blushing.

"This confirms your serial killer theory," she says. "Can't wait to see the Owl's face when we spring it on him."

"He'll say it's just coincidental."

"What'll he say when we bring Lester Tarsis in?"

"He'll call a press conference. Spin it like he ran the investigation."

"That won't work," she says. "Everybody knows it was your idea. He'll have to give you the credit . . ."

She's so happy for me.

And all I can think about is Bree.

BAD NEWS

Jonas gets his dinner at El Pollo Loco. He orders the ten piece, legs and thighs, two large sides—pinto beans and cole slaw—extra flour tortillas, plus a Califresco burrito, and a one-liter Pepsi because he doesn't want the pretty Latina cashier to think he's eating alone. Kills a bottle of Smoking Loon Cabernet and nods out in his Barcalounger watching the Dodgers game. A gas bubble in his side wakes him in the bottom of the fourth. He staggers doubled over to the couch. Next thing he knows his phone is going crazy and the postgame show is on.

It's Walsh.

"The sting didn't work."

The pilot light burns in his sternum. He's got the red wine headache, the stiff neck from sleeping on his face. The blinking. The tic under the left eye.

What's next, a stroke?

"What happened to your honey pot?" he asks.

"Veasy arrested her for an attempted sale before she could grab him for the same thing."

"So he knows we're after him."

"No. He thinks they took him for a weed head they could flip to get Roger Greenspun."

"Okay then, no harm done."

"Better than that," Walsh says. "The honey pot says Veasy cuffed her, showed her up, pretty much blew her cover on the boardwalk. She wants another shot at him."

"But he knows she's a cop."

"She thinks she can win his confidence."

"She'll have to screw him. That's the only way to get him to drop his guard."

"She says she'll do what she has to do. On her own time. This is personal with her."

The tic subsides. "That's almost good news," he says.

"Not quite . . ."

The tic returns.

"Cheri Tingley texted Sheila Rogers," Walsh says. "Don't miss the morning squad meeting, she said." He tries a joke. "All these women working on their own time. Why can't they get shitfaced like cops are supposed to?"

Police work makes strange bedfellows.

He knows the answer, but wants to hear it from Walsh.

"Since when is Rogers reporting to you?"

The boast in the voice confirms it. "We're kinda . . . friends . . ."

He tries to picture them together. Walsh, the Chicago transplant, seventeen years on the job and watching the pension clock. Big-bellied, shambling. Broken capillaries popping up under his eyes. Rogers, skinny, thyroid-eyed, nail-biting mother of three. Her husband is a FedEx guy. She does domestic disputes, parent-child complaints.

Is it two lonely souls communing? Or do they just get it on in an empty office at odd hours? Tight little ass. Does she take the top? Is she a spinner? A screamer?

"Any idea what's gonna happen at the meeting?" he asks.

"Tingley says Veasy's gonna show proof he's got a serial killer."

Jonas starts blinking again. The tic is jumping under his left eye. His eyebrows twitch like they're about to fly off his head.

CYBER NOIR

"Color film will soon be an artifact, a relic from a simpler time," Jay says. "High Def will run its course. People will find it too revealing."
   ("won't hide their flaws.")
   "The future will return to black and white. Grays and shadows . . . Everything concealed . . ."
   ("the return of the dirty secret.")
   Jay orders the shots—"A-Camera tight on my face in the shadows, B-Camera across my hands to the computer screen. Make the room deep-space black. Give me a bounce from the tensor lamp off the blue eyeball of the iMac. Catch my white fingers typing, the gray highlights of my beard, the shadowy hollows of my staring eyes . . ."
   ("rolling . . .")
   "The future will be billions of people alone in dark rooms," Jay says. "Black letters on a white screen . . . What is the color of an electron?"
   ("incredibly zen . . .")
   Jay types "Seth Tarsis" on the Google bar.
   "In the future an invisible madman will easily find his prey. The computer is compatible with all mental states. It is dys and mal as well as multifunctional . . ."
   ("is somebody writing this down?")
   Google has two pages: PRODUCER'S SON ARRESTED FOR BURGLARY . . . Top billing goes to Kenneth Shuster, son of Oscar-winning producer Robert Shuster, who broke into the pharmacy section of a Rite Aid. Seth Tarsis, son of TV producer Lester Tarsis (*She, Queen of the Jungle*) was arrested along with him . . .
   Lester gets another credit in *Variety* . . . "Seth Tarsis, son of veteran syndie satrap, Lester Tarsis . . ."
   Finally, a mention of "tearful mother Claire Tarsis . . ."
   Jay's Google search finds one Claire Tarsis in the whole U.S.A. One address: 118 Charleville, Beverly Hills. Lester's old house in the flats.
   He clicks on a site called THEWHOLESTORY.com, which promises to "search all public records." For $39.99, charged to his Visa Platinum, he gets the vital stats on Seth Tarsis—SSN, mobile, e-mail address,

school reports about his abuse of medication, referrals to rehab facilities. Juvenile records are sealed, but Seth's attorney and court-appointed psychologist are listed.

"They should call this site THE WHOLE TRAGIC STORY," Jay says.

("painfully true.")

Seth's mug shot is posted on CelebrityBrats.com . . .

"Big nose and overbite," Jay says. "He's Lester's son alright."

BRAINWATCHING

On the street the cop lights flashing.
In the room I draw the blind.
Twisted wrecks of neurons crashing
In the junkyard of my mind.

Veasy loads the trumpet mouthpiece with Roger's Love Colors and lights up. Soon the nightmare will come up like a scene in a movie. Starting with cop lights in the blue morning air.

Wisps of dawn
Enshroud her.

Cops and neighbors staring down at something on the ground under the trees in Cloverdale Park. Stepping aside to reveal little Nina Encarnación, little brown body trussed, brown eyes staring past him.

Wisps of smoke
Can't cloud her.

He'll fish Robert Browning out from under the bed. Pick up *My Last Duchess* and start from the top. Read and read until the image fades.

But this time the nightmare doesn't come. Instead, there's the rumble of Rollerblades and that cop, Bree, pops into his mind. Skating around him . . . Around and around . . . Scornful and pointing . . . "You're clueless . . ."

Am I cured
Or is this a new torture to endure?

Veasy sits up.

Teleport time.

He steps out of his body and goes to the computer. Stays on the bed—the room is small enough for him to be in two places at once.

He watches himself bending to the flickering screen. The Task Force shouldn't be online. It should be a secret agency, working with informants and undercovers. But there it is in bold caps, LA COUNTY NARCOTICS TASK FORCE. Names and phone numbers, institutional history . . .

Everybody has to have a website.

Can't be confidential

In matters existential
Be self-referential
And you'll be deemed essential.

It's after eleven, but he knows Bree is there, hair fluffing, long legs crossed, telling her story to the night supervisor. Cops walking by to peek into the cubicle.

He calls the 800 number. It's picked up promptly.

"Los Angeles Narcotics Task Force, hold the line please." Female voice—they make the women work the night tour. This has got to be the snitch line. It's always busy . . .

She comes back on.

"Thank you for waiting. May I help you?"

"I'm looking for Bree."

She's there, the pause gives it away. "This is the Los Angeles Narcotics . . ."

"I ran into Bree on the Venice boardwalk tonight. If she's there I'd like to talk to her . . ."

"There is nobody here named Bree . . ."

"Maybe it's her street name. Tall, hot blonde . . ."

"What is this in reference to, sir?"

"Just tell her it's Roger Greenspun's friend."

"If you'll wait a moment, please . . ."

He's on hold. Doris Day is singing "que sera, sera." Bree and the night tour brain trust must be steaming up the cubicle trying to figure out how to handle him.

A sting is blown
Better bury it fast
Cops go Keystone
When they cover their ass.

The bosses will want to control the damage. Take Veasy's name off the assignment sheet, delete the e-mails and the searches they made on him.

But Bree will want revenge.

Never met a pretty girl who could take a joke.

She'll say he's a classic marijuana megalomaniac, who can be trapped by his own vanity.

Or is that what I would say?

But she has to be careful making her case. If she lobbies too hard they'll take her off the street until she calms down. They may decide she's a loose cannon and transfer her out of the task force.

If she would come to the phone he would tell her not to get emotionally involved. He would tell her about Nina and she would understand.

But she won't talk to him. And now his cell is going off. Mineo on Caller ID.

"The hospital says Mrs. Brownlee is okay to talk. They're waking her every few hours. Gonna give her a brain scan in the morning. Can you get over there right away?"

"Sure."

Veasy's e-mail dings. "I just sent you Sandusky's mug shot," Mineo says. "It's not a legal lineup, but if she IDs him we can talk to Jonas about phone taps and extraditions . . . Take Tingley and a nurse in with you when you show the old lady the pictures so they can corroborate."

ACT THREE

"The night was never long enough," Jay says.

He's reheating Zack's pizza. Laying out the bagels and cream cheese from the morning's production meeting. Entertaining the crew with coffee and war stories as he waits for sunrise.

"Studios wanted to finish the episodes in seven days, even if it meant working eighteen hours, paying triple overtime, and forcing turnaround time. The crews were called back a few hours after they wrapped . . ."

("slave drivers.")

"It was tough on the actors. They'd get frazzled, blow their lines, miss their marks, fight the ADs. You had to retouch their eye bags before every shot. The smart actresses would refuse to do close-ups . . ."

("survivors.")

"Lester told me to put a fill light on the camera for the ladies. I said it won't match the rest of the shots. Nobody'll know the difference, he said. I told him the actors were exhausted. What are you, a Communist? he said."

("he didn't give a shit.")

"Union rules stipulate you have to feed the crew every six hours." "That put the director in the middle. If you didn't finish the night's work the studios would blame you. If you drove the crew too hard they would find a million ways to slow you down . . ."

("we would never do that to you, boss . . .")

"Daytime shooting was no problem. When the sun went down you could blast Ten Ks and make midnight look like high noon . . ."

Can't use the broken pot so Jay holds the cups under the spout to catch the coffee.

"Night exteriors were brutal. The crew got a half hour to eat, but stretched it out to forty-five minutes. Then, they would dawdle getting back to the set. Energy levels scraping bottom . . ."

("we're fresh as daisies.")

"You had four hours of black. After that, the night would start to fray and the blue would show through. You'd work fast, hoping to make that last shot before the blue went gray around the edges . . ."

("all that aggravation for an episode of Knight Rider?*")*

"And in the end Lester was right," Jay says. "Nobody did know the difference . . . Nobody cared . . ."

He points out the window. "There's the gray. Slushlight we called it. Dishwater sky just before dawn . . . CAMERA . . . Follow me down the hall into the bathroom . . ."

("following.")

"My pharmacopeia runneth over," Jay says. "Gives you a warm feeling to know you won't outlive your meds."

Jay uses his toothbrush handle to mash an Oxycodone, an Ambien, and a Placidyl and puts the powder in a piece of tinfoil.

"Thank God for the drug culture," he says. "Makes homicide so much easier."

("that line will be tweeted and retweeted and . . .")

"Thank you . . . And now, CAMERA CAR: follow my Mercedes down Olympic Boulevard to Beverly Hills . . ."

WHY THEY PAY THE BIG BUCKS

Dr. Pine, Lester's urologist, is sick of his job. "I could water ski on the river of urine I see every day," he told Lester at his last checkup. "What do you think? Good image?"

"Off-putting," Lester said.

Dr. Pine said he wanted to change careers and become a standup comedian. "There's never been a comedy urologist before."

"With good reason," Lester said.

The doctor was undeterred. He tried out jokes during the rectal exam.

"That's either the world's largest prostate or I found that Titleist I hit into the rough."

"I'm going to use two fingers this time. In case you want a second opinion . . ."

And when he stopped laughing:

"Funny? Should I keep it in? The joke, not my finger."

"Take them both out."

Dr. Pine sulked while Lester was wiping the cream off his rectum.

"You're going to be getting up twice a night to piss for the rest of your life. It's what you get for living this long."

"And if I live longer?"

"You'll come to a point where you have congestive heart failure and can't piss at all. Then we'll give you diuretics and a diaper . . ."

"What should I do until then?" Lester asked.

"Sit down when you pee at night," Pine said. "You could get micturition syncope—fainting while urinating—fall and crack your head on the toilet bowl . . . Don't drink anything up to four hours before you go to bed, not even when you brush your teeth. Studies show that men who are sexually active have a lower incidence of prostate disease. I know it's hard for you older single guys, but try to have more sex . . ."

"If I have any more sex I'll have the healthiest prostate in the poorhouse," Lester said.

He's cut out the second Diet Coke with dinner. Brushes his teeth dry. It doesn't help. He's up at two and five every morning like clockwork.

He was never a dreamer, but now he has pointless encounters in his sleep. People he doesn't know walk by him and make cryptic remarks in empty rooms with abstract paintings on the walls.

He called Doctor Pine. "I walked out of your office into an Antonioni movie."

"The Cipro has a recently discovered adverse effect," the doctor said. "It might interfere with your sleep patterns and cause vivid nightmares . . ." And then, after a mirthful wheeze: "I have nicer drugs for people who laugh at my jokes . . ."

The dreams are never scary, just exasperating. Now he surfaces from a party in a disco in the '70s . . . He's on a crowded dance floor, strobes blinding him, trying to avoid wildly flailing couples.

The phone on the night table is flashing a voice mail. Five o'clock sharp. Only two possible calls—Claire that Seth has been arrested again, or Owen in New Zealand telling him he's fired.

"Lester, you awake?"

It's Owen.

That down-under twang usually gives Lester palpitations, but now he's relieved that it's not about Seth.

"Sorry mate, I never know what time it is in LA. Have time for a chat?"

"For you, always."

There's a slight, breathy chuckle. "Yeah, I'm sure . . . Well. Here's the long and the short of it. We've lost Slovakia and Slovenia."

"I thought they were the same country."

"We have to make some drastic cuts if we want to come out of next season with tea and crumpet money," Owen says.

"We're pretty lean as is," Lester says.

"We can get leaner with one fell swoop. Save fifteen K a week . . ."

That's Lester's salary. He's being fired.

"Did you read Toledano's script?" Owen asks.

"Who?"

"Zack Toledano."

It takes Lester a second. "The postproduction runner?"

"Very professional. Shootable length, feel-good story about She's long-lost mum. Funny, we never thought about the mum angle before . . ."

"We? Since when did you have any input into the scripts?"

"You should read it. Kid's got the show down as if he's been writing it for years. Very complimentary little note about you. How he's studied your style and has learned a lot from his association with you . . ."

"He gets me pot for the weekend . . ."

"I'd like to shoot it for episode eleven," Owen says. "Get rid of Lippman's Tarzan tripe about silent tribes shooting blowguns and melting back into the jungle."

"We cleaned that up in the second draft . . ."

"Have him rewrite O'Meara's liberal shit about evil warlords . . ."

"That's being changed as well. Sean's first drafts are always a little preachy . . . I send you these early drafts as a courtesy . . ."

"What does this kid Toledano make?" Owen asks.

"The job is budgeted at eight hundred, but we got him for six . . ."

"Give him twelve and put him on staff."

Lester wonders if he's still dreaming. "I thought you wanted to get leaner."

"We will. The kid can replace Lippman and O'Meara."

"You want me to fire them?"

"They're both making six grand a week. Add the residuals and there's your fifteen with a few dollars to spare."

"Fine, but who's gonna write the show?"

"Toledano is, with a big assist from you."

"You could fire me and save eighteen Gs."

"The thought occurred, to be honest, mate. But the foreign boys love you. Oboya in Gaborone, Pistov in Podgorica . . . They both asked me, is Lester going to run the show again? Two fucking thugs, sell their mothers, but won't hear a discouraging word about Lester Tarsis . . ."

The distributors from Botswana and Montenegro. Lester had taken them to Koreatown for naked sushi when they came to LA for the American Film Market. They slurped sake out of Thai navels and swore eternal fealty.

"You've got fourteen weeks from the time the show goes on hiatus to start cranking out the next thirteen," Owen says. "You and the kid can probably get five or six ready before we start shooting . . ."

"You'll have to pay the kid his residuals," Lester says.

"He's not a Writers Guild member," Owen says. "Just move him out to Wellington, he can join our New Zealand branch. No residuals, no benefits, but they sign a lot of Greenpeace petitions . . ."

"What if he won't go?"

"Raise him a hundred. Tell him how beautiful the Maori girls are. Ask him where he's working after you fire him . . ."

Noah Lippman's face pops into Lester's head. Squinting and sweating and flinching as Lester gives his notes. His sons are jocks. Every summer he pays for Magic Johnson's basketball camp with his residuals . . .

Sean scuffing in his cargo shorts and vintage tees. Bleary from pot and wine. War stories about Nicholson and Beatty . . .

"These guys have been with me for seven years," Lester says.

"They had a good run for two dried-up hacks," Owen says.

"They'll never work again."

"Fortunes of war, mate. C'mon, put a little pepper in your pecker. You've fired hundreds, so I'm told. You're an infamous bastard you are . . ."

STAKEOUT IN
BEVERLY HILLS

"You've heard of the Homes of the Hollywood Stars," Jay says. "This is the Homes of the Hollywood Has-Beens."

Jay drives down Olympic Boulevard and turns left onto Spalding. The crew is following in a camera car.

"Hold the roll while I drive around the block," Jay says.

("holding the roll . . .")

"This is where the poor, huddled masses of Beverly Hills live," Jay says. "Nobody's on the corner selling maps for these losers. If it were India it would be the district of the Untouchables, and I don't mean the show with Robert Stack . . ."

Jay turns right on Charleville. "Here'll you find the showrunners who ran their shows into the ground. The actors who came off a long run on a hit series—fifteen years ago—and haven't worked since. The writers who made a living writing unproduced scripts until they had been hired and fired by everybody in town and ran out of places to fail . . . The smalltime agents whose clients can only work $100-a-day nonunion jobs . . . The directors who went crazy after their one hot picture, overspent on drugs or women or crooked business managers—sound familiar? The occasional upstart like Lester who's making millions in the low-rent end of the business—porno, cheap slashers, direct to foreign video, TV syndication—but can't buy a welcome from the aristocrats north of Wilshire. Let us not forget the colony of divorced wives like Claire living on community property. And abandoned children like Seth who have just enough money to kill themselves on drugs. One thing about this town: if you know the address you know the story."

He points to a split-level, lime green stucco walls, flat tar roof, louver doors, slatted plastic shades . . .

"Chez Lester Tarsis . . . He bought this house when Seth was born. A year later he walked out and moved into a condo on Ocean Avenue. Claire's been here ever since, bringing in a new guy every couple of years on Lester's nickel."

A Lexus, a Tundra, and a dusty Corolla are jammed into the narrow driveway.

"The junker belongs to Seth. All banged up and parked against the fence. So many speeders they wouldn't let him take Internet Traffic School . . ."

("know the address, know the story.")

Jay turns right on Bedford.

"I made almost every mistake in the book, but that's one bullet I dodged—I never had a kid."

("close call.")

"Most of the guys I knew were getting nailed. If it wasn't an abortion or a paternity or a palimony, it was like a shotgun marriage kinda thing. Jon Pfeffer knocked up this little blonde makeup girl and left his wife and three kids to start a new family. A year later she dumped him for Jack Cornford . . ."

("the composer?")

"She traded up, good career move. Meanwhile, Pfeffer's wife had become a lesbian and his kids wouldn't talk to him. He got strung out on booze and Valium and spent three months at Betty Ford. Got out and went straight to Cornford's house in Palos Verdes. Banging on the door, threats—they got a restraining order. Ignored it and stalked the little blonde in the Southcoast Mall. Bit a security guy. Ducked jail by checking into rehab at Second Chances in Laguna Niguel. Hung himself in the shower a few nights later . . ."

("a family would have interfered with your work.")

"Totally. But it's funny that no woman ever tried to sandbag me into marriage. Blackmail me, trap me, guilt me with a kid . . . Something . . ."

("they knew you were too smart.")

("couldn't be manipulated . . .")

("wouldn't ruin your life over a piece of ass.")

Jay turns back onto Olympic.

"Get a wide shot of me pulling me into the bus stop," he says.

("rolling.")

"Now ZOOM IN to me behind the wheel, checking my watch."

("done . . .")

"INSERT of the watch showing five-thirty . . ."

("solid establishing sequence.")

"Thank you . . ."

Jay turns off the motor. "I can sit here by a meter. Big street, I'm invisible. There's no parking before eight A.M. in Beverly Hills so if I park in front of Lester's house now, I'll draw the security guys and then the cops. At eight all the service trucks show. The gardeners, plumbers, pool guys, dog groomers. I can slide in behind them. Wait for Seth to show."

PHOTO OPS

Come be the alchemist of my soul,
Anoint my forehead with droplets of gold.
In my ears sigh a lover's blessing,
Close my eyes with silken caressing.

A cold shower douses the vision. Bree skates away, waving over her shoulder. The golden droplets turn into an icy needle spray. The silken caress is a loofah that's starting to chafe.

Veasy doubles up on the Visine, scrapes a razor across his face, and brushes his teeth until his gums bleed. Wipes the foggy mirror for a better look and decides:

"I'm straight enough."

He gets a text from Tingley. "At the hospital with Mrs. Brownlee. Downloading Tarsis pic off IMDB."

There's a pot of week-old coffee in the fridge. He throws it down, cold and black.

Prints out Olin Sandusky's mug shot.

Gets another text from Tingley as he gets into his '01 Malibu. "Hurry, the window's closing."

She meets him outside the ICU. "They found a subdural hematoma. She was on blood thinners so they have to wait for the cardiac surgeon to come and assist at the operation. We've got a few minutes before they start to prep her."

They find Mrs. Brownlee in a tangle of IVs. Veasy strokes her hair.

"From snow white to tombstone gray."

A West Indian nurse hovers as they try to wake her.

"Mrs. Brownlee . . . ?"

No response.

The nurse shakes her shoulder.

"Wake up sweetie, the poh-lice wants to talk to you . . ." Shakes her again. "C'mon honey, Doctor Waring will be mad with me if you go to sleep. You don't want me to get in trouble, do you?"

Mrs. Brownlee's eyes open wide, like a ventriloquist's dummy. Bright blue, they fix on Veasy. "Did you find the man?"

Veasy leans close. "We brought a picture. Can you tell us if this is him?"

She gropes like a blind woman. The nurse finds her glasses on the table and eases them over her ears. Tingley holds Sandusky's mug shot in front of her.

She tries to sit up. "I remember the eyes. He had a little beard under his lip and a mustache, but I remember the eyes . . . It's him."

She falls back. The nurse slips off her glasses. "Okay honey, just rest up now. Doctor will be here soon . . . Tomorrow, you'll be walkin' into bingo like nothin' happened . . ."

Veasy mimes a silent "thank you" to the nurse. His hands shake as they walk down the corridor.

"That's not a positive ID."

"We'll need an updated photo," Tingley says.

"Married fifty-seven years and this is how they spend their last day together," Veasy says. "Terrorized by a bungling thug . . ."

Tingley takes a closer look. "Little too much herb last night?"

"Little too much world today."

"Would it do any good to tell you that the marijuana distorts your perceptions of reality?"

"You mean if I didn't smoke weed Olin Sandusky would have gone to the right house and Mr. Brownlee would be alive today?"

"No, but you wouldn't be all red and shaky about it."

"You mean I'd be a realistic professional? Just the facts, ma'am?"

"I mean you'd be a cop," she says. And then with a look of revelation. "That's what's wrong with you. You're not really a cop."

"Impersonating a police officer is a pretty serious accusation . . ."

"I mean . . ." She struggles to find the words. "You're not objective . . . You take things to heart . . ."

"I'm okay most of the time. But I can't predict my feelings."

Tingley hands him a photo of Lester Tarsis. On a set, surrounded by an unsmiling crew.

"How do you feel about three producers stalked by a serial killer?"

He shrugs. "Purely an intellectual exercise . . ."

RAISING THE STAKES

They've been shooting the cars on Olympic Boulevard for hours. Wide shots, close-ups, different angles. The crew is puzzled.

"Think I'm just wasting film out here?" Jay asks.

("we know you have a reason, boss.")

"It's for a time lapse MONTAGE on the traffic flow," Jay says. "A few cars at dawn, thickening and speeding at seven as the drivers try to beat the building traffic. Slowing and lurching by eight. Horns, brake lights blinking, veins bursting . . ."

("rush hour.")

"Put it all together into one sequence showing the passage of time through traffic."

("revelatory!")

"Thank you," Jay says. "Now we're ready for the next sequence. PAN OFF the road and rack focus to me."

("retro style.")

Jay starts the Mercedes. "Let the car go out of frame."

He turns onto Charleville right in front of Lester's house and noses between "Gala Pool Service, Green and Chlorine Free" and "Dapper Dogs, Eco-Friendly Pet Grooming . . ."

("great parking job . . .")

"The only thing I learned in Brooklyn," Jay says. "I can sit here until two A.M. and nobody will look twice. But I don't think I'll have to . . ."

A black Escalade stretch limo has pulled up alongside them. A kid stumbles out of the back door and blinks as the air hits him. Short and skinny with a big nose.

"Spitting image of you know who," Jay says.

The Esacalade pulls away with the door still open. The kid trips over the curb. He's got his house key on a lanyard in his back pocket.

Jay opens the passenger window and calls:

"Seth . . ."

The kid comes over, warily.

Get him framed in the window.

("he walked right into the shot.")

Same size reverse of me. Intercut between us.
("done.")

"Your dad sent me to get you," Jays says. "Take you to his office."

The kid squints into the Mercedes. Dusty, old newspapers and McDonald's wrappers . . . *Suspicious* . . .

"Why?"

"He says he's got some money for you," Jay says. "Wants to give it to you personally. You know, make sure you get it."

The kid's undecided. "He didn't tell me anything . . . I'd better tell my mom I'm going . . ."

"Partying all night, huh?"

The kid loosens up. "Yeah. She's probably waiting for me . . ."

"Want to take a little ride, first?" Jay says. "Get some fresh air, you know, so you'll look a little better . . . Polish your eyeballs . . ."

He eases the vial out of his pocket. The kid's eyes go right to it.

"Yeah, maybe I should . . ."

He gets in the car. Jay pulls out onto Charleville.

"I'm Jay Braffner. I directed a picture your dad wrote. *The Mad Bomber* . . ."

The kid is looking at the vial.

"Ever hear of it?"

Shakes his head. "Don't think so."

Jay hands him the vial. He hunches over and pours a little powder onto his thumbnail.

"Go ahead, I got plenty," Jay says.

The kid snorts into one nostril. Then reloads and snorts into the other.

"Smooth, no bite," he says.

"Pharmaceutical," Jay says. "It's the cut that makes it sting."

"Cool," the kid says, handing it back.

"Go ahead," Jay says, "it'll help you deal with your mom."

"They haven't invented the drug that can do that," the kid says.

"You've got your father's sense of humor."

The kid takes another hit.

"Speak to your dad lately?"

"Called him yesterday."

"He never answers calls at his office."

The kid loads up again.

"He talked to me . . ."

("nicely done.")
Thank you . . .
"I'll just drive around the block a few times until you get your head straight," Jay says.

The kid takes another hit. Then he puts his head back and closes his eyes.

"Okay . . ."

RED HERRING

Do carpenter ants have little saws
  That dangle from their mandibles,
  To cut into our maple floors
  And wangle bosky edibles?
They're in the conference room of Universal Extermination. Veasy
is looking at the plaques, the banners, the Little League photos, Coach
of the Year, Man of the Year from the California Conference of Pest
Control . . .
  "Do tool belts dangle from their feet
  As through our house they're stealing
  Searching for a morsel sweet
  In the oak beams of our ceiling?"
Tingley waves him into silence. "I can't hear . . ."
She's on the phone with Mineo. "We need a newer shot of
Sandusky with a soul patch. Did they do an exit photo when he
left prison?"
  "Parole officers sometimes take a cell phone shot of their new
clients," Veasy says.
  A sharp knock and a fat, pale man with thinning red hair and a very
blue suit comes through the door.
  "Detectives Veasy and Tingley?"
  "I'm Veasy. You the lawyer?"
  "Is it so obvious?" The lawyer offers a damp, red hand. "Gerald
Corley . . . Mr. Burg called me in to see if I can help . . ."
  Veasy shows him the photo of Lester Tarsis and the film crew.
  "We'd like to show this to the crew that was working on the Kessel
house. See if they recognize anybody . . ."
  "Like who?"
  "The murderer."
  "Is this officially a homicide investigation?"
  "Every death is a homicide until proven otherwise."
  "Interesting view of the world, Detective. Anyway, the men have
already given me affidavits that they saw no one."

"That was for the civil action," Veasy says. "This is a possible criminal matter in which they could face a charge of lying to a police officer."

The lawyer smiles, unfazed. "That's a federal charge and wouldn't apply."

Veasy smiles back, unrepentant. "Can't blame a guy for trying. But seriously, Counselor, if you're concerned about defending a negligence lawsuit, wouldn't it be better if you could show that a murderer hid from your crew while they were making their final inspection?"

"Not necessarily, Detective."

"Well, wouldn't it be better if you let me talk to them before I turn Mr. Burg in for hiring undocumented workers?"

"That might be better."

The lawyer goes to the door. "You want to see them one by one?"

"Bring the whole crew in. We can get this done in ten minutes . . ."

Tingley gets a text. "Mineo can't find an updated photo of Sandusky."

"Portland PD might have something," says Veasy.

The lawyer comes back with three nervous young Mexicans in blue uniforms.

"Chill, *guerros*, we're not checking socials," Veasy says. "Just want to see if you recognize anybody in this picture. So let's do this one by one . . ." He picks out the youngest and shows him the photo.

"Recognize anybody?"

The kid sneaks a look at the lawyer who nods quickly.

"It's the man who came out of the house that day," he says.

Veasy looks at the lawyer. "There was a man in the house?"

The lawyer glosses smoothly. "The boys saw someone they didn't know, but thought he was just a new man . . ."

"Mr. Burg didn't tell us that."

"They didn't bother to tell Mr. Burg. As I said, they just thought . . ."

"That he was a new man, I know. You don't skip a beat, Counselor . . ."

"Just trying to help."

Veasy shows the photo to a skinny kid in an oversized uniform. "Hey *gordito*, see anybody you know?"

The kid looks and nods. "That's him . . . He came out the back door and said he thought he heard someone in the house, but it was just a dog barking."

"And you thought he was a new guy in the crew."

"Yeah, he was wearing a uniform. Had a clipboard."

"Love the clipboard," Tingley says.

"Yeah, that is a nice touch," says Veasy. He waves the photo at a chubby guy with a round face and a mop of black hair. "Hey *jefe*, let's make it unanimous . . ." Points to Lester. "This the man you saw?"

Jefe shakes his head. "That's not him." He points to another man in the photo. "That's the man I saw."

It's a big, wild-haired man in a safari jacket with a director's viewfinder around his neck.

"Let's get this straight," Veasy says. He waves the two others over and points to Lester Tarsis. "Him?"

"No . . ." The three shake their heads. They point to the big, wild-haired man in the safari jacket.

"Him."

LIGHTING THE FUSE

The kid is snoring and dribbling out of the corner of his mouth all the way down the 10 Freeway. He starts to stir and sniffle as Jay pulls onto a quiet street by the Santa Monica cemetery.

PUSH IN on Braffner.

("pushing in . . .")

Jay winds the duct tape around the kid's ankles without waking him. But when he tries to ease his hands behind his back the kid pulls away, instinctively . . .

"Wha . . ."

Jay slaps him hard on the side of the head, knocking him into the window.

"Quiet Seth. I don't wanna hurt you, but I'll kill you if I have to."

("Hammett line.")

"Thank you," Jay says.

The kid's lip is bleeding. Jay twists his arms back and wraps the duct tape around his wrists.

The kid blubbers.

"I didn't do anything to you."

"Sins of the father, Seth," Jay says.

He winds the tape around the kid's head, covering his mouth.

"Breathe through your nose, you'll be okay."

He pushes the kid onto the floor and takes side streets to his house. Pulls onto the driveway. Short trip to the back door. No one's ever around, but it's early morning. Someone might be making coffee in the kitchen. Looking out the window . . .

("safer to pull into the garage . . .")

"But it takes a lot of screen time," Jay says. And decides: "We'll risk being discovered. It'll add suspense."

Jay drags Seth out of the car and picks him up like a baby. He's so flimsy. No sinew. Already wasting away from drugs. He looks up at Jay with docile eyes. Like a little dog.

It hurts Jay inside.

"You're all skin and bone, Seth," he says. "Gotta eat more, work out. Toughen up . . ."

The kid doesn't move. No fight in him. No fear. Like he's waiting for the end.

"Follow me," Jay orders.

("following . . .")

He carries the kid into the house and down the hall to the guest room.

"I guess you've just learned how dangerous this world can be, Seth," Jay says.

He dumps the kid on the bed.

"Take it from a guy who knows. Don't get so wasted that you lose control. You've got enemies. People you think you can trust are plotting against you . . ."

("bonding with the captive.")

("changing his life.")

("whatever's left of it.")

TAKING CONTROL

Jonas hears a whimper and realizes:

It's me.

If he wasn't in the locker room he'd cry out in frustration.

I'm out of touch for an hour and World War III breaks out.

He doesn't like to keep his phone in a fanny pack around his shorts when he does cardio. It leaves an itchy sweat rash. So he left it in his bag.

But when he came back from the treadmill the message beep was going crazy behind the locker door.

He had three voice mails from Mineo.

"Hey Boss, Veasy's got a tentative ID from Mrs. Brownlee on the home invader. The guy's based in Portland so I was thinking maybe we should send Veasy up to talk to him . . ."

Then: "second unheard message:"

"Hey Boss, Veasy's got a wrinkle on this Kessel termite thing. The exterminators saw a guy leaving the house before they turned the gas on. They ID'd him from a photo of some TV producers . . ."

And finally: "third unheard message . . ."

"Hey Boss, two mutilated bodies found in the trunk of a car at Santa Monica beach. Male and a female . . . Decapitated . . . Heads in garbage bags. Vehicle is registered to Alison Sobel, the psychiatric social worker, who was reported missing. Tried to get Walsh, but he wasn't answering. Couldn't get you so I called the LAPD forensics. Didn't want to wait too long on the physical evidence . . ."

The one fucking day I leave my phone . . .

The correct move was to call in the FBI. They'd collect evidence in an "advisory capacity," and Jonas would run the investigation as local law enforcement. Now LAPD is going to control the case. He'll be the junior partner, the beach cop in his yokel blues sharing a press conference with the sleekly dressed LA Homicide Detectives.

Gotta get a handle on this.

He calls Mineo.

"Anything new?'

"We got a tentative ID on the female in the trunk," Mineo says. "It's Alison Sobel."

"So soon?"

"One of the responding officers found a wallet next to the body . . ."

His head jerks so violently he almost drops the phone. "Nobody's supposed to touch a body once the victim is confirmed dead . . ."

"It's a kid on the midnight to eight. You know how it is when you find your first body. He got excited . . ."

"Now he's contaminated the scene. We're gonna look like hicks . . ."

"I'm on my way down there to seal the area . . ."

Jonas looks in the gym bag for his meds, but remembers he didn't bring them.

"Where's Veasy?"

"Going out to that producer's office in Hollywood . . ."

Christ, did another one turn up dead?

"What producer?"

"Lester Tarsis. He's in a photo with the man the three exterminators say they saw outside Dave Kessel's house . . ."

"What three exterminators? When did all this happen?"

"Yesterday afternoon. Tingley got a lead on this guy Tarsis. He was a person of interest for a hot second, but now they think it might be this other guy in the photo . . ."

"What other guy? What photo? Why was I kept in the dark on this?"

Shrill. Shows weakness . . .

That second of silence means Mineo is taking a breath, counting to ten.

"Nobody's holding out on you, Chief," he says in measured tones. "Things were breaking quickly . . ."

Careful . . . He's squad commander. Can find a million ways to sabotage me.

"I know that, Lieutenant. Let's just say there was a breakdown in communication."

More silence.

His way of telling me to fuck off without saying it.

"Let's take a breath and catch up. Get all the relevant officers in my office for a briefing at ten . . ."

"I don't know where Walsh is. Veasy might be out in Hollywood by now. With traffic and all . . ."

"Okay, we'll make it ten-thirty. Just get 'em in here."

ELOISE
WORKS A MIRACLE

"The time is right."

The voice comes in the night. She sits up in bed, the words ringing in her ears.

Twelve Women of God.

"I'm on wheels, Eloise," Lester said to her yesterday.

"I'll pray for you," she promised. But she didn't say for what so it wasn't really a lie. She actually prayed hard for the show to end. Lester would be alone, no one to take care of him. He'd turn to her and she'd save him. There's a neglected audience out there—a billion Christians worldwide, hungry for meaningful programs. With her ideas and his expertise they'd change the world.

Twelve Women of God was a miniseries she had written as her senior thesis in Religious Filmmaking at Missouri Methodist. She'd forgotten about it during these hectic two years. But now she understood.

It was meant for Lester.

She had called it *Thirteen Women of God*, originally. Twelve hours about the twelve great heroines of the Old Testament with an added thirteenth about Mary, the mother of Christ. But Professor Cunliffe, who had been a staff writer on *The Guiding Light* for twenty-seven years advised a change of title.

"Thirteen has evil connotations," he told her. "But twelve is a holy number—the tribes of Israel, the disciples of Christ, the steps to sobriety."

So she changed it to twelve and made *Mary* an encore episode.

It was a huge success. Professor Cunliffe read excerpts from it in class as an example of scene construction. The theater department dramatized it for their annual show. Bishop Wellman praised her at graduation.

"It is young filmmakers like Eloise Gruber who will bring God into the living rooms of millions of Americans."

Professor Cunliffe recommended her to his good friend Albert Jessup, who made religious videos in San Diego. Jessup praised the script to the skies. At dinner in Chili's he took off his shoe and stroked her foot under the table as he promised to raise the money for a first-class production. He was a jowly man with bits of loose skin under his eyes who made chewing noises like her grandfather. She knew what he wanted and was willing to make the sacrifice, but worried that he might not be sincere. While she was praying for guidance, God put a job notice on Craigslist—"Personal assistant wanted for TV producer . . ."—and sent her to Lester, her eternal soulmate.

Now the voice in the night has enlightened her. God has arranged for Lester to be fired so he can be free to produce the show. This is her mission. This is why God sent her to California. She weeps with gratitude.

Lester isn't a religious man, but Eloise is confident that God will send her the right pitch to sell him. All she has to do is open her soul to receive His wisdom.

She prays all night. Before dawn the word comes that the script needs an epigraph. A theme to grab Lester's attention.

She closes her eyes and opens her Bible.

A miracle!

God has sent her to Proverbs, Lester's favorite book. Her finger rests on:

"Favor is deceitful and beauty is vain. But a woman that feareth the Lord shall be praised."

Yes! Yes! A perfect theme for the series, but also a message to Lester of the kind of woman he needs in his life. She types it in red letters in 18-point Herculanum and slides it in the cellophane window of a Morocco binder.

Way too excited to sleep, she hops into her Jetta and heads out onto the Ventura Freeway.

On damp, gray mornings like this she always thinks back to Reverend Morrow's sermon on the Sunday after the tornado leveled their town and killed the four Talbot kids. "Missouri is God's country," he said. "God reveals His power in the rains He sends to flood our land, the winds to rend our houses. Then, in the depths of our despair, when shaken in our faith, when we howl our grief, He sends the glorious sun to dapple the mountains. To inspire us with the hope and strength to rebuild and praise Him for His abiding love . . ."

Los Angeles is not God's country. Satan troubles your sleep with vague premonitions. He sends the morning gloom to mildew your spirit, the sun to blind you, the fumes to rise like brimstone, stinging your eyes and choking the breath out of you. In the afternoon he blows a chill breeze of foreboding . . .

Satan fights hard to keep people from bringing God's word to the world. But Eloise will not be discouraged.

As she pulls into the parking lot she sees Lester's BMW in his space. *Why is he here so early?*

He'll be scowling in that muggy office. This is not the best time, Eloise knows. But it's been two years and she can't wait a moment longer.

The lights are off. Maybe he left his car overnight.

Eloise turns on the lights and the AC. The fluorescents pop and she sees Lester walking around Noah Lippman's dark office. His hair is flying out in wings from the sides of his head and his eyes are wide, as if seeing things for the first time.

"You believe this place?" he says. "Noah's refuge . . ."

He looks positively prophetic.

Tears of gladness well up. This is truly the moment that God ordained . . .

"It's like a family room in here," Lester says. "The vacation shots, graduation pictures, the trophies his kids won."

She wants to comfort him.

"You accumulate things in seven years, Lester."

"Noah has no happiness in his own home . . ."

"He loves his sons . . ."

"He's been hanging from a ledge for seven years. Now the rocks will crumble and he'll plunge into the abyss . . ."

"God will provide."

"He'll provide a garden apartment in Culver City. Arlene will dump him and take his precious kids away. He'll blame himself and give her everything without a fight. His only consolation will be to have coffee in the Farmers' Market with the other outcasts. Sitting at the counter in Du-Par's, gray and pouchy in baggy green golf pants, reading the papers, coffee and a plain bagel . . ."

She's never seen Lester like this. So sad, almost sorrowful.

"Seven years and I never set foot in their offices, either of them," he says.

He brushes by her into Sean's office.

"Sean keeps his Oscar here, you believe that?" he says, hefting the golden statuette. "This is his real home, too. He only sleeps in that place in Los Feliz . . . Look at these photos. Jack and Warren, he calls them, because he did a draft of a buddy cop movie for them . . . Bob Rafelson, Dennis Hopper, Hal Ashby . . ."

"Sean was friends with a lot of stars," Eloise says.

"Not friends. These are production stills, taken on sets. He never really made it with the A-crowd because he was always being rewritten and he wasn't psycho enough to be a mascot. You can get some mileage if you're a tragic Hollywood burnout like Jay Braffner. Sean was just another mediocre writer who got a break and couldn't make it stick. Booooring, there's a million of them around town . . ." He shows her a pool party photo of a blonde in a bikini. "Sharisse, his second wife. She gave him some heat, got him invited places, but it was only because Jack and Warren wanted a shot at her. After six months she realized she was the attraction. She took off with the flavor of the month Bertolucci's DP, Vittorio Vitruvio. Cameramen outrank writers. Women want physical, not metaphysical. Who would you rather be with, a fashion plate who took pretty pictures of you or a neurotic *kvetch* who whined about the world?"

"I'd rather be with you, Lester," she says.

He doesn't hear her over his torrent of words.

"They had no careers left when they came to work for me. This show was the last stop before the cemetery. It's kept them on life support for seven years, but now we're pulling the plug . . . They'll never work again."

He usually speaks in terse sentences like dialogue in a scene. Now he's doing a monologue. He's moving faster than she's ever seen. She has to hurry after him into his office before he slams the door.

"No Tarsis memorabilia here," he says. "Nothing for the yard sale after my death. I was never nominated for anything so no plaques. I never made a movie with a star so no production stills. Never married a hot little Hollywood hand-me-down so no wedding pics . . ."

He sits at his desk opening and closing drawers.

"Nothing . . ."

"You don't need a desk anyway," she says. "You use the conference table."

"No pictures of my son because I thought I didn't like him until yesterday . . ."

Now the big surprise. The moment she's been dreaming about . . .

"Lester . . ."

She puts her hands on his shoulders. Bends and kisses him lightly on the lips.

Oh God, he's so surprised. Look at his darling little face. But suspicious, too . . .

"What's this about, Eloise?"

"About something I've been wanting to do for two years . . . Wait . . ."

She runs to her desk and brings back a copy of *Twelve Women of God.*

"Oh, a script."

Lester gets that Mexican-food look.

"You learn fast, Eloise . . ."

His vanity is wounded. How adorable.

"It's not about the script, Lester," she says. "I'll prove that to you in a minute. But just take a look. I really believe that everything, even the sad destiny of Noah and Sean, is part of God's plan to bring these stories to the world."

He opens the binder and reads the epigraph.

"This is from Proverbs."

She exults.

"Yes. Yes . . ."

"What's *Twelve Women of God?*"

"It's a miniseries, Lester. Twelve hours about the twelve great heroines of the Old Testament. I know what you're thinking— 'CORNEE'—but there's a huge untapped Christian audience out there that is hungering for this kind of programming. A person with your experience could inspire trust and support in the Christian investment community. With the support of the churches we could syndicate the series in a thousand markets worldwide and sell millions of DVDs . . ."

Lester sniffs the script.

"I'll bet Walmart has a boxed set like this," he says.

"They don't," she said. "I checked."

He taps the vein in his forehead (a good sign).

"You have titles for the episodes?"

Her face heats up so fast she thinks she's going to faint like she did on those warm spring days in high school when she had her curse . . .

"My grandma had this book, *Famous Women of the Old Testament* . . ."

"And you stole the idea from that . . ."

"I didn't . . ."

"Don't apologize. Theft is the mother of success. A thief is the first person to recognize the potential of an idea. You guys stole your religion from us, and made it a huge hit. Shakespeare stole his plots. Darwin stole his theory . . . When was it published?"

"1882."

"Public Domain, it's clear then . . ."

He flips the pages, looking at the titles.

"*Eve, The Mother of Us All.* How about *Eve, The Sin and The Serpent?*"

Her heart is doing flip-flops. "That's a lot better, Lester . . ."

"Here's a good one: *Rebekah, The Beautiful but Deceptive Wife.* We'll just make it *Rebekah, The Beautiful Deceiver . . .*"

He checks the list. "*Jephthah's Daughter: The Consecrated Maiden.* What did she do?"

"Her father promised God that if he won a battle he would sacrifice the first person who greeted him after his victory," Eloise says. "It turned out to be his daughter. He didn't want to kill her, but she made him keep his vow. She asked for a few months to bewail her virginity and then returned to be sacrificed . . ."

"Bewail her virginity," Lester says. "Tough scene to write . . ."

"Not for the Christian audience. They suspend disbelief."

Lester reads another. "*Witch of Endor: The Enchantress of Samuel's Ghost . . .*"

"She was a medium," Eloise says. "She conjured up the ghost of the prophet Samuel for King Saul. The ghost told the king he would be killed in battle the next day . . ."

"Wow, that Bible's some book. Hot babes, ghosts and battles . . ."

A little bit of that old cynicism showing through, but Eloise knows he's sold.

"Local stations are always looking for family stuff," he says. "If I brought this pitch in they'd laugh me out of the office. But they just might buy it from a skinny, freckle-faced, Bible-Belt Baptist . . ."

He's such a tease.

"Methodist," she says. "And I'm not so skinny . . ."

She sits on his desk and bends to kiss him again, flitting her tongue around his lips until he shudders and opens his mouth. Pressing her breasts against his chest.

"Let me take a pill," he says, rising.

She pushes him back. "You won't need it."

She could unbutton her blouse, but decides it would be sexier if she just lifted it over her head like those teasy girls on the porn sites.

Lester sits back in his chair with that little half-smile that she loves. "I usually pay for this."

"Never again," she says.

She had stayed outside that lingerie store on Hollywood Boulevard for an hour before going in. The clerks hadn't looked twice when she brought up the crotchless panties. But Lester's eyes are popping out of his head.

"Like me?" she whispers.

"Why did you wait so long?" he asks.

"The time wasn't right."

Under the desk like Mamie Van Doren in "The Untold Story of a Movie Legend . . ." There's a bump. Somebody stuck some gum or putty on the bottom . . .

A knock.

She ducks down. Lester sits up and grabs the phone. The door opens. Stupid Zack . . .

"Lester, got a minute?"

"I'm on a call, Zack . . ."

"I'm sorry to bust in, but I had the weirdest conversation last night . . ."

"I know all about it."

"You know?" He sounds surprised.

"Just give me a half hour to get up to speed. Wait in the cutting room, okay?"

"Okay . . ." He sounds doubtful. The door closes.

She unzips his fly. "What does he want?" she says.

"To talk about his script, what else?"

She reaches into his pants . . .

Golly, it's true what Aunt Sylvia said about big noses . . .

Another knock. "It's like Grand Central Station in here," Lester says. He picks up the phone again. The door opens.

"Morning Mr. Tarsis, Detective Veasy, La Play . . ."

"I know . . . Morning, Detective Veasy . . ."

"If you've got a minute I'd like to show you a photo. See if you can identify someone for me."

"Be glad to. Just let me finish this call."
"I need this right away . . ."
"With you in a second."
The door closes.
Lester pats Eloise on the head.
"Now you know why producers have desks."

THE FUSE IS BURNING

"Ten forty-five," Jonas says. "Veasy's late."

"They probably hit traffic coming from Hollywood," Mineo says.

How dumb do they think I am?

"Traffic goes the other way this time of morning," he says.

"Maybe there was an accident," Moritz says.

They're always making excuses for him.

Even Walsh chimes in. "All you need is some guy changing a flat and the looky-loos slow down like it's the most amazing thing they've ever seen."

You too, Walsh?

Walsh looks away like a kid caught in a lie.

Covering his bases. Doesn't want it to be obvious that he's my mole . . .

Tingley rushes in, blushing. "Morning . . ." Tucking her blouse down into her slacks.

Christ! Did they pull off the road for a quickie?

"Where's Veasy?" he asks.

"Getting coffee."

Twenty minutes late and he has the balls to hold things up. Don't show impatience, it's what he wants.

"I won't keep you people long," Jonas says. "Just want to update the status reports on the current cases . . ."

Veasy comes in with a coffee.

"Morning . . ."

"Nice of you to join us," Jonas says.

A smirk.

"Nice of you to have me."

Can't beat him with sarcasm. Just stick to business.

"Okay, let's get organized."

He turns on his mini recorder.

"Aren't you going to give date and time?" Veasy asks.

Ignore him.

"I understand there was some movement on the home invasion . . ."

"We've got a suspect," Veasy says. "We're pretty sure . . ."

Mineo raises a hand to shut him up.

Do they think I don't see these things?

"As I told you this morning, Chief, Veasy and Tingley developed some information from a partial license plate ID."

That "as I told you" is a signal to Veasy not to punch up his story. Do they think I don't know that?

Jonas looks through the printouts.

"I don't see this information mentioned . . ."

Tingley jumps in. "We didn't have time to update our reports. Things were breaking on these producer, uh . . . deaths . . ."

"Let's stay with the proven crime for a moment," he says and turns to Tingley. "Fill me in."

She gets busy with her memo book.

Nobody can look at me this morning.

"Housekeepers reported a red van in front of the victims' house," she says. "Oregon plate, partial ID."

"What's a partial ID?"

"They recalled a number and a letter . . ."

"Tingley and Veasy used the information they had to develop a list of owners," Mineo says.

Good officer, supporting his squad. Or maybe he's banging her, too.

Jonas swivels back to Tingley.

"And on this list there was only one person with a criminal record, I assume."

"Only one, sir," Tingley says.

"Okay, who is this person of interest?"

Head down, she reads from her notes.

"Olin Sandusky, forty-three, Portland resident, eleven arrests, two burglary convictions. We pulled his mug shot and got a tentative ID from the victim, Mrs. Brownlee . . ."

"Why tentative?"

"The mug shot has him clean shaven. Mrs. Brownlee said the man had a beard and soul patch, but she was sure it was him; she could tell by his eyes."

"So we have an elderly woman with poor eyesight in shock from a beating making a tentative ID based on an old photo," Jonas says.

"As I told you we'd like to send somebody up to talk to this Sandusky," Mineo says.

"We'll need an updated photo for a positive ID before we start taking planes to Portland. Meanwhile, if we don't have enough to hold Sandusky for extradition maybe it's better not to let him know we're working on him."

"We should move on this," Veasy says.

"What's the hurry?"

"Sandusky's lawyer is the victim's son-in-law."

"I thought the Brownlees didn't have any children . . ."

Veasy nods like he knew that was coming.

"I'm talking about the Keene family, on 21st Place."

"Oh yeah, your theory about the bungler, I mean burglar, who went to the wrong house."

"Yes sir," says Veasy. "I think the lawyer's wife and her brother hired his client, our suspect—excuse me, our person of interest—to hit their parents' house . . ."

Take a pause to focus attention.

"Do you have any evidence that he targeted the wrong house?" Jonas asks.

"None. Can't establish motive because the wrong house was burgled. That's why I feel we should shake things up."

"But the lawyer knows you have no leverage . . ."

"We can scare him," Veasy says. "Remind him that Sandusky is a two-time loser who will give his wife up unless she flips on him first."

"Have you considered the possibility that this Sandusky didn't do it?"

Veasy has no problem with eye contact.

"He did it," he says.

"This is all based on a hunch, right?"

"He did it," Veasy says.

Jonas turns to Tingley.

Does she not see what a total marijuana monomaniac this guy is?

"Well, I don't have your telepathic gift, Veasy. Best I can do is request Portland PD to do a routine interview with Sandusky . . ."

"And see if they can sneak a DNA sample," Veasy says.

Mineo gets up quickly. "I'll call Portland . . ."

"It can wait until after the meeting."

Mineo sits down slowly.

Pregnant pause . . . Ironic smile . . .

"What's this breaking news you had on your serial killer, Veasy?"

"We spoke to the exterminating crew at David Kessel's house," Veasy says. "They say a man wearing one of their uniforms came running out just before they turned on the gas . . ."

Walsh taps his nose with his finger.

Warning me that they have something.

"They picked the man out in a TV crew photo," Veasy says. "Lester Tarsis, a producer, identified him as Jay Braffner, a director who had worked with the three decedents . . ."

Don't twitch. Please don't twitch.

Veasy grins like a poker player about to turn over a Royal Flush.

"Braffner is a notorious Hollywood head case," he says. "According to Tarsis he had a grudge against the three dead guys for ruining his career. Had to be removed from a production office after threatening them. Seven DUIs, drugs and weapons in the car. One head-on with a gasoline truck, killed a young actress. One comatose underage female at his house, more drugs found. Violated probation, two nonappearance warrants. Three stints in rehab. Flipped his car on the PCH. Attacked the arresting officers and had to be put in restraint. Was finally committed to the psycho ward at Harbor Medical. Released as an outpatient a few weeks ago . . . Now he shows up at Kessel's house, pretending to be a member of the tenting crew."

Should have taken a pill. Walk to the window so they can't see the twitches.

"We'd like to show Braffner's photo around the Helfand and London locations," Veasy says.

This could be huge. Take control. Show leadership.

"Good idea," Jonas says. "Canvas the neighbors, housekeepers, see if we can get someone else who saw him. Mineo, coordinate this . . ."

"Okay, Chief . . ."

Hold on! A connection they all missed!

"Harbor Medical . . . Isn't that where Alison Sobel worked? Did we ever get a list of the patients she was going to visit?"

Walsh checks his notes. "Jay Braffner was her last stop."

NO TIME FOR BACKSTORY

This is the happiest day of Eloise's life. She hid in the office while Lester went out and spoke to the cop. She felt like the "other woman" in all those old movies.

Lester came back a few minutes later.

"The cops think Jay Braffner killed Dave and Mitch and Gary, you believe that . . . ?"

And sat down at his desk. "Now where were we?"

Now, naked and kneeling on the dusty floor, she puts her head in Lester's lap, as he tells her how he created *She* . . .

"I knew network TV was dead for guys like me," he says. "Best we could do was line produce somebody else's show, if we were lucky . . ."

He's leaning back, eyes closed.

"The future was in syndication." "Simple stories that would work in all cultures. Good guys and bad guys and half-naked women with just enough plot to work in the softcore lesbian stuff . . ."

She's never seen him so completely relaxed. He runs his fingers through her hair, giving her little chills as he strokes the nape of her neck.

"Jon Pfeffer was teaching a seminar at USC. One of his students had an idea for a series based on *Green Mansions*, the novel about the beautiful white girl living in the jungle, swinging through the trees in a loincloth, talking to animals, fighting evil natives. Pfeffer thought it was the stupidest pitch he had ever heard. Kid doesn't understand material, he told me. But as soon as I heard the idea I knew it was exactly what I was looking for."

The phone rings.

"I'll get it," she says and reaches onto the desk.

"Lester Tarsis's office . . ."

It's Mrs. Tarsis. "I have to speak to Lester right away . . ."

"I'm sorry, but Mr. Tarsis . . ."

"Don't blow me off you little bitch. Tell Lester it's about his son . . ."

Lester sits up. "I'd know those dulcet tones anywhere . . . Put her on speaker . . . What is it now, Claire?"

Her voice screeches through the speaker.

"Is Seth there, Lester?"

"I'm in the office, Claire . . ."

"He was supposed to be home hours ago . . ."

"Don't worry, he's probably passed out somewhere . . ."

She's sobbing. "I'm scared, Lester. He always comes home . . ."

"Except when he's in jail . . ."

"Doug saw him this morning, outside the house talking to an older man in a beat-up old Mercedes . . . He thought he was coming in so he went back to bed, didn't think anything of it. But when we woke up and he wasn't here . . ."

"Did you call his phone?"

"He never calls me back, never answers my texts."

"What about his friends?"

"I posted a message on his Facebook page. He'll be furious when he finds out . . . Could you call the Shusters and the Levins? They never come to the phone for me."

"Let's give it an hour. If he's not home by then, I'll call . . ."

"Is this a trick to get rid of me, Lester?"

"I'll call in an hour, Claire. I promise . . ."

Gulping sobs subside. But then, suddenly, a cry of anguish.

"This kid has put me through the wringer every day of his life, Lester. Between the jaundice and ear infections and the asthma and the drugs and arrests . . ."

Lester gets that Mexican-food look again.

"I know he's a burden, Claire."

"I ask myself: is this God's punishment for all the evil things I did in my life?"

Lester covers his eyes.

"You're not evil, Claire, you're just dumb."

"You're such a comfort," Claire says. But she laughs through her sniffles. "I thought I was rid of you, but Seth grew into a little Lester. He looks just like you . . ."

"Poor kid."

"He's sharp like you, too."

"Sharpness is not an asset in a dull world," Lester says.

Another knock. Zack again.

"I need a minute, Lester . . ."

"Where were you before?"

"I ducked out when I saw you talking to that cop. It's pretty urgent . . ."

"As soon as I finish this call . . ."

The door closes.

"Still there, Claire?" Lester says. "I'll call in an hour."

"You promise, right?"

"We just played this scene, Claire. Goodbye . . ."

He signals to Eloise to cut off the squawk box. In the silence she hears the slight whistle of breath in his nose.

"Claire and I are misfits, we deserve what we get," he says. "The real question is why did God punish Seth by giving him parents like us?"

Eloise puts her head back on his lap.

"Not interested in my tangled affairs?"

"I heard better stories in the Ozarks," she says.

He likes that. She knew he would. "That's what I always say to writers," he says. "Tell me something I don't know . . ."

The phone again. Eloise checks the ID.

"Unlisted . . . Bet it's Mr. Braffner again . . ."

"Not now," Lester says. And she disconnects.

"So where was I?" he says. "Oh yeah, I hear a great idea that the late unlamented Jon Pfeffer is too dumb to steal. I rent *Green Mansions* with Audrey Hepburn . . . almost unwatchable. I get old episodes of the '50s series *Sheena, Queen of the Jungle* . . . Irish McCalla, big blonde in leopard skin. Perfect.

"I concoct a show about a mysterious beauty who lives in the Amazonian jungle. Give her super powers, second sight, visits from the spirits. She cavorts in a leopard loincloth fighting human and supernatural villains. I write up a pitch, twelve story ideas, and bring it to Peter Leibowitz at Alliance Syndicating. He laughs me out of the office, but his weasely little assistant David Owen grabs in the parking lot. Fuck Leibowitz, he says. Bring me a piece of ass and I'll sell the show all over the world, he tells me.

"A few weeks later I'm in a strip joint out by the airport. There's a mean, dirty blonde pole dancing on the bar and cursing out the customers. Finola Newton. Six feet tall and seven feet of it legs . . . She was the Captain of the Australian Olympic Women's Volleyball Team. Cover of all the magazines. Made a triumphant arrival in LA, complete with agent, manager, and modeling contract. It didn't happen for her, usually doesn't. Three years later she's humping a pole in El Segundo.

"You gotta be a sick degenerate like me to understand Finola. She's the woozy slut in the airport bar, who you have to have. You get her loaded and squeeze into a stall in the men's room with her. The best sex you've ever had in a minute and a half. She's every man's wet dream and I have her for seven years with an option for seven more."

"I take her to Owen. He understands her too and raises the money for a pilot. We're booked onto seventeen U.S.A. stations for our first season. Finola goes viral. They're jerking off from Naragansett to Nairobi. We're on forty-three stations next year, not counting the hundreds we have worldwide. I keep the language simple. She's in constant jeopardy, tied to a tree, wrestling in the mud with an evil cutie, frolicking in a steamy mountain pool with giggly native girls, murmuring magic incantations taught to her by an ancient cave shaman, who is invisible to everyone but her. Work in a smirky lesbo moment, frequent bondage, tilting the camera up from crotch to boobs and then back to crotch again . . . We're huge. Owen is one of the richest men in New Zealand and he doesn't have to shovel sheep dip to make his pile. I get nine years and eleven million dollars out of it before he pulls the plug. So now I'll be the richest guy in the unemployment line . . ."

"No you won't, you'll reinvent yourself as a producer of faith," Eloise says. "It's the same concept—simple stories that work in all cultures. Good guys, bad guys . . ."

"And twelve half-naked women of God," Lester says.

Another knock. He grabs the phone and says "come in."

Zack again.

"Lester, this is important . . ."

Lester pushes Eloise further under the desk.

"Just finishing up this call, Zack."

He turns for a quick look at Eloise's discarded clothes on the floor. Zack must have seen them, too.

Eloise is aflame with defiance.

So what? Marilyn did it. And Jayne Mansfield . . . Joan Crawford made dirty movies . . . We Hollywood girls do what we have to do . . .

Lester gives her a fatherly kiss on top of the head. Zips himself up and goes around the desk.

"David Owens is a big fan of yours, Zack . . ."

Zack sounds shocked. "He is?"

"I haven't read the masterpiece myself. If you give me a half hour . . ."

"That's great, man. That's . . . Wow . . . I mean I didn't even want to talk about that. I wanted to tell you about this weird experience I had with Jay Braffner last night . . ."

"How could it be anything but . . . ?"

"I mean scary. Like frightening . . ."

The door closes. Eloise comes out from under the desk. Lester's chair is still warm on her naked buttocks. She hits voice mail and hears Jay Braffner's friendly voice.

"Hi, this is Jay Braffner. Seth Tarsis is here and he really wants to talk to his dad. Hold on . . ."

Then a boy's halting, trembly voice.

"This is Seth Tarsis. When I call back please put my father on the phone . . ." A cry of fear . . . "Please . . ."

CLIFFHANGER

Jonas calls his staff together.

"Let's set up a conference call with all the players."

He gets Lester Tarsis, Zack Toledano, and Eloise Gruber on the line from Hollywood. Doctor Robert Goff and his staff from Harbor Psychiatric Services. Cindy Pertner and her attorney from the Straight Path Clinic where Braffner did two stints. He has his people—Walsh, Tingley, Mineo. LA Homicide sends a Sergeant Elfand who is assigned to the Sobel case.

They all sit at the table, iPads open.

Except Veasy. He scrunches himself into a chair in the corner, muttering and tapping on his iPhone.

What's he gonna do now? Recite a poem?

When everybody is patched in, Jonas begins:

"We've got a very delicate situation here. I'm hoping we can come up with some plan to resolve this and keep everybody safe . . ."

Mumbles of approval.

"Good idea to move carefully." That's Doctor Goff.

"What's your history with Braffner, Doctor?" Jonas asks.

"We had Jay for over a year on a court-ordered commitment. Then his insurance plan changed coverage schedules and he had to be discharged pending readmission as a private patient . . ."

Tarsis cuts in shrilly:

"You mean you let a dangerous lunatic out on the streets because his insurance lapsed?"

Goff replies with clenched patience. "If you let me finish, sir. We had to release him pending the results of a competency hearing. We needed a court order to seize Jay's assets and pay for his treatment by direct withdrawal from his account . . ."

"This maniac is holding my son hostage and all you care about is getting his money . . ."

A chair scrapes as if Goff was getting up. "I don't have to listen to this, Chief Jonas . . ."

"Afraid you do, Doctor. For a little longer."

Tingley is watching with obvious admiration.

She sees how calmly I take control.

"Okay, let's see if we can figure out what's going on here," Jonas says. "Mr. Tarsis, you say that Braffner was in your office last week."

"Yes, my assistant saw him . . ."

"What was he doing, Ms. Gruber?"

"He was putting something on Mr. Tarsis's desk, I think. He said he was an actor and wanted to drop off a resumé . . ."

Southern accent . . . Sounds like a cute little blonde.

"Okay and then what happened?" Jonas asks.

"Well, Zack came in and chased him out," she says.

"The guy was giving me the creeps," Toledano says. "I know Lester doesn't like actors in the office so I told him to leave . . ."

New York punk.

"And you saw him drive out," Jonas says.

"Yeah. He was driving a beat-up old Meredes 450. Same car I saw in his driveway last night."

"You say Braffner has been calling you for several days, Mr. Tarsis."

"Yes, my assistant spoke to him."

"Did he tell you the purpose of his call, Ms. Gruber?"

"No, he just said he was an old friend of Mr. Tarsis . . ."

Veasy pipes up from the corner.

"Any more information on the other victim, Sergeant?"

Mineo shakes his head with a helpless gesture. Tingley looks distressed.

Be patient.

"What other victim, Veasy?" he asks.

"The kid in the trunk, Roy Farkas. How did you ID him, Sergeant?"

Sergeant Elfand flips through his notebook.

"Got a print match from three arrests," he says. "We're running the DNA now, but that'll take a week . . ."

"What were the arrests for, Sergeant?"

Elfand looks at Jonas for approval.

Let him rave. Let everybody see what I'm up against.

He nods and Elfand goes back to his notes.

"One for menacing. His ex-girlfriend got a restraining order . . . One for a raid at a meth lab . . . One after an ATF Facebook surf picked him up trying to sell Semtex . . . Unlicensed possession of RDX plastic explosive . . . pending . . ."

"We'll get back to this, Veasy," Jonas says. "Ms. Pertner, you had Mr. Braffner as a patient on two occasions. Do you think he's dangerous?"

"Film directors can be charming and persuasive," she says. "Some might say even manipulative and deceitful. Jay convinced us twice that he was rehabilitated . . ."

Veasy blurts:

"Any personal background on Farkas, Sergeant?"

In his own world. He hasn't even been listening.

"Not yet," Sergeant Elfand says. "We're waiting for a positive ID before we notify the family."

"Let's put that on hold, Veasy," Jonas says. "Mr. Toledano, you say you visited Mr. Braffner . . ."

"To do an interview, yeah . . . House was filthy with food boxes and coffee cups, photos stacked up . . . He was acting crazy, talking to himself like he was directing a movie . . . Like close shot here and camera follow me here . . ."

"Sound familiar to you, Dr. Goff?"

"Jay told us he was setting up a movie and was hoping to start shooting as soon as he was released. That's not unusual in this town. Everybody has a script or is working on a movie. Call it a dream or a self-sustaining delusion, but some of those movies actually get made . . ."

Tarsis cuts in again:

"You're acting like he was perfectly normal. Did you hear what the kid said? Jay was talking to an imaginary crew in his head . . ."

And then Toledano, hysterically:

"There was blood in his kitchen. Blood on the counter, a big bloodstain on the floor . . . A bloody rag in the sink . . . He said he had killed a rat. But there was a shoe under the table. A Nike shoe sitting in a puddle of dried blood . . . I was scared . . . Big guy with a broken coffee pot chasing me down the hall . . ."

"He's already killed Dave and Mitch and Larry," Tarsis says.

"Why are you so sure it's him?" Jonas asks.

"He's doing scenes from the show . . . The termite gas. The drowning in the pool. The locked car . . ."

"But you wrote those."

"He thinks I stole them from him. He thought everything we shot was his idea . . ." And then, tearful with frustration: "Am I speaking Esperanto here? The man is out of his fucking mind . . ."

A choked whisper from the assistant. You can hear Tarsis breathing through his nose, struggling for control.

"Look, my son has asthma. He never goes out with his inhaler, okay? Something like this could trigger a fatal attack . . ."

Christ! He's gonna kill this kid!

"What did Braffner say to you, Ms. Gruber?" Jonas asks.

"That Seth was with him and really wanted to talk to his dad. And that he would call back. Then he put Seth on and he"—she breaks off to compose herself—"and Seth pleaded with me to put Lester on the phone when he called back."

"When did he say he was calling back?" Jonas asks.

"Oh my God, Lester . . ." More hysterics . . . "He didn't say . . ."

"Okay, we'll send someone out right away. If he calls, be calm and responsive. Keep him on the line . . ."

"NO!"

Veasy jumps and runs to the table.

"Everybody punch up Roy F-A-R-K-A-S on YouTube," Veasy says.

They all go to their iPads and start tapping.

Unbelieveable! After all this they still trust him.

"Sit down, Veasy, or get out," Jonas says.

Veasy grabs his iPhone off the table. Jonas jumps up, fist balled.

Knock him on his ass!

"Gimme that . . ."

Veasy jumps back, typing like mad.

"Please, boss, just take a look at this." He shoves Jonas's iPhone back at him.

Jonas sees a kid in an Afro at a worktable in a windowless room . . .

"My name is Roy Farkas," the kid says. "And this is my show . . ."

A big title flashes across the screen: "HOW TO BLOW THE SHIT OUT OF ALMOST ANYTHING."

Veasy pleads: "Whatever you do, Mr. Tarsis . . . Please don't talk to Jay Braffner."

MARTINI TAKE TWO

The kid is shaking and squeaking like a frightened puppy. Bronchitic wheeze, nose running . . .

"This is not an attractive look, Seth," Jay says. "It'll make the audience uncomfortable."

He's crying and coughing and retching so hard Jay can't get a word in. So he sticks a towel in the kid's mouth. Just to shut him up so he can explain the scene.

"Noir is style, Seth," he says. "You're playing it real."

He runs out to the living room and brings back *The Noir Encyclopedia*. Opens to the entry on *Out of the Past*.

"The noir character never loses his cool, even in the face of death, Seth."

Shows him still shots of Mitchum, Kirk Douglas . . .

"Noir violence is meticulously choreographed. The noir victim stays in character until the end. Many noir victims have a premonition that their time is up and go to their death with a certain amount of tragic grace . . ."

Shots of dark streets, shadowy rooms.

"See the silhouettes, the splashes, the transition from light to dark? Faces in mirrors, shadows in an empty room. It's a cold, detached world. No tears, no whining. A certain kind of sniveling bad guy is allowed to sweat in a harsh light before he dies, but not a young hero like you, Seth. The sound is part of the story. No blubbering or hacking coughs . . . Cool music, bop-swing. Cigarette cases click open and snap shut . . . Voices are unique. Notice the precision of movement. Even down to the style of smoking. The vamp holds the cigarette between her full rouged lips and bends to the flame of a gold lighter, illuminating her face, glistening in her eyes . . . The hero blows two streams of smoke from his nose. Watch how Bogey and Mitchum hòld cigarettes . . . Or Rita Hayworth in *Lady of Shanghai* . . . Tragic grace, Seth. That's what I want from you."

No use. Even behind the towel he can hear the muffled begging: "I didn't do anything to you. Please don't kill me . . ."

This is not what people want to see at the end of an intricately plotted thriller.

"Shut up, Seth!"

Snot drips out of the kid's nose onto the towel.

It's disgusting.

"You're making it ugly, godammit."

Slams Seth on the forehead in frustration. The kid bounces on the bed three times. Then, his eyeballs go up in his head.

That's no good, either. He can't be unconscious for this scene. He has to speak to his dad, then hand the phone over to Braffner.

It's so infuriating. How many times has this happened? Biggest scene, payoff scene, scene you've been painstakingly working up to, and you're at the mercy of a balky actor who flatly refuses to do it the right way.

"THEY KILL THE MAGIC!"

Is that Jay Braffner shouting himself hoarse?

Is Braffner pounding the wall so hard the whole house is shaking?

"CUT!"

"Momentary meltdown people," Jay tells the crew.

Silence. They're embarrassed for him . . .

"Don't use this shot," Jay says. "Delete Seth and his entire arc. Drop all the scenes with him, he's off the picture. We'll find a crisp noir way to get Lester to the phone."

No response from the crew.

"Any suggestions?" Jay asks.

Did they step away out of concern for his feelings?

"There's a lot of pressure on a set. Once in a while you blow. But I'm back and ready to finish the day."

No answer. Must have given them a "ten" while he rehearsed with Seth. That's it, they're on a break.

No need for them to be here. He's not going to film this last moment with Seth. Like that nosy social worker. A few twists of the towel and we're back on schedule.

"You're wanted on the set, Mr. Braffner."

A strange voice. New man on the crew? At the door, hard to see in the gloom. Suit, tie, flunky smile . . . Studio exec? Looks like Chris Reeve . . . Who's the lady? On the *zaftig* side, but in the right places. Script girl? Wardrobe person? Invite her into the trailer for a drink at wrap . . .

Don't take any crap from the suits.

"The crew better be ready," Jay says. "I don't want to stand around while they're fiddling with lights and touchups . . ."

"They're ready, Mr. Braffner. Just waiting for you, sir."

The suit holds out the handcuffs.

Must be for the new ending.

"It's an honor to work with you, Mr. Braffner," he says.

"Thank you," says Jay.

FEEL-GOOD FINISH

Jay gets the star treatment.

They throw his jacket over his shoulder so no one can see the cuffs. People come out of their houses as they walk him to the car. An elderly man applauds.

"You've got friends around here," the suit says.

They drive into the dazzling sun down the California Incline. A pregnant girl is begging at the bottom.

"That girl has been panhandling here for thirty years," Jay says.

The radio is squawking. The suit has a brief, whispered conversation.

"We're setting up a big entrance for you, Mr. Braffner," he says. "You're gonna be front-page, top of the hour tonight. E! channel is updating your bio, movie bloggers crashing your Wikipedia bio . . ."

"I never cared about publicity," Jay says. "Other guys created a persona for themselves. I was all about the work."

The script girl slides over and presses her warm thigh against his leg. "I was a big fan of yours without ever knowing your name."

He presses back so she knows he got the message. "That's the fate of a TV director."

Is that a "fuck me" smile? Haven't had one for years.

("it's the sexual power of celebrity.")

The crew is back.

I thought you had wrapped.

("never . . . what's next boss?")

Change of plans. The story is beginning to tell itself. It's morphed from simple revenge to an exploration of the shifting boundary between fiction and reality.

("that's so today.")

CAMERA in the front seat, pointing back at Braffner.

("done.")

And . . . ACTION . . .

"You know the first thing I noticed about California?" Jay says.

The script girl looks adoringly into his eyes. "What?"

"That everybody was smiling. Where I come from, if you smile at a girl you don't know she calls a cop . . ."

She has a sweet laugh. "It can't be that bad."

"Where I come from dreams were for crazy people. You had to finish school, get a job as a gym teacher. Give up this stupid idea of being a filmmaker."

"Where is that?"

"Anywhere but here . . ."

Push in for CLOSE-UP of the big speech.

("pushing in.")

"Where I come from, you drag your ass through the freezing slush onto a stifling subway car full of demoralized people, each reliving some private hurt, and by the time you get off you're totally defeated . . ."

("that is so freakin' eloquent.")

"Out here, there's always a feeling of possibility," Jay says. "No matter how bad your week has been, as soon as you hit the PCH, the golden light comes through your windshield, the surf sparkles off Malibu and Chet Baker starts playing in your head. You're free . . . Anything can happen . . . You might get a big offer. Might fall in love . . ."

Helicopters circling. TV news guys standing on platforms. Reporters rush the car. Cops push them back.

The script girl smooths the collar of the safari jacket.

"What's your name, honey?"

"Cheri . . ."

"You do wardrobe, too, Cheri?" he asks.

"Little bit of everything."

Out of the car.

Overlapping voiceovers. "Why did you kill your friends, Jay . . . ?" "Over here, Jay . . ." "Wanna send a message to your fans, Jay?"

Suit whispers. "Stay strong and silent. Project an air of mystery . . ."

Good note. Keep the head down, enigmatic smile.

CAMERA is my eyes.

The crew is ecstatic.

("this is gonna be the best picture you ever made!")

"Thank you," says Jay.

DISSOLVE TO THE PRODUCER

Paparazzi are swarming in the hospital lobby. They come at Lester, cameras flashing. "Mr. Tarsis, did you know Jay Braffner was . . ."

Security guys blaze a trail for him to the elevator. There's a cop outside Seth's hospital room.

"It's a media feeding frenzy," he tells Lester. "One of 'em bribed a nurse to put him on a gurney like a patient and wheel him past the room just so he could get a shot of your son."

Seth looks so small and forlorn among the pillows. But he's rigid under the covers and won't hug Lester back.

"I'm okay, Dad. They won't let me out of here until you give permission."

A resident takes Lester aside.

"A few alarms went off on his bloodwork so we gave him a full physical. He's got scarring on his lungs."

"He had pneumonia as an infant," Lester says. And realizes: *God, I forgot all about that.*

"Does he smoke cigarettes? Marijuana?" The resident lowers his voice and looks toward Seth. "This is one kid who should not party. He's underweight, asthmatic, doesn't have the constitution for it. This is the kid we find OD'd in the dorm bathroom after his buddies have gone off to the beach . . ."

Seth is staring at the TV, lips tight like he is trying not to cry.

"I know what the doctor said, Dad, you don't have to repeat it."

"You should think about it, too, Seth . . ."

"You don't have to worry, I'm never gonna smoke again or get high or do any of that shit ever again . . ."

"That's good. We'll start over when you come live with me . . ."

"I'm gonna work out every day. Doug wanted to teach me how to surf. I said I didn't wanna be no retarded surfer dude. He said do you wanna be the little bitch in the crowd who they give free drugs to so they can make fun of him when he pukes himself and passes out? I hated him for saying it, but he was right . . . Nobody fucks with Doug.

He doesn't take shit from anybody, not even Mom . . . This would never have happened if I listened to him . . ."

Suddenly, Doug is the macho role model. No talk of moving out.

"I'm gonna get serious about Krav Maga, Dad, not just take it for PE credit. One of the cops told me I can get a carry permit because of what happened . . ."

"Seth . . ."

Seth pushes him away, voice hard, vengeful eyes on an invisible tormentor.

"Don't worry, Dad. If anybody ever touches me again, I'll fuckin' kill 'em."

In twenty minutes the crowd in the lobby has turned into a shrieking mob. Four security guys and a squad of La Playita cops form a flying wedge to get Lester to the door. Camera guys on the couches jump up, trying for a shot . . . "Can we get you for five minutes, Mr. Tarsis? Just five minutes . . . ?"

He gets a text from Noah Lippman. "In the waiting room . . ."

They're all there—Eloise, Sean, Zack, too. Even Elliot.

The cops stand outside keeping the press at bay. Reporters bang on the window, shouting and waving.

In seven years Lester has never touched the writers. Now they rush up for hugs. Noah, sweat, slime, and coffee breath . . . Sean, scruff and old leather seasoned with cannabis. They were worried about him. They're his friends; he never thought of them that way.

Eloise gives him a chaste shoulder brush with a complicit smile. Zack's eyes are big, still in shock after his near-death experience, but he manages a quick pat. Elliot shakes hands, eyes downcast.

"Glad you're okay . . ."

"If this had been one of my kids, I would have dropped dead on the spot," Noah says.

"Me too, if anything happened to Melanie," says Sean.

"Your wife?" Eloise asks.

"My labradoodle."

"I mean, we always knew Jay was crazy," Noah says.

"TV crazy," Sean says. "Not real-world crazy . . ."

"He was gonna blast the office to kingdom come, Lester," Noah says. "The police dog sniffed out the explosive in the phone and under the desk . . ."

"Now you know why I don't take calls," Lester says.

"That cop saved our lives," Sean says.

"The cop and Josh warned me about Jay . . ." And before Zack can correct him: "Just a little levity, Zack."

"We can joke about it now," Noah says, "but it would be a nightmare if we were dead . . ."

"Arlene would be picking out the appropriate black mourning thong," Sean says.

Can't fire these two clowns. It would be sending them to their doom.

"We're all here," Lester says. "Might as well have a staff meeting."

"Can't, no coffee," Sean says.

Eloise runs out. "I'll get some from the machine."

"See if they have flavored cappuccinos . . ."

"I'm serious," Lester says. "We've got a big issue."

They get quiet. Elliot covers his face and shakes his head.

"I knew this was coming . . ."

"Owen says the show is losing money. He wants to cut the weekly budget."

"Didn't I tell you?" Elliot says to Zack. "Tuition's overdue. I'm underwater on the house . . . My timing is impeccable . . ."

They look at him. They're doing the calculations, seeing who'll make the cut.

Eloise comes back with the coffees. "I got you a raspberry cap, Sean."

"California hemlock," Sean says.

Noah licks the stress crud off his lips. "So give us the bad news, Lester."

"Don't keep us hanging, Lester," Sean says. "Who's on wheels?"

"Hold on, let me enjoy the moment."

He looks around the room, actually brimming with good cheer. "You guys are okay for next year," he says. "I'm out."

They're stunned.

"But you created the show," Zack says.

"Owen did the math. With me gone he'll save about nineteen-five per show, counting script fees, residuals, expenses."

"Oh well," Sean says, "better you than me."

"That's what I always detested about you, O'Meara, your honesty."

"C'mon Lester, you'll be okay with your pensions and IRAs and tenements in Northridge. We're the ones who need the job."

"You'll die broke anyway," Lester says. "Only it'll take a year longer."

They brighten.

"A lot can happen in a year," Sean says. "I've got a few spec scripts out there . . ."

"I can pick up another series," says Noah.

Elliot is cheer-proof. "Next year at this time I'll be in exactly the same situation I am now, only deeper in debt."

"Wait a second," Noah says, starting to worry again. "Who's gonna run the show?"

Lester gives it another beat.

"Zack is."

Everybody gapes.

"ZACK?"

Zack blinks.

"Me . . . ?"

"You made films in film school, I assume."

"I had two entries in the Rio Student Film Festival . . . Won a Selznick Fellowship . . ." ·

"Don't give me your resumé, I might change my mind. It's the same process. You'll get the scripts from these two geniuses. Take a few stupid notes from Owen so he can feel he's part of the creative team but make sure the shows finish on budget, that's what he really cares about. Recut everything Elliot does, but don't fire him. He's the only editor who'll work overtime at a flat rate . . ."

"I'm grateful to grovel," Elliot says.

"Fire the New Zealand production manager for stealing, which I'm sure he is. Throw a dart at the crew list once a month and fire the name it hits . . . Oh yeah, and if you want job security, take the foreign distributors to Koreatown for naked sushi when they come to town . . ."

Sean's up and pouting.

"I don't know about you, Noah, but I'm offended."

"I'm humbly grateful," says Noah. "I'm parked on that grovel driveway right next to Elliot."

"How does this *pisher* get the job over one of us?" Sean asks.

"Because you've never cut a show in your life, Sean," Lester says. "Or mixed one or sweated over budgets and schedules. Because you sit in your office with the door closed, smoke a joint, and jerk off in front of your Oscar . . ."

"I ran two shows, Lester," Noah says.

"You're not up for the eighteen-hour days, Noah. You're needed in the bosom of your family for Little League and AYSO and band practice. You don't want to be scrolling through thirty hours of dailies at two A.M. worrying about who Arlene is shtupping . . ."

They're not buying . . .

"Tell the truth for once, Lester," Sean says.

Eloise makes a tiny gesture, a signal for him to at least be kind.

"In seven years Owen has never said a nice thing about your work, either of you. But he loves Zack's script. I think I can sell him the idea of Zack as exec producer at $1200 a week and keep you both on at your inflated salaries. How about it, Zack?"

Zack strokes his stubble. "I'm keeping my options open, Lester," he says. "I'm submitting my exclusive interview with Braffner to various media outlets. I call it a killer's last words. I'm thinking maybe something big will come of it."

"Zen master ask what is sound of a worm turning?" Sean says. "Chalk on a blackboard."

"You'll be the biggest thing on the Web," Lester says. "Millions of views. Tweets, calls, e-mails. Next day everybody'll be watching a goat shtup an orangutang and you won't even get a blowjob out of it. I'm offering you one of the last jobs left in old media. Real money, a credit your parents can understand and access to hordes of desperate females."

Zack wants to stay hot a little longer. "Can I sleep on it?" he asks.

"By tomorrow morning fifteen guys will be begging for the gig at a grand."

"I'll take it," Zack says.

"Whew . . ." Noah wipes his forehead. "The suspense was killing me."

"But I gotta warn you guys, I've never been a fan. I'm probably gonna totally rewrite you."

Sean checks his watch. "New world's record. Kid's on the job thirty seconds and already he's a dick."

Noah shakes the sweat off his Lakers cap. "I feel like the governor gave us a reprieve . . ."

Sean still isn't sold. "Why are you taking the bullet for us, Lester?"

"I'm done here. I've explored all the artistic possibilities of syndicated TV. I want to spend more time with Seth, although it looks like he's gonna join the Navy Seals. I'm working on an interesting project with Eloise . . ."

Sean gives Noah the I-told-you-so look. "Top secret or can you share?"

"Biblical story. *Twelve Women of the Bible* . . ."

"*Of God*," Eloise corrects.

Sean snickers. "Right in your wheelhouse, Lester."

"Lester can do anything, Sean," Eloise says.

"Lester or Pfizer?"

Eloise takes Lester's arm with a proud smile. "Christians are an untapped billion-dollar market. They've been ignored, but their time is coming and Lester's going to be on the cutting edge."

Is that a trick of the California sun or is a halo glowing over her head?

CUT TO THE COMMANDER

Jonas downplays the arrest. "We're questioning film director Jay Braffner in the deaths of . . ."

He's the no-nonsense professional. Just another day of solid police work at the LPPD.

Orchestrates the press conference. Calls the squad in to stand behind him. "Everybody who worked the case." LA Homicide at the end of the line.

Puts Veasy and Tingley right behind him.

Be magnanimous.

"After our initial hunch, solid investigative work by Detectives Veasy and Tingley established that these deaths were not accidental . . ."

International coverage. He's relaxed in the interviews. Gets plaudits from all over. Even City Attorney Streeter. "Saw you on TV last night, you looked great." Headhunters call for his resumé. Big security jobs open all over. The BBC wants to take him step by step through the process. The initial suspicions, the clues. Walk the scenes of the murders, feature him . . .

Then Tarsis releases an emotional statement.

"If it wasn't for Detective Veasy, my son would be dead today . . ."

Like a school of fish they veer away from him to Veasy and Tingley. They love the hook: the cop who writes poems to clear his mind.

"Let's hear one," they shout.

His cute lady partner, Tingley, warns, "Keep it clean."

And Veasy recites:

"A serial killer,
A Hollywood thriller.
Makes the big news of the day.
The media's in heaven
Twenty-four seven
Then the novelty fades away.
But a cop's story is never-ending.
Another case is pending
Another creep to put away."

They make him repeat it for Fox and CNN. Then the foreign stations. Al Jazeera does an interview.

Now the BBC wants Veasy and Tingley to do the show they pitched to Jonas. They don't even have the class to call and explain.

Have to be a good sport.

Twitching as he dials. He gets Tingley's voice mail. "Hey Cheri," he says. "Just wanted to thank you for your great work. This is gonna be a big boost for the department. Hope the FBI won't seduce you away from us. Seeya tomorrow and congratulations again."

This is not a Cabernet moment. He recorks the wine and cracks the Smirnoff.

It's on every station. Ten seconds of him and the rest on Veasy and his stupid poem.

The phone. If he hears one more time how great that whacky detective is . . .

A female. Valley girl? "No names," she says. "Saw you on TV. Know the case. Had an encounter with that weedbrain the other night. Did Detective Walsh brief you about our conversation?"

It's Bree, the undercover from the LA Task Force. Smart . . . She knows her phone is safe, but isn't sure about his.

"Still got it in for him?" he asks.

"Worse than ever. I was just watching him on TV. I mean, you call that poetry? Doesn't sound like anything we studied in school."

"He ad-libs them," Jonas says. "Like a rapper. They love him. He makes better TV than a boring professional. He's colorful, good-looking . . ."

"I'll take you over him anytime. You were great on the tube, the way you gave them all the credit. That's real leadership . . ."

"It's how I do my job . . ."

A moment of anxious breathing. Then . . . "Still want to nail this clown?"

"Worse than ever," he says.

"Wanna talk about it?"

Am I gonna get a shot at the honey pot? Am I gonna get a chance to bat where Veasy struck out?

"Anytime," he says.

THE NOIR HERO GETS
THE GIRL

Arrests go by in a flash.
  Shaky hours in afterspark.
  Then suddenly you crash,
  Alone in the dark.
The walls are closing in again. Veasy texts Tingley.
  "Sic transit gloria,
  The ancients knew it all.
  I chased that butterfly euphoria
  Into a brick wall."
She calls back.
  "What happened?"
  "We lost our witness. Mrs. Brownlee went into cardiac arrest on the operating table."
  "I can't believe you went back to work after all this excitement."
  "I had a premonition. Old woman, bleeding on the brain, shock of her husband's death, how long could she have? So I wanted to try for one more ID with an updated photo, but it was too late . . . Have to move on this."
  "Can't it wait until tomorrow?"
  "No time. The Finkelmans have to do something about Olin Sandusky. Jared knows Forensics are all over the Brownlee house, raising prints, taking DNA off the bodies. He's got a ten-day window before they ID Olin. He knows Olin will offer his wife, his brother-in-law, and him for a deal. He can stake Olin to a long vacation or . . . He's got gangbanger clients. Olin is a five-hundred-dollar drive-by . . ."
  "Okay fine, but what can you do about it tonight?"
  "Get a court order to cover his phones."
  "Jonas won't wake up a judge for this, Veasy."
  "Then I'll call Streeter . . . Or I'll take a little trip to Portland and have a chat with Olin . . ."
  "Slow down Veasy, for God's sake, you can't do that."

She knows I'm breaking down.

"Aren't you happy? You made a major arrest. Saved a boy's life and maybe others as well. The YouTube of your poem has gone viral, 614,567 hits . . ."

"Most of them were me looking at myself. Anyway, that case is done. Now I'm looking at the murder of two harmless old people . . ."

"Calm down. Take some of your medicine."

"Ran out. My boardwalk buddy is blown. Can't cop on the street. I am a public servant, after all."

"Will a coupla drinks ease the pain?"

"They'll have to . . ."

"Oh God, Veasy, can you try to relax?"

"I can try."

"Okay, look . . . I'll bring you some. My mom gets it for her glaucoma. Stay home. I'll be right there . . ."

She's worried. Afraid for him. She's a nice, warm person. Likes the sex and cuddling and snacks and all the homey stuff that goes with it. Thinks he'd be a good guy to throw a football around with her son.

"That'll make you an enabler," he says. "Take away your deniability."

"Just this once."

Another call. Unlisted number. "Hold on a second, Cheri . . ."

It's the tress tosser. Cold blue voice goes with the eyes. "Remember me?"

"Bree, the Blade Runner . . . Anybody ever forget you?"

"You look cute on TV . . ."

"The camera loves me."

"I'm outside your house on Windward. See me?"

She's under a streetlight, jeans and Nikes, mane tied with a red ribbon.

"You're underdressed."

"I'm off duty. Wanna hang out?"

"Why?"

"I'm curious. Aren't you?"

Casual. Offering herself without giving up her dignity. But something's going on. Pretty girls don't forgive. Maybe she was reshuffling her emotions from the night before and felt something. Maybe Jonas is watching through her eyes.

Interesting . . .

"Hold on a second . . ."

Back to Tingley.

"Can't let you take the risk, Cheri . . ."

She's not fooled. "Got a better offer on the other line?"

"Not better . . ."

"So what is it?" she asks. "Do you like walking on a tightrope or do you just want to fall to your death?"

"Both, I guess . . ."

BLACKOUT

THE END